Entangled

K. Elliott

PUBLIC LIBRARY
EAST ORANGE, NEW JERSEY

This novel is a work of fiction. Names, characters, places, and incidents are the product of the Author's imagination and are used fictitiously. Any resemblance to actual persons, living or dead, events, locales is entirely coincidental

Urban Lifestyle Press
P.O. Box 12714
Charlotte, NC 28220

Library of Congress Control Number: 2003105695

E
Y
Elliott

Acknowledgements

I would like to give thanks to God for giving me the ability and determination to write a novel. Secondly I would like to thank my parents Otis and Margaret for bringing me into the world. I would also like to thank Irene Honeycutt for introducing me to poetry and language and encouraging me to write. Also I would like to thank Sharon Fincher for her help and support and all my friends and family for there are far too many to name but you know who you are. The true ones. I would like thank Nicki Smith for your time and input. LaDonna Meredith for assistance with editing and proofing. Special thanks to Hybrid Design for the layout and design. Antoine Scott of hi-rezgraphix for the hot book cover, Carl Weber and Vicki Stringer for advice about the industry I would also like to acknowledge Terri Woods, Shannon Holmes and Sister Souljah, and other writer's who paved the way in this new genre dubbed Street Life fiction. My researcher Chris DiGiovanni. Shana Wilson for her insight. My wonderful Editors Chandra Sparks Taylor you are truly a gifted woman and it was a real pleasure working with you. Lastly I would like to thank my cousin James Billy Sims (Rico). I don't use the word genius lightly because I haven't had the pleasure to know many people that I would consider a genius, but in you I see true brilliance, true artistry, and thanks for helping make my story the best it can be. I am praying for your return home. I dedicate this book to the memory of my Aunt Annie Adams. RIP to my friend John "Duke" Davis.

$13.95
10/6/08
MJ

m CHAPTER 1 m

MONDAY, JUNE 2, 2002. The Greyhound bus moved slowly up I-95. Jamal Stewart sat in the back of the bus in a corner by himself occasionally gazing at a little girl who sat across from him with a woman he believed to be her mother. Jamal had just completed a five-year sentence with the Bureau of Prisons in Coleman, Florida, and the little girl across from him was the first child he had actually seen in a long time. He hadn't done a lot of things in a long time: He hadn't seen dogs, he hadn't chewed bubble gum, he hadn't driven a car, and he hadn't been with a woman. He smiled at the little girl who was waving at him.

Finally the woman stood and shoved the little girl to the front of the bus while looking at Jamal coldly. His attention shifted to the cars on the interstate. The shapes and sizes of cars had changed, everything looked futuristic. He had not seen or heard from his own mother in five years. He tried not to think about her, but ever since he was told of his release date he found himself thinking about her.

Five years, he kept saying to himself. He wasn't bitter about his incarceration, in fact, he was glad it had happened. It gave him a chance to just sit back and reflect on his life and learn a great deal about people. He had lost contact with a lot of his so-called friends, some of whom he hadn't heard from since the U.S. Marshals had picked him up for drug conspiracy, but everything was fine now since he was finally free. He had entered prison at the ripe age of twenty-three, still a boy. He was twenty-eight now and very much a man, a muscular 230 pounds.

Eight hours later, at the Charlotte, North Carolina terminal, his best friend, Dawg, greeted him as he stepped from the bus. "What's up, Playboy?" The two men embraced.

Steven Davis had been Jamal's friend since childhood. A tall, lanky, light-skinned man; his facial features resembled a Doberman, thus earning him the nickname Dawg.

They had met during a fight in kindergarten over an Incredible Hulk action figure. Neither had won the fight but mutual respect was gained and they had been best friends ever since. Since Jamal's mother was on drugs, and he had not heard from his father since he was a child, Dawg was the only person Jamal could count on for money and support during his incarceration.

"I'm finally here," Jamal said.

"How does freedom feel?" Dawg asked.

"Ain't no feeling like this, not even getting your first piece of ass—nothing can compare to having your freedom back."

"I can't believe how big you've gotten," Dawg said, looking at his friend from head to toe. A very handsome man, Jamal had a cocoa complexion, and his hair was in thick black braids.

"Yeah, man, I did nothing but pump iron and read books the whole time I was down."

"Nigga, you read books? You never got me to send you nothing except for the Robb Report and Dupont Registry."

"Yeah, I needed those magazines to keep me focused on what I wanted to accomplish out here." Jamal had spent countless hours looking at the lavish mansions and luxury cars in the magazines. One particular house plan, a glass-front mansion, he would stare at before he went to bed at night. He would have Dawg forward the plan whenever he transferred to a different prison. It was customary for the Feds to move an inmate from one place to the next, depending on sentence length, and while in transit, Jamal's house plan would usually get misplaced.

"So what you trying to accomplish?" Dawg asked.

"I just want to live. I guess I'm going to need to get a job first and then go from there."

"A job? Come on, man, you haven't gotten soft, have you?" Dawg said, staring at his friend oddly. "I mean, a job is not going to give you the lifestyle that you have been used to and you damn sho ain't going to be able to afford that damn house that you want to have built."

Jamal thought about the counselors' warnings, given before his release. They had told him that his friends would assume that he would be the same person he was before he left. Jamal knew Dawg remembered him as a big-time hustler who refused to settle for second best. Before he was locked up he had become accustomed to everything—luxury cars and apartments, expensive jewelry and furs. He knew Dawg was right; he couldn't afford the mansion with a regular job. He couldn't live the lifestyle he was accustomed to—not working for someone. Jamal was the same person he was before he left, which was scary. He would do what he had to do to get the things he wanted, even if it meant dealing drugs again.

They got into Dawg's white BMW and sped off to the mall. Once they arrived, Dawg handed Jamal a wad of cash. Jamal found himself looking at some high school girls on occasion, and Dawg warned him that they were jailbait. Jamal had to keep reminding himself that he was a grown man now, not the twenty-three-year-old who had left so long ago, though every other girl seemed to be giving him the eye.

Dawg caught him up on the latest fashions and trends before taking Jamal to a condo, rented in downtown Charlotte. Dawg had started renting it a month earlier because he figured Jamal would need somewhere to live when he was released.

"How do you like it?" Dawg asked.

"Man, I love it," Jamal said, looking around. The condo was simply decorated with basic black leather furniture, fine African art, and shiny hardwood floors. It offered a perfect view of the city.

"Come here and look," Dawg said as he motioned Jamal toward the living room window. "You can see Ericcson Stadium from here," he said.

"How much is this thing running you a month?" Jamal asked.

"Twenty-two hundred dollars a month."

"How in the hell am I gonna afford this?"

"I know you got some money stashed somewhere," Dawg said, grinning.

It was true. Jamal did have some money stashed, but it wasn't a lot. After he'd caught the drug case, he had to pay lawyers and bondsmen. He'd also left some money with his mother, but since he had not seen or heard from her, he assumed she had spent the money on crack. His then live-in girlfriend also had some money that belonged to him, but she'd run off with it shortly after he got sentenced. He was actually down to his last ten thousand dollars. He was broke as far as he was concerned. "I ain't got enough money to afford this place."

"Well, this means we got to go back to work. You still have your connection's numbers out in California?"

"Yeah, but I ain't gonna call him just yet. I'm going to enjoy myself a few weeks. You know, get some pussy and get reacquainted with the city."

"I hear that. Well, this place is all yours. It's getting late. I gotta go scoop this honey I've been chilling with. Watch some TV," Dawg said, pointing to a forty-two-inch plasma television. The two men hugged.

* * *

A few days later, Jamal had finally gotten used to his freedom. He had finally had sex again, and he felt rejuvenated. After passing the driver's license test, without even studying the driver's handbook, he decided to retrieve the money he had stashed before going to prison. It was buried underneath a railroad track on the west side of town, where he figured it would be safe. The money was exactly as he'd left it, in PVC pipes, still in thousand-dollar stacks. He decided he would get himself some transportation but nothing too extravagant. He went to a dealership and test-drove a winter-green Ford Expedition with cream leather seats. He absolutely loved it. The salesman frowned when Jamal told him he didn't have a job—until Jamal produced a wad of cash as a down payment.

"I believe I can get my sales manager to work something out," the man said as he dashed into the sales office. Fifteen minutes later he returned with a contract already drawn up. Jamal signed the proper papers, received the keys then drove off the lot.

* * *

Dream Nelson's childhood bedroom led to a huge terrace that provided a splendid view of the neighborhood. Dream sat on the terrace drinking Evian bottled water and skimming through Honey magazine. The sun shone brilliantly, thus making Dream's beautiful skin a shade darker. She was naturally beautiful, smooth dark skin and perfect white teeth. Her hair was so long, most people thought it was a weave.

Oak Crest Park was a beautiful integrated neighborhood full of two-story and split-level houses with perfectly manicured lawns. A friendly neighborhood, it was not uncommon to see children with lemonade stands on the street corners. Oak Crest Park primarily consisted of doctors, attorneys, and educators. Dream's mother was a high school teacher and her father was a principal who was approaching his thirtieth year as an educator. Dream had chosen to follow in her parents' footsteps by becoming a history teacher.

After high school, she had initially wanted to be a doctor but decided against it because she didn't want to be in school for an additional eight years. She simply didn't have the patience. Besides, she enjoyed her job. It definitely didn't pay the most money, but she got satisfaction in helping her kids. They loved her because she made learning fun and easy. She was only twenty-four, and she related more with her students than some of the older teachers who often turned up their noses at her when she walked by. Some of them complained that she dressed too provocatively, citing her skirts were too short and her clothing too tight. Someone even suggested to the principal that she didn't wear underwear, which was a complete lie. She wore thongs, not to turn on teenage boys, but she couldn't stand the thought of panty lines, besides she was young and sexy, and those hags hated the fact that they didn't have the body to wear sexy clothes.

Summers always seemed to come and leave so fast, Dream thought, particularly this summer, though there was nothing spectacular about it. She had spent most of it just hanging at her parents' house and working. She had gotten a job as a geometry tutor for the Sylvan Learning Center. She'd had to brush up on the subject, since she taught history during the school year, but somehow she would manage to fake it enough to get by. This summer marked the first one she didn't spend with her boyfriend, DeVon, who was incarcerated for vehicular homicide. Though DeVon and Dream didn't have much in common, they were deeply in love. She didn't know why she was attracted to the bad-boy types; it seemed that all the thugs and convicts were immediately drawn to her.

Keisha Ferguson, her best friend, would tease her by saying she was a thug lover. Dream would taunt Keisha by saying Keisha liked the pretty boys with feminine qualities, the kind who didn't want to get their hands dirty. It was true. Whenever they went out, all the roughnecks would step to Dream, and the pretty-boy-model-types would be drawn to Keisha. Dream and Keisha had been best friends since high school, and they had attended North Carolina Central University together. Keisha was the one person Dream could trust with secrets.

Dream had finished reading Honey. She'd begun to snooze when her mother walked out onto the terrace. "Dream, baby, I didn't know you were still here," she said with a warm smile. At forty-five, Janice Nelson had the body of a twenty-five-year-old thanks to diet and exercise. Her silky dark brown skin was wrinkle-free.

Dream was startled after hearing her mother's voice. "Mama, what time is it?"

"It's six o'clock. If I had known you were gonna be here this late, I would have cooked dinner for you."

"Don't worry about me, Mama. I got food at home and I can cook, you know." Dream smiled.

"I know you can cook, but ain't nothing like one of Mama's home-cooked meals."

"Well, maybe you should cook. Daddy says he never gets a home-cooked meal until I come over."

"Child, you know your daddy can lie, don't you?" Janice said, laughing. "Besides, I'm trying to get that man to back away from the table. Your daddy done got kind of chunky."

"Mama, don't talk about Daddy when he's not here to defend himself."

"I'm just saying men, always want you to look your best. Why can't we require the same thing? See, right now, it's all good 'cause you're young, and you don't need to work to keep yourself looking good. Those young boys you're dating, they all still have flat stomachs. You just wait until you get in your thirties."

"I'll still look good."

"Yeah, thanks to me you got good genes, but I don't know about that boyfriend of yours. He's gonna be the reason for some ugly-ass kids." Janice laughed.

"Mama, you need to stop."

"When was the last time you visited that hoodlum?"

"DeVon ain't a hoodlum. He just made a mistake. In fact, he's very intelligent. One of these days I'm going to let you read some of the letters he has written."

"I don't have the time to be reading anybody's jailhouse poetry. I prefer Nikki Giovanni, myself," Janice said before going back inside the house.

Dream knew her parents weren't fond of DeVon, but they had never liked any of her boyfriends. They would prefer she date an executive, or an attorney in some fancy law firm, or at least someone with a college degree. Her parents were like most people in this country, equating a college degree with intelligence. Dream had tried dating those straight-laced academic types, but she could not seem to get into them. Their conversations were boring and their dates were predictable—most of the time it was dinner, a movie, and back to the apartment to listen to some jazz artist of whom she had never heard. Dream preferred hip-hop. She liked the bandana-wearing, diamond earring-sporting thug; the kind who would do eighty miles per hour on the freeway at night; the guys who would be ready to defend her if someone disrespected her. She liked the guys who didn't necessarily play by the rules but took chances. She didn't know why she liked that type, she just did.

* * *

The visitation room at White Mountain State Prison was filled to its capacity. The visitors were mostly African-American and Hispanics, sprinkled with a few whites. Some of the women wore their best clothing, while others came in jeans with big plates of food for their husbands or boyfriends. The children ran rampant playing, happy to see their fathers.

Dream wore white skin-tight Capri pants and a red midriff shirt that revealed a hint of her belly. DeVon loved it when she dressed sexy, and she enjoyed trying to please him, but she knew she had to dress tastefully because of the sex-crazed inmates. DeVon had told her about a case where one of the inmates had masturbated in front of a female correctional officer.

Dream sat at a table in the far right corner of the visitation room, out of the view of the correctional officers. DeVon always suggested she sit there so he could fondle her without the officers noticing. While waiting for DeVon to arrive, she read several chapters of a Terry McMillan paperback to pass the twenty or thirty minutes it usually took DeVon to arrive at the visiting room. The inmates wore green hand-me-down army clothes and black boots. Though the clothes were really gaudy, most of the guys still tried to look their best for visitation.

DeVon finally came out. He was a tall, pecan tan-colored man with a neatly trimmed goatee. He smelled of Obsession cologne—created by an inmate of course. Dream hugged him as soon as he approached the table. They made small talk and Dream noticed something seemed to be bothering him.

She had been with him for twenty minutes and he had not attempted to touch her; something that was usually the highlight of the visit. She tried to rub his hand underneath the table before he moved it.

An inmate walked up to the table. "How about a picture for you and your girl?" he asked.

"How about you getting the hell away from this table?" DeVon said.

"What in the hell did you say, punk?"

DeVon stood up from the table and squared off with the inmate. A heavyset correctional officer with huge, ape-like hands got between them. "You, go over to the other side of the room," the correctional officer ordered the photographer.

"I ain't even do shit," the inmate protested before throwing his hands up in disgust.

"The other side!" the officer said while pointing. When the man was halfway there, the officer motioned for DeVon. "One more outburst like that, Mr. Williams, and I'm gonna recommend that your visiting privileges are taken away. You understand me?"

DeVon nodded before returning to his seat.

"What was that all about?" Dream asked.

"The guard was loud enough, I know you heard what he said."

"I know what the guard said. I wanna know what your fuckin' problem is. Why did you go off on the camera man?"

"I ain't got no problem. You're the one with the problem."

"What the hell do you mean?"

"Do you know Corey Mitchell?"

"Yeah, Corey and I dated briefly at West Charlotte High School."

"That's not all you did together," he mumbled.

"What do you mean by that?"

"Seems to me, you and Corey did a bit of role-playing. I mean, you used to play model, while he played photographer, right?"

Confused, she asked, "What are you getting at?"

"You know Corey is locked up here."

"No, I didn't know this."

"Yeah, he is, and he has some pretty explicit shots of Ms. Goody-Two-Shoes."

"I don't know what you're talking about, and whatever pictures he has have got to be more than five years old."

Suddenly she remembered the pictures. One evening after school Dream and Corey had gone to his house to make out, and he took some Polaroid pictures of her lying across his bed wearing only her panties. "What is the big deal?" she asked.

He stood from the table and the entire visiting room's attention seemed to shift.

"The big deal is that I didn't know I was dealing with a ho."

"I'm a what?"

"You heard me," he said, turning his back toward her. "I'm outta here."

"So you just gonna call me a ho and leave, huh?"

"Watch me," he said as he made is way toward the double doors of the visiting room that led to the prison yard.

ɱ CHAPTER 2 ɱ

It was 4:30 A.M. and DEA Agent Mark Pratt had finished his last set of push-ups and was just starting his second cup of coffee. He hadn't slept later than 5:00 A.M. since his freshman year at the Citadel, a military college located in South Carolina. Mark was grateful for his education at the Citadel. It made him more objective and more disciplined, which prepared him for his career as a Drug Enforcement Agency officer. It was his discipline that kept him looking young. An almond-complexioned man, he had a baby face with serious eyes. His body was well-defined.

Mark had joined the DEA nine years earlier at the age of twenty-five. The years had passed so quickly. Though his job was hard work, there was never a dull moment. He had been on drug busts that took place as far away as Miami. He had been part of undercover operations that had lasted for several years and he had always wanted a career that would make a difference in people's lives. He had come from a long line of preachers dating all the way back to his great-grandfather. His father was the pastor of Greater Mt. Sinai Baptist Church. With a twelve-thousand-member congregation, it was the second largest African-American church in Dallas. Mark admired his father and tried to pattern his life after Pastor Fred Pratt. Though he was miles away, Mark always called him for advice.

Son, always try to do what is pleasing in the sight of the Lord, his father would say. Mark's brother, Barry, was a youth minister; Mark chose a career with the DEA.

Though most of his friends supported his career decision, some weren't too enthusiastic about him working for the government, particularly the DEA, which had a reputation for targeting blacks and Hispanics. Some even said the so-called drug war was a useless battle—a conspiracy to destroy the black man's existence. Mark never denied that some of the blacks were pawns in this seemingly endless war. Some of his colleagues liked the profession because they knew they would always have a job. Mark wanted more than job security, he dreamed of a day when every drug dealer would be off the streets and the addicts put in treatment centers. If his dreams were to come true, he would gladly look for another job.

At 4:45 his phone rang.

"Good morning," Mark answered.

"Yeah, is this Agent Mark Pratt?" the voice asked.

"Yes, it is," Mark answered reluctantly. He knew the call was work-related but he wasn't scheduled to go in to work for almost another four hours; he had planned on taking a morning jog.

"Agent Pratt, I'm Trooper Doug Morgan with the North Carolina Department of Highways. My captain asked me to give you a call about a situation we could possibly use your expertise on."

"Who is your captain?"

"Mike Lowman."

Mark and Mike Lowman were good friends. Mike's son had played on Mark's Little League baseball team a couple of summers ago. Mark had seen Mike a few weeks earlier at a gas station, and Mark had given him a card with his home number scribbled on the back.

"Where are you?" Mark asked.

"The state trooper's office on Highway 49."

"Give me a chance to shower, and I'll be right over."

Mark didn't particularly like going to the state trooper's office. The state troopers were comprised of a lot of good 'ole boys, and many of them weren't too fond of black DEA agents. Mark had been pulled over a couple of times by officers he believed to be racist. In a couple of instances, if he hadn't put his hands up in plain view he would have probably been a statistic.

He showered and brushed his teeth, and twenty minutes later he pulled into the parking lot of the state trooper's office and parked near the back door. He walked up to the door and tapped lightly. A tall, thin white trooper, with an elongated face and thinning gray hair opened the door and blocked the entrance. "Yeah, can I help you?" the man asked.

Mark frowned. He hated these rednecks with their Robocop mentalities. "Yeah, I'm here to see Trooper Doug Morgan."

"Yeah, I'm Doug Morgan," the man said.

"I'm Agent Pratt," Mark said, extending his hand.

Doug paused before speaking, "You sounded different on the phone," he finally said.

Mark was used to people, whites in particular, saying this. People oftentimes attributed proper enunciation with someone being white. He considered his oratory skills a plus in his field. He was equally gifted at speaking street slang, and he spoke Spanish fluently, thus enabling him to go undercover easily. "Yeah, a lot of people say I sound differently over the phone."

Mark followed Doug through a set of double doors that led to a small conference room. Sitting at the table was a small black man who looked to be in his mid-forties, wearing gold earrings in both ears. Doug shut the door and introduced the man to Mark. "Mr. Ruffin, this is DEA Agent Mark Pratt."

Ruffin shrugged as if he could care less.

"What's going on in here?" Mark asked.

"Ain't shit going on but this cracker keep harassing me 'cause I drive a nice car," Ruffin said.

"There's no need for the profanity," Mark said.

"I didn't harass you. I pulled you over because you were swerving," Doug said.

"What gave you the right to search my car?" Ruffin asked.

"I searched your car because I saw you shove something underneath the passenger seat."

"It was only money. Y'all act like a black man ain't supposed to have shit."

"How much money?" Mark asked Ruffin.

"Why don't you ask your fellow law enforcement officer," Ruffin said.

"Eighty-five thousand dollars," Doug answered.

Mark's eyebrows rose. "Where were you going with that kind of money?"

Ruffin dropped his head, staring at the floor. "I ain't gotta answer that question if I don't want to," he said.

"He's a fuckin' doper, that's what he is. I ran his record. He already has two prior drug convictions," Doug said.

"Let me see the money," Mark demanded.

Doug left the room and reappeared with two manila envelopes. He handed them to Mark, who took the money out and spread it on a conference table. The money was in stacks of thousand-dollar bills, held together by rubber bands.

"Mr. Ruffin, since you don't want to talk about your money, take a last look at it," Mark said.

Ruffin raised his head and made eye contact with Mark. "Y'all mu'fuckas gonna give me my money back!" he shouted.

"We might give you the money back if you give us an explanation for it," Mark said.

"What kind of explanation y'all want?"

"What were you doing with it and where were you going with it?" Mark asked, stuffing the money back into the envelopes.

"I ain't no snitch," Ruffin said.

"I know you ain't no snitch, you're a fuckin' doper with a drug record dating all the way back to 1982," Doug said.

"That ain't no dope money," Ruffin said to Mark. His eyes were red and pleading for understanding.

Mark wanted to believe Ruffin but his knowledge and expertise wouldn't let him. Mark turned from Ruffin's gaze. "Legally, Mr. Ruffin, I can't hold you for possession of money."

"I know. You gotta give me my money back," Ruffin said.

"Wrong. This money is going to the district attorney's office. Someone from that office will be in touch with you. You have a right to dispute the seizure."

Ruffin rose from the table. "Can I go now?"

"That's totally up to Mr. Morgan," Mark said.

"He can go," Doug replied.

As Ruffin headed toward the double doors, Mark called out to him, "Ruffin, I'm going to be keeping an eye on you."

"Well, do your job," Ruffin replied.

* * *

Jamal awakened around 7:00 A.M. He would look for a job today. He figured he would at least try to be legitimate. He had seen many of his friends get out of prison and come right back for hustling, but he didn't really want to get caught up in his previous lifestyle. He remembered how much he hated prison. He would often say that if he could get out, he would work two jobs. McDonald's even. He just didn't want to go back to a dreadful cell. If that didn't work, he would go back to what he had been accustomed to. He had to survive. This was his rationale.

Jamal had been to at least thirty different places looking for work. They all wanted to know where he'd been for the last five years. McDonald's wouldn't even hire him. One man, Paul Angel, owner of Angel's Courier Service, had actually hired Jamal before learning of his past. Jamal and

Angel had chatted for twenty minutes. They'd discussed everything from current events to sports. Angel showed Jamal pictures of his son and daughter who both attended the University of North Carolina at Chapel Hill. Angel even encouraged Jamal to go back to school and get an education. "Who knows? If you get the right schooling, you might end up running this business for me once I'm not able," Angel said, smiling. "When can you start?" Angel asked as he extended his hand to Jamal.

"Today," Jamal replied. They continued their discussion in the small office.

Angel's jaw dropped as soon as Jamal informed him that he'd just been released from prison. "You've been locked up before?"

"Yeah, I did five years in prison," Jamal said.

"For what?" Angel asked as he stood and paced.

"I was locked up for selling drugs," Jamal said, suddenly realizing he should not have been so honest.

"I'm sorry, Mr. Stewart, but we can't use your services," Angel said, unable to hold eye contact.

Jamal felt like an idiot for even trying to play by the rules. His plan was to be wealthy. He wanted a mansion, exotic cars, and at least a half-million dollars in cash. He chuckled to himself for having the notion that a regular-paying job would help him reach his goals. He got into his truck and decided to call Angelo, his California drug connection.

Angelo answered on the first ring. "Hello."

"Angelo, this is Jamal."

"Oh my God, when did you get out?" Angelo asked.

"Almost a month now," Jamal replied.

"I knew it was about time for you to get out," Angelo said. "What have you been up to?"

"Trying to find work, but I ain't having no luck. Whenever I tell somebody that I just got out of prison, they don't want to have nothing else to do with me."

"Well, guys like me and you ain't cut out for working for nobody else. Besides, you know the white man ain't trying to deal with no black ex-convict, so why don't you come on out here to see me? I'll put you back to work."

"I'll be on the next flight to San Diego."

* * *

When Jamal and Dawg stepped off the plane, they took an escalator to the first floor of the airport. Angelo was there to greet them. He was a thin man with a wavy gray ponytail. He looked to be in his mid-fifties. He hugged Jamal. "Man, it's been a long time," Angelo said, happy to see his old business acquaintance.

"Angelo, you remember my friend, Dawg, don't you?" Jamal asked.

Angelo and Dawg shook hands.

The three men hurried to baggage claims and grabbed the luggage from the conveyer belt before heading to the parking lot where a blue Chevrolet Suburban transported them to Northern San Diego County. Angelo pulled into the driveway of a beautiful ranch-style, stucco house, nestled among eucalyptus trees. The inside of the home was richly decorated, and furnished with beautiful, green, Italian leather furniture. The floors were made of marble tile and a huge aquarium was built into the wall. A small octopus swam wildly as Jamal and Dawg looked on, very impressed. Angelo led them into a room in the back of the house, set up with a huge round table in the center. The three men took a seat. Shortly afterward, two women joined them.

"Fellas, I want you to meet my girls," Angelo said.

"Hey, guys, I'm Connie," one of the girls said. She was tall with skin the color of coffee. Her hair was short and stylish. "This is my friend Jennifer," she said.

Jennifer was tall and looked biracial. The girls shook hands with the guys, and the meeting began.

"Well, I think everybody in this room knows what we're here to discuss, so I'm gonna get right down to business," Angelo said. "My man, Jamal here just got out of prison, and he wants to make some money. I'm gonna help him as much as I can because I know he is a stand-up guy. I feel like I owe him because when he went to prison, he could have been a bitch and brought me down. I would have died in prison, so I appreciate this man. Besides he's like a son to me," Angelo said.

Jamal was surprised Angelo had such strong feelings for him. Angelo was right. Jamal could have given the Feds information and never served a day in prison. The two men had met while Jamal was in high school, at a downtown hotel where Jamal worked. One day Jamal overheard the hotel manager saying that he believed Angelo was into some type of illegal activity. Shortly thereafter Jamal told Angelo what he'd overheard, and the two had been friends ever since. "Yeah, I definitely need to make some money, but I don't want you to think you owe me anything," Jamal said.

"Then let's just say I feel obligated. Plus I feel like I should make your transition back into the game as smooth as possible. So, I got a proposition for you. I think you might want to hear what I've got to say," Angelo said.

"I'm game for anything that's gonna put some money in my pockets," Jamal said, placing his forearms on the table.

"Okay, this is the plan: I got a friend living in Charlotte. I've known this man for years. He's willing to pay $25,000 for a kilo of cocaine."

"Where do I come in at?" Jamal asked.

"I'm getting the kilos for $13,500. I'm going to give them to you for $18,500, and you can pass them on to Ruff and make $6,500 off the top."

"Your man is okay, ain't he? I would hate to see my boy get caught up in some more bullshit," Dawg said.

Angelo stared at Dawg coldly. "I understand you, but this guy is cool. Trust me. Nothing is going to happen," Angelo said before a smile materialized on his face. "Besides, he gets rid of dope faster than anybody I know."

"So, basically, my job is to be a runner for you?" Jamal asked.

"If that's all you want to be, that's fine, but I'll give you your own product on consignment, I mean, however you want to do it. That's on you."

Jamal smiled broadly. "That's what I want to hear. I need to make some money. I ain't accustomed to being without it. When will the plan go into effect?"

"As soon as you leave, the girls will make the delivery the next day."

"Well, hell, I'm leaving tomorrow. I like California and all, but I need to get this money."

m CHAPTER 3 m

TWO DAYS LATER, with four kilos attached to their girdles, the girls had gone through the airports undetected. The plan to get the product across the country had been successful. As soon as Jamal and Dawg got the product in their possession, Jamal called Ruff and got the directions to his home. It took thirty-five minutes to get to Ruff's house from Jamal's downtown condo.

Ruff lived near the Piedmont Courts housing projects, a neighborhood notorious for drug dealing and murder. Young boys were huddled on street corners, drinking and rolling dice, while prostitutes and drug addicts paraded up and down the street. Ruff's place was an enormous one-level home that stood out prominently in such a poverty-stricken neighborhood. A Lincoln Navigator and a Mercedes Benz were in the driveway. As soon as Jamal and Dawg reached the porch, a man opened the door. "I'm Ruff," he said, his smile revealing gold teeth. "Come on in. Have a seat."

Dawg sat beside Ruff on the sofa, and Jamal sat on an ottoman on the other side of the room. Ruff's home was simply decorated with earth-tone furniture and plush beige carpeting. Prison photos on the coffee table taken while he was locked up made it obvious that Ruff was no stranger to law enforcement.

"Angelo said you were gonna have something for me," Ruff said.

"We do," Dawg said

"Where is it?" Ruff asked.

"Now you wouldn't expect us to come over here with it on us before meeting you and feeling you out?" Jamal said.

Ruff smiled again. "Yeah, I see what you mean, but if you trusted Angelo and he sent you to me, he evidently feels that I'm okay, wouldn't you say?"

"He told us that you were cool but, you know, I still like to feel people out myself," Jamal said.

"I understand. So how long is the feeling-out process gon' take?" Ruff asked.

"As long as I need it to take," Jamal said.

"Well, I ain't got all year to be fuckin' with you cats. The fuckin' police just took $85,000 from me. I need to get back to work quickly. You know what I mean?"

Jamal and Dawg rose at the same time. "Have your money counted. I'll be back in about thirty minutes," Jamal said.

"I guess that means you boys trust me," Ruff said.

"Naw, this means we trust Angelo," Jamal said.

* * *

Three days later, TGI Friday's parking lot on Independence Boulevard was empty, except for the black pickup truck in the back of the restaurant. Jamal and Dawg waited in the front with two kilos underneath the seat. A 9mm handgun rested at Dawg's waist.

Jamal glanced at his watch. It was 3:15 P.M. and already his prospective customer was late. "Do you think we ought to get the hell out of here?" he asked.

"Let's wait another fifteen minutes," Dawg said, looking over his shoulder, scanning the parking lot.

"I don't like waiting in no empty parking lot," Jamal said. "If it wasn't Rico we were waiting on, I would have gotten the hell out of here a long time ago." Rico was a former associate whom Jamal had dealt with before going to prison.

"Yeah, I know what you mean," Dawg said.

Jamal turned to Dawg. "Is Rico still cool? I mean, you haven't heard anything about him robbing anybody, have you?"

"Naw, Rico is cool, as far as I know." A blue Lexus with chrome rims pulled into the parking lot. Jamal and Dawg recognized Rico immediately.

Rico pulled up beside the Expedition and asked Jamal to follow him.

Nervously, Jamal and Dawg both looked the parking lot over before following the Lexus. About a half-mile later they reached an apartment complex. Rico sprang out of the Lexus and signaled for Jamal and Dawg to come in behind him. Dawg moved the gun from his waist to his pocket.

Once they were inside the apartment, they felt there was no immediate danger. A short Hispanic woman with a round ass was inside.

"Rosa, these are my friends, Dawg and Jamal," Rico said. The woman nodded and smiled.

"Now get the hell out of here and let me and my friends do business."

After Rosa left, Rico hugged Jamal. "I'm glad you're home, man, that's real."

"You ain't the only one. Hell, I'm glad to be home," Jamal said.

"So what do you have for me?" Rico asked.

"I got what you want. It's some good shit."

"Cool, because it's been kind of hard to get the good shit lately, and I need to serve my people in the 'hood," Rico said.

"Well it's here. I got two bricks, and I'm going to need $50,000."

"I got forty. I can pay you the rest in a couple of days."

"Okay. I'll let you deal with Dawg from now on because I got to make sure we keep getting what we need."

"I see you're playing the big-man role already," Rico said, laughing.

"I don't want to be the big man. The big man is the one who gets all the prison time. I want to be the one who gets all the money."

Jamal showed Rico two brick-like packages. They reminisced for a few minutes before counting the $40,000.

* * *

Dream was still upset by the way DeVon had treated her in the visiting room. He'd acted like an adolescent about some pictures she'd taken years ago. She blamed society for the double standard between men and women. It was acceptable for a man to engage in any kind of undesirable act, and society would forgive him. Bill Clinton, Jesse Jackson, and Jimmy Swaggart had all been involved in sex-related scandals. Initially the media was in a frenzy, but after a couple of months, the hype died down; the country forgave them, but the poor women involved were scorned.

She wondered why men always dwelt on the past. She had never tried to investigate DeVon's previous relationships. She was certain that she could easily dig into his past and come up with some skeletons, but she had no desire to. She wasn't concerned about his past love life. She didn't know whether she still loved DeVon. She missed him terribly though, and she needed to talk to someone. She decided to call her best friend, Keisha Ferguson.

Keisha picked up the phone on the first ring. "What's up, girl?" she screamed, which meant she must have looked at the Caller ID.

"Nothing much here. Just needed someone to talk to," Dream said.

"You sound down. What happened?"

For the next twenty minutes, Dream told her all the details of her visit with DeVon. Keisha listened without interruption, and when Dream finished talking, Keisha commented, "He's so damn childish."

"That's exactly what I said," Dream replied, but she wasn't exactly surprised that Keisha had taken her side, after all, they were best friends, and they did think alike.

"You know what? You need a vacation, girl. You haven't been anywhere but to that damn prison, to work, and to your parents' house. Why don't you come with me to South Beach this Fourth of July weekend?"

"A vacation like that must be expensive," Dream said.

"Well, I already have a room reserved. All you need to do is get an airline ticket."

Keisha was right. Dream hadn't been anywhere all summer, and a trip could be soothing. Dream thought about it for a couple of minutes before deciding she would go. "I'll search the Internet for a deal."

"Call me back and let me know what you come up with," Keisha said.

* * *

Jamal had dealt with Ruff for about three weeks, and had made nearly $50,000 in profits. Not bad money for less than a month of work. When he was in prison, he had heard that high-tech was the wave of the future, with some jobs making as much as $150,000 a year. He preferred pharmaceutical sales. There was no money like drug money, he thought. He had made enough to get the new E-Class Benz if he wanted. He had enough to buy some cheap real estate. He could even buy into a fast-food franchise. He decided to wait before he spent his money foolishly.

Fourth of July weekend was coming up, and since this was his first summer of freedom in five years, Jamal decided he and Dawg would fly to South Beach for the weekend. Rappers, hustlers, and women from all over the United States would be down in Miami, and Jamal knew it would be live. I have to be there, he told himself. He had Dawg call Oceanside Car Rentals and reserve two convertible Porsches.

* * *

Mark Pratt had been following Ruff since the day the $85,000 was seized. Ruff hadn't tried to contact the D.A.'s office to reclaim the money. Trailing Ruff had been a very arduous task. He was a very busy man who was into all sorts of things—most undesirable. A typical day for Ruff usually included a few gambling houses and a strip club. Ruff had even gotten locked up a couple of times for other petty charges while Mark had him under surveillance. Two things were certain: Ruff was definitely a womanizer with at least three different girlfriends who were much too beautiful to be involved with a character like him. Secondly, Ruff was definitely involved in illegal drugs. Mark had observed Ruff accepting money from at least three people a day. He could have busted Ruff a long time ago, but he didn't want to go for a small amount. He wanted to catch him on the day he picked up from his suppliers. The more drugs, the more leverage Mark would have to make Ruff break down and inform on his connection.

* * *

U.S. Air Flight 341 departing from Charlotte for Miami boarded at Concourse C, Gate 18. There was a long line. Most of the patrons were African-Americans in their twenties and early thirties. Jamal and Dawg stood at the very back of the line, each wearing a Hawaiian shirt, shorts from the Sean John summer line, and a new Cartier watch. Their row was close to the back of the plane. A young lady sat in the seat next to the window. Jamal took the middle seat and Dawg sat on the aisle. The woman turned and greeted Jamal. "Hello, I'm Keisha," she said.

"I'm Jamal."

"Nice to meet you," she said. They shook hands.

"Same here," Jamal smiled. He noticed she was looking at his Cartier.

A booming voice filled the plane, directing passengers to turn off all electronics and to make sure their seat belts were fastened and seats were upright. Five minutes later they were in the air. Jamal and Keisha talked nonstop during the fifty-five-minute flight. She told him all about her trip to Cancun the year before, and they discovered they had even attended the same high school, but he was a couple of years ahead. She even told him she was an accountant.

"I'm impressed," he said.

"Yeah, I just passed the CPA exam last month," she said, pulling a card from her purse. "Take one of my cards." The card read: KEISHA A. FERGUSON, CERTIFIED PUBLIC ACCOUNTANT SPECIALIZING IN PAYROLL AND BOOKEEPING.

Jamal found Keisha very attractive but thought she might be a gold digger. He felt she would be better as a friend.

"So, Keisha, are you down here by yourself?" Jamal asked.

"Well, my girlfriend, Dream, is flying in later this evening."

Jamal came to the conclusion that her girlfriend was probably attractive as well because good-looking women usually hung around one another. "So what are you girls doing tonight?"

"I don't know. I got the itinerary from the Internet. There are so many parties going on. We haven't decided where we're going yet."

"Maybe we can hang out tonight," Jamal said.

"Well, give me the card back, and I'll write down the number to the hotel for you."

* * *

Hector, the young Hispanic man at the counter of Oceanside Car Rentals looked afraid when Dawg stared coldly at him. Dawg and Jamal were told that there was only one Porsche left.

"I can g-give you a Grand-Am for half price," the man said, while staring at Dawg's huge hands.

"I don't want no damn Grand-Am. I want what the fuck I reserved!" Dawg yelled.

A crowd of people looked on curiously and the man began to sweat profusely before loosening his tie. "Sir, I don't know what else to do to accommodate you," Hector said.

"Go get your damn manager," Jamal demanded.

The manager was also Hispanic. His nametag read Pedro. "What seems to be the problem?" he asked politely.

"The problem is, I reserved two Porsches and your man is telling me you've only got one," Jamal said.

Pedro told Hector to step aside as he scrolled through several screens on his computer. "Mr. Stewart, I can give you a black convertible Jag for half price."

Jamal decided he would take the Jaguar, though he would rather have the Porsche. He knew the Jaguar would be better than getting stuck driving some low-budget Grand-Am while all the athletes and rappers ruled the strip in exotic toys. "I guess we'll take it," Jamal said, "but I want you to know that I know you got that damn Porsche, and you probably gonna give it to some white mu'fucka."

Hector gave Jamal a tight-lipped nod. His facial expression indicated that he really didn't want any trouble from the two black men. Hector made a phone call and had the two vehicles brought to the front door.

Jamal and Dawg left the airport racing until they were about ten miles away from the beach where a long line of cars was at a standstill. Forty-five minutes later, they were pulling up to the Doubletree Hotel on Collins Avenue.

m   CHAPTER 4   m

KEISHA WAS DRIVING A blood-red convertible when she arrived at ground transportation. Her hair was down, and she wore expensive Versace sunglasses. She jumped out of the car and hugged Dream as if they hadn't seen each other in years.

"You are playing your part," Dream teased.

"I wouldn't have it any other way," Keisha said as they loaded Dream's bags into the car and sped off.

When they reached the beach, it overwhelmed Dream. She couldn't believe how many people were actually on the strip. The crowd was predominately African-American and there was an excess of police officers—crowds and police seemed to go hand in hand.

People from all over the country were there. Rappers were promoting their albums and movies. Every other person was passing out a flyer, announcing a party, fashion show, or another social gathering. The strip was breathtaking. Palm trees and the ocean on one side of the road, shops and restaurants on the other. Expensive cars like Bentleys and Ferraris filled the streets. Scanty clad model-types walked the strip as guys with camcorders recorded their every movement. Dream had been on the strip for ten minutes and she absolutely loved it.

Their hotel was on James Avenue, fifteen minutes away from the main strip, but with the massive crowd cluttering the street, it took them almost an hour to get there. The Crest Hotel was an ordinary stucco building with three levels. Their room was very spacious, equipped with two full-size beds and hardwood floors. The bathroom was tidy with a huge oval tub in the center, contemporary meets classic decor.

The plane ride and the heat had worn the girls down. They sat on the bed and talked for a few minutes and before they knew it, they both were snoozing.

The phone rang at 9:30 P.M. Dream answered it, still half asleep, "Hello."

"Hello, can I speak to Keisha?"

"She's asleep. May I ask who's calling?"

"My name is Jamal. She met me on the plane. Would you let her know that Steve Francis, the NBA nigga, is having a white linen party at Club Onyx? It's supposed to be happening."

"I will. What did you say your name was?"

"Jamal, and what's yours?"

"Dream."

"Hope to meet you at the party," he said before hanging up.

* * *

Dream dozed for a few more minutes before finally getting out of bed. She decided that it was time for them to get ready if they were going to go out. She reached over to Keisha's bed and nudged her. "Girl, wake up. I know you didn't come all the way down here just to sleep."

Keisha sat up on the edge of the bed and refocused. "Hell, it's so many different parties going on, I don't know where to go," she finally said.

"While you were asleep, some guy named Jamal called. He said you met him on the plane. He asked me to tell you about a white-linen party some NBA player is having."

"Oh yeah, I met Jamal and his friend. They were real cool. We should hang out with them since they're from Charlotte."

"Sounds like that party might be worth looking into. I brought some linen, what about you?" Dream asked.

"Yeah, I brought some linen pants."

"Good, because that's the party I want to go to."

"Me, too," Keisha replied, "because I know it's going to be a lot of brothers there with serious money."

Dream rolled her eyes teasingly. "Girl, you know our mamas ain't raise no gold diggers. Besides, you just became a CPA; you're about to be rolling in money."

"You're right. Our mamas didn't raise no gold diggers, but we didn't grow up struggling either, and I'm not about to start at this stage of my life."

"You know you got a lot of competition out there?"

Keisha rose from the bed and sashayed across the room. "Yeah, it's always like this, but honestly, do you think I give a damn about the competition with a body like this?" she said as she traced her silhouette.

"You're a ho," Dream said, giggling.

"No, I keep it real." Keisha winked.

* * *

Keisha called Jamal and they met in front of Club Onyx. Jamal's eyes met Dream's and they held the stare for a long time before she extended her hand. "Hey, I think we spoke on the phone," Dream said.

"Yeah, we did." Jamal tried to answer her as calmly as possible but he was lost in thought. He wanted her to be his wife. She was stunning. Her eyes were radiant and her skin was dark and smooth. She wore a tight white linen skirt, and it contrasted with her skin artistically.

The line for the party had extended all the way to the middle of street. Jamal decided immediately he wasn't going to be waiting in anybody's line for hours. He had come to South Beach to have a good time and that's exactly what he was going to do. He pulled one of the bouncers to the side. "Listen, man, how much is it going to cost for me and my friends to cut the line?"

"Two hundred dollars apiece, three hundred for VIP," the bouncer answered.

Jamal pulled out a handful of hundred-dollar bills from his pocket, peeled off twelve, and handed them to the bouncer. "Take us to VIP," he ordered.

The huge bald-headed man grinned while quickly stuffing the money in his pocket. He then shoved several people out of his way to make room for the group.

The club was crowded with people, almost on top of one another. Jamal asked Dawg to take Keisha to the dance floor so he could be alone with Dream. Jamal led Dream to the outside patio, and they sat facing the crowded South Beach streets. He was so taken by her beauty that he wanted to leave for Charlotte with her tonight. "You know I really dig your name."

She smiled. It was a corny line, she thought, but she had been hearing it all her life. "Thank you."

"So, Dream, where are you from?"

"Earth," she said teasingly.

He smiled. He liked a woman with a sense of humor.

"I'm from Charlotte, North Carolina," Dream said.

"Me, too. I've never seen you before."

"Well, I've never seen you before, either, but that doesn't mean that you aren't from Charlotte."

He hesitated before speaking. "I lived in Orlando for a while before returning home this year." The Federal prison had been close to Orlando but he claimed Orlando assuming it might impress Dream. It sounded worldlier.

Her eyebrows rose. "Really?" she asked, pretending to be interested.

"So what do you do in Charlotte besides posing as an absolute beauty queen?"

She blushed. "I'm a history teacher."

He couldn't believe she was a teacher. He had expected her to say something like modeling or a makeup artist not teaching. She didn't strike him as the teacher type. He knew if he were in school, he would find it hard to concentrate in a classroom with her, though he wouldn't mind her teaching him a few things. Jamal didn't know what else to talk about. She was the most beautiful woman he had been in contact with since he had been released from prison. "Would you like something to drink?" he asked.

"Seltzer water."

"You don't drink alcohol, huh?"

"I don't drink around people that I don't know."

He laughed out loud before disappearing inside the club. He spotted Dawg at the bar with a bottle of Moet in his hand.

"What's up, Soldier?" Dawg asked.

"Nothing, man, I'm just out on the patio chilling with that Dream chick. The fine-ass woman is a damn teacher."

"Well her friend is acting like it's all about these tall-ass NBA niggas but she don't even know we got money like these mu'fuckas. That's cool, though, 'cause I got these two bisexual women from Miami on my jock."

Jamal laughed.

"Well, don't wait up on me 'cause I'm in for a long night," Dawg assured him.

When Jamal returned to the patio, he found Dream sitting with perfect posture. When she stood to receive her drink, he noticed how well-proportioned her body was. Her breasts were small but delicious looking. Her ass was round and firm, and when she turned to the side he could see that she was wearing a thong. He became aroused immediately. He handed her the seltzer water. "Did you miss me?" he asked.

"Yeah, I counted the seconds you were away," she teased.

She took her position back on the bench and he sat beside her.

"So, Ms. Dream, do you have a man?"

She turned from his gaze. "Kinda."

"How can you kinda have a man?"

She turned and faced him again. "Let's just say we're not exactly getting along right now."

"What's wrong?" he asked before taking a sip of his Corona.

"Long story."

"I got time."

She put her legs across his lap.

He stared at her well-defined calves and his arousal returned.

"Let's just enjoy the moment, the mood and the moonlight," she said.

Two hours later the crowd on the patio had grown dramatically. Dream and Jamal sat talking about everything while holding hands. The pale moonlight fell down on their faces.

* * *

The next morning, Jamal woke up with Dream on his mind. Though there were thousands of fine women at the beach, he wanted Dream. Her beauty went beyond the skin. She wasn't just another pretty face. Her conversation was seasoned with substance, and he felt connected to her in a way that he could not explain. He showered, got dressed, repossessed the Jaquar from the valet, and slipped in his Tupac CD. Tupac was like religion to Jamal. He loved what the rapper had represented before passing away. Tupac was a young black man who was from the slums, a man who was not supposed to make it but did, against all odds. Jamal felt in some ways he and Tupac's lives were parallel.

Jamal was bouncing to the music when he picked Dream up in front of her hotel. When she got in, he put the top down and her hair blew fiercely as they drove off in the direction of the Bal Harbor Area shopping mall. He drove impatiently, maneuvering his way through the jam-packed streets. He would glance down occasionally at her beautiful brown legs, and when she would catch him, they would laugh.

Bal Harbor was full of specialty shops like Gucci, Chanel, and Fendi. When they entered the mall a woman in her sixties sporting breast implants and Donna Karan sunglasses carrying many bags was leaving.

"There are a lot of rich people down here," Jamal said.

"I see," Dream said, admiring the trendy-looking stores.

For the next hour and a half, they visited at least six different stores, and Jamal purchased at least one item out of each store. Dream noticed each time he paid with cash.

"I want to buy you something," Jamal said as they left the Versace store.

"Why do you want to buy me something? You hardly even know me," Dream said.

"Because I've never met anybody like you. I'm feeling chemistry here. Besides, I've spent so much money on myself. I'm kind of feeling guilty for just splurging in your face."

"You don't owe me anything, Jamal. Honestly, I'm okay."

At Tiffany's he noticed her looking at a diamond-encrusted gold watch. Dream didn't want to try the watch on but the saleslady was so adamant, she finally agreed.

"It's ravishing," the saleslady said.

"It's the bomb," Jamal replied.

"Expensive is what it is," Dream added.

"We'll take it," Jamal said, and the saleslady quickly retrieved the watch and headed to the back room to box it up before Dream could challenge her. Jamal pulled thirty-four $100-bills from his pocket and placed them on the counter.

As night fell, Dream and Jamal strolled the beach barefooted as the ocean waves pounded the shore vehemently. The seagulls sounded off like a high school trumpet player. A half moon hung low, and a few stars decorated the night sky. Lost in thought, Dream reflected on her last visit with DeVon. Though she was having a good time with Jamal, she couldn't help but think of DeVon. It was Sunday night, and it had been nearly one month since she had seen him. She felt guilty for not visiting, while at the same time she was having the time of her life. She decided to send DeVon a postcard but quickly dismissed the thought. After all, it was he who had cursed her out and left her in the visiting room feeling like a fool.

Jamal had been quiet for most of the walk. He was just enjoying the night and her presence. Finally he broke his silence and caught her off guard. "Dream, do you believe in God?"

She stopped in her tracks and turned toward him. "Of course I do. I believe in Jesus. What about you?"

He turned toward the ocean and inhaled the saltwater aroma. "Sometimes I do, sometimes I don't know what to believe."

"Sounds like a lack of faith to me," she said.

"Not necessarily a lack of faith but a lack of understanding. I mean when I look at the ocean and the stars, I know there is a creator, but when I see one group of people prosper so much more than another group, I can't help but wonder why God would allow that. Why would He allow anyone to suffer? Why would He let kids in Africa go hungry? There are just so many questions I have that I need answers for. Honestly, to me, hell is being broke here on earth."

Jamal's eyes were misty when he finished, and Dream could tell he had been questioning the concept of God for a while. She didn't have the answers for him. Finally, she took his hand and they continued to walk in silence.

"So, Dream, are you gonna work your little situation out with your man, or are you gonna free up that time for me?"

She laughed. "You're definitely straightforward."

He smiled boyishly. "That's the only way I know to be."

"To answer your question, Mr. Jamal, it's not that easy. There's a lot to the relationship. It's more complex than you could imagine."

"So, does this guy know you're down here in South Beach?"

"He doesn't know where I am."

"Aren't we wild?"

"No. It's not what you think. He's locked up."

"Oh, I see why things are complicated."

"Let's not talk about him right now."

"That's fine with me," he said, placing his arm around her waist.

* * *

In her hotel room, Dream lay on her stomach as Jamal massaged her back. Jamal couldn't believe that he was actually in her room. Either women were more gullible than they used to be, or his lines were more polished. A rerun of The Cosby Show was playing on television, but his eyes were fixated on her ass.

"Lower shoulders please," she said.

He maneuvered her shoulders gently. He felt the erection returning, so he shifted his attention to the television. "You know, I never liked this show."

"Why not?"

"It's too far-fetched."

"What's far-fetched about it?"

"A doctor married to a lawyer? Come on. How many black people do you know like that?"

"I know quite a few professional people married to each other."

"Oh, really?" His erection began to reduce.

"Yeah, as a matter of fact, the guy who lived next door when I was growing up is an engineer and his wife is an attorney."

There was a long silence and it seemed as though the volume on the television increased. Dr. Huxtable was confronting Theo about marijuana he had found in Theo's schoolbook. For the first time since they had met, Jamal realized that he and Dream were from different classes. He thought about Tupac's lyrics. Jamal's family tree consisted of drug dealers, thugs, and killers, while Dream's social circle was made up of attorneys, doctors, and teachers. He had expected the next question to come much sooner.

"What do you do for a living?" she asked

He hesitated, thinking of an answer. "Let's just say I have to hustle to get my money." He wanted to lie but decided not to. He knew Dream was smart enough to realize he didn't have a regular job because of the way he had been throwing money around. Besides, he figured, a lot of good girls liked thugs.

Dream turned over on her back and her eyes met his. "I don't want to know what you're involved in. I can imagine, though. I've dealt with your kind before."

Jamal was relieved that she clearly wasn't going to hold the fact that he hustled against him. He really liked Dream, and he didn't want to have to deal with a scared little girl. He was what he was, and he didn't want to change for anybody until he felt he had enough money to stop and live comfortably. Hustling was how he was eating, and anybody affiliated with him was going to have to accept it. "You know, you're cool as hell," he said.

"Where did that come from?" she asked, smiling.

"You accept me for me, and I like that because, I mean, here you are, this teacher from obviously a better background than mine, and you still ain't judging me because I'm a hustler," he said.

"Jamal, I have a question for you."

Now he figured she was probably going to pry. He hadn't anticipated another question, but whatever it was she wanted to know, he would tell her. "What do you want to know?"

"Will you cuddle me?" she asked softly.

"Cuddle you? What do you mean?" He honestly didn't know.

"Get up under the cover, silly, and hold me."

He kicked off his size twelve Nikes and slid underneath the cover, placing an arm around her waist. Her body was warm and soothing and his erection formed fast. His erection was pulsating against her ass. He knew she liked it. It was agonizing to have an erection and not be able to penetrate her. He liked the feeling nevertheless.

* * *

On the flight back to Charlotte, Jamal tallied up the cost of his trip. From airline tickets and rental cars to the mini-shopping spree he and Dream had at Bal Harbor, the total came to around $10,000. He called Angelo as soon as he got off the plane.

m CHAPTER 5 m

MARK WAS STAKED OUT across the street from Ruff's house posing as a BellSouth telephone repairman. He had been there about a half hour when a white BMW drove up with a young black man behind the wheel. Mark noticed the man using a cell phone. A minute later, Ruff came out of the house and walked up to the vehicle. Ruff handed the man a black leather bag in exchange for a small brown box, after which the man drove off. Mark's surveillance experience told him that Ruffin had just scored, and the young guy in the BMW was his supplier. Mark immediately called the office and asked for help.

Forty-five minutes later, Jeremiah Tolliver pulled up beside Mark in a BellSouth telephone truck. Mark wasn't particularly fond of Jeremiah, but he was the only one available to come out and help.

"What's up, Mark?" Jeremiah asked, extending his hand.

"Nothing much, just needing a little help with this surveillance."

"Which house are you watching?" Jeremiah asked as he looked across the street.

"The one with the lavender siding."

"So, he's a doper, huh?"

"I'm pretty sure he is," Mark replied. He then told Jeremiah about the money that had been seized, Ruffin's drug history, and the exchange between Ruffin and the guy in the white BMW.

"Did you get the guy's license plate number?"

"Yeah, I ran it already. The car belongs to Steven Davis. He lives on Lake Norman."

"Lake Norman? This guy must have some serious money," Jeremiah said.

"He has an apartment."

"Even so, apartments ain't cheap on the lake. He's probably pushing some heavy dope."

"We'll have to check him out later."

"Do you think he has drugs in the house?" Jeremiah asked. His blue eyes were intense.

"I'm pretty sure of it," Mark said, nodding.

"Let's get an informant to go in and make a buy from Ruff, get a search warrant and bust his ass."

"It's not that simple. Ruff is from the old school. He ain't gonna go for it unless . . . "

"Unless what?"

"Unless we get a woman to go along with the informant."

"Why do we need a woman?" Jeremiah asked.

"I've been watching this man for a while now, and he likes beautiful women."

"Well that's what we'll do then. We'll get a woman and come back tomorrow. Hopefully he won't sell out before then. In the meantime, let's get some info on this Steven Davis character."

* * *

Steven Davis had never gotten into much, according to his record—a few simple possessions of marijuana and a charge for assaulting a female, which was dismissed. He had one brief stay at the county jail for child support, about four years ago. But according to his record, he was far from a hardened criminal. Mark and Jeremiah examined his mug shot. "I'll tell you what, he definitely is an ugly S.O.B.," Jeremiah said, chuckling.

"No, he ain't gonna win no beauty contest no time soon."

Jeremiah looked at a printout of Steven's arrest record. "Are you sure this is the guy that was in the BMW? I mean, he's a petty criminal according to his rap sheet."

Mark shrugged. "Honestly, I couldn't see him from where my truck was parked, but I think this is the guy."

"Let's ride up to Lake Norman and see if we see the BMW."

* * *

Lakeside Condominiums was a luxurious gated community. Jeremiah presented his BellSouth ID to the security officer and the man promptly opened the gate. Mark spotted the BMW as soon as they entered the parking lot. Steven Davis lived in Apartment 4, overlooking the marina. "Let's ask one of the neighbors about Davis," Jeremiah suggested.

"Not yet. The purpose of the visit is to see if Davis lives here. Let's wait a few minutes to see if he comes out and leads us to something concrete." Mark stared at Jeremiah. "This is my show. I don't need you to mess nothing up. We're gonna do it my way or no way at all. You got that?"

"Well you're not the only one out here. I thought we were working together."

"Shhh. Not now, listen up."

Jeremiah had just parked the truck in the corner of the parking lot when Steven came out on the balcony, shirtless, pants sagging. His oversized blue and white striped boxer shorts were exposed. He held a cordless to his ear and shouted obscenities into the phone.

"I ain't paying no child support. I don't give a damn how far it gets behind. You won't let me see my daughter and you got some other mu'fucka raising her; do the best you can," Steven said, looking over at the BellSouth truck. He quickly ducked inside his house and slammed the door. He emerged fifteen minutes later and jumped in the BMW.

Mark and Jeremiah followed him to a high-rise apartment building downtown.

"I wonder who lives here," Jeremiah said.

"I don't know. We'll just have to wait and see. Let's hope when we bust Ruffin he tells us who lives here."

* * *

After not hearing from DeVon for nearly five weeks, Dream finally received a letter from him.

July 8, 2002

Dream,

Baby, I'm sorry for the way I acted in the visiting room. Please try to find it in your heart to forgive me for the embarrassment that I caused. I'm under a lot of pressure in here. I've been locked up for the past year for some bullshit, and it's starting to get to me. Imagine for a second having your freedom taken away, and in my case I have to live with the fact that my carelessness killed someone. Baby, I'm not asking for sympathy, just understanding. I will always love you, and I miss you dearly.

Love always,
DeVon

The letter was moving, but Dream was not in a forgiving mood. She'd been humiliated and didn't know whether she could ever go back to the prison to visit DeVon. She didn't want to show her face there. She crumpled the letter before tossing it in the wastebasket. Maybe in a few more weeks, she told herself. She was having too much fun being single.

She thought about Jamal. Though she had only known him for a few days, he made her feel like they had known each other for years. His personality was vibrant and lively. She felt so at ease around him, it was scary. He was clearly rough around the edges, but she was attracted to that part of him.

Jamal didn't break his neck to open doors, and he didn't appear to be awestruck by her appearance like some of the other men she had gone out with. The only thing that really bothered her was the fact that he hustled for a living. She had dated hustlers in the past, but they'd been small-time weed dealers who had dealt just to support their habits. Even though Jamal didn't say exactly what it was he was into, Dream could tell he was big-time. She wanted to keep seeing him, but she didn't know what her family and friends would say if they ever found out. She would talk to Keisha about her dilemma.

* * *

Stacey Matthews was both Black and Native-American. A tan-colored lady, her hair came midway down her back. She was twenty-nine years old and very appealing. Originally from Arkansas, she had been with the DEA for eight years and had spent the last two years in Charlotte. Stacey would be paired with Tony Jennings, an informant in his early thirties, from Ruffin's neighborhood.

Tony had been busted with two kilos of cocaine and had immediately become an informant to avoid a prison term. He was indebted to the agency. Whenever the DEA needed him, they would call him. He had dark, dirty skin and a scruffy beard. He had the appearance of a junkie. On the day of the buy, Mark placed a small recording device under Tony's shirt.

"Can I put this thing in my pocket?"

"No. The sounds will be muffled," Mark replied.

"Well why don't you put the thing on the broad?" Tony asked.

"Cause you're the fuckin' no-good doper who got caught bringing the poison in the neighborhood," Jeremiah said.

As much as Mark despised Jeremiah, he hated people like Tony Jennings more. They were the people pushing the dope to kids, the poor and elderly, making a once strong and mighty black race fragile and reckless. "Listen, Tony, we need you to get Ruff to sell you a couple of ounces."

"He's not going to sell me anything. You know word on the street is that I'm working with the DEA."

"That's why she's gonna be with you," Mark replied.

"What am I gonna use her for?"

"She's gonna be your girlfriend," Mark said.

Tony looked at Stacey's ass and smiled, revealing brownish-yellow teeth.

"This is only make-believe," Stacey said.

Tony was about to respond when Mark grabbed his shoulder and spun him to attention. "Tony, here's the plan: You're gonna knock on Ruff's door and tell him you're looking for something to party with."

Mark smoothed Tony's shirt out so the device wouldn't look too bulky.

* * *

At 11:30 A.M. Mark and Jeremiah arrived in the BellSouth truck and pretended to be working. At 11:46 Stacey and Tony drove up to Ruffin's house in a dark blue Cadillac Deville. Tony knocked on the door while Stacey stood two steps behind him.

Ruff opened the door wearing a green terry-cloth robe. "What in the hell are you doing at my door?" he asked.

"I need to talk to you for a second," Tony replied.

"Get away from my door. I don't want to have anything to do with you."

"Come on, Ruff, man. You know I ain't trying to make no trouble for you, man."

"Yeah, right. Mu'fuckas like you don't give a fuck who you bring down."

"Listen, man. I got money," Tony said, flashing thirteen crisp hundred-dollar bills.

"I don't give a fuck about your money."

Tony leaned toward Ruff and whispered. "Hey man, I need something to give this broad, so we can party all night."

Ruff looked at Stacey for the first time. He smiled and she smiled back. "Is that your girl?"

"Something like that. But hell, you can have her. Just let me get something to get high with."

Ruff took one more look at the beautiful Stacey and said, "I know I'm gonna probably regret fuckin' with you. Y'all come on in."

* * *

"A hustler!" Keisha said. "Why didn't you tell me this in Miami?"

"I don't know. It just slipped my mind with all the hoopla," Dream replied.

"Girl, you know you should have told me that."

"Yeah. He said he was a hustler," Dream said as she took a sip from her lemonade. She had visited Keisha because she needed someone to talk to. Jamal had called her several times since returning from Miami, but when she saw his number on the Caller ID, she let his call go to voice mail. She really wanted to see him again, though.

"Did he say what kind of hustler he was?"

Dream placed her glass on the coaster in front of her. "What do you mean?"

"I mean, there are all kinds of hustles out here. He could be doing a lot of different things like washing cars, selling clothes, promoting concerts—all these things fall in the category of hustling. My point is, hustling doesn't necessarily have to be illegal," Keisha said.

"Well, Keisha, I don't know exactly what he does for a living, but I very seriously doubt if the brother was washing cars he would be able to buy me a watch like this." Dream held her arm in the air showing off the watch.

"How much did that thing cost?"

"A little more than $3,000."

"Damn. And just think I was the one he sat beside on the plane. I should have batted my eyes a little harder," Keisha teased.

"I didn't ask him to buy me the watch."

"Yeah, I believe your boy might be big time. Are you going to go out with him?"

"Should I?"

"I can't answer that for you. All I can say is, don't let your parents find out what he's into if you do decide to go out with him."

"Oh, hell no, never that," Dream replied.

Their eyes met as Keisha took a quick sip of her drink before saying, "You really like this guy, don't you?"

Dream tried hard to contain her smile, but it materialized like moonlight on a summer night.

"Look at you, blushing. You don't have to say anything. I know what that look means. I've known you all of my life. What about DeVon?"

"What about him?"

"Girlfriend, you've got some major issues," Keisha said.

* * *

Tony and Stacey had purchased an ounce of cocaine from Ruff. Stacey had to promise she would come back to see Ruff before he would let her out of the door—and that's exactly what she did. At 12:45 P.M. the next day, Stacey, Mark, Jeremiah, and five other DEA officers raided Ruff's residence with a search warrant issued by the federal magistrate.

When they kicked the door in, Ruff shouted, "What in the hell is going on here?" He stood in the middle of the living room wearing only a pair of white Fruit of the Loom underwear.

Jeremiah grabbed Ruff by his neck. He slammed him on the floor face down before cuffing him. "Stay down or I will blow your fuckin' brains out."

"Where's your damn search warrant?" Ruff asked.

"Mr. Ruffin, I told you before I left that I was coming back to see you," Stacey said, laughing.

"Bitch, you set me up!"

"Where's the rest of the dope?" Mark asked.

Ruff turned from Stacey to Mark, and they made eye contact for the first time since the day Ruff's money had been confiscated. "You're the mu'fucka responsible for this shit?" Ruff asked.

"No, you're the motherfucker responsible. Where is the rest of the dope?" Jeremiah yelled, applying pressure on Ruff's back with his knee.

"Fuck you. Do your job," Ruff said.

Mark had radioed for the K-9 unit, and within minutes, a German Sheppard ran rampant through Ruff's house before stopping in front of the kitchen cabinet area. Mark opened the cabinet underneath the sink and recovered two wrapped packages. He held it up and showed it to Ruff, who was speechless. The life had just been sucked out of him.

* * *

Ruff sat motionless in the middle of the interrogation room with a blank look on his face, still handcuffed. This wasn't the way his book was supposed to end. He had envisioned his departure from illegal activities many times. He would be living on a Caribbean island with pretty young girls all around him fulfilling all of his sexual desires. He finally looked up at the many DEA agents surrounding him. "I can't believe this shit." he said.

"Well, believe it, Mr. Ruffin," Jeremiah taunted. "You're going down for a long-ass time."

Ruff dropped his head without responding.

"Ruff, look at me," Mark said in a friendly tone.

Ruff raised his head, and their eyes locked. "What do you want? Ain't you done enough?"

"I want to help you, man."

"I already told you, I ain't no informant."

"So you would rather do twenty-five years and be a hero for some guys who don't care anything about you?" Mark asked.

"I ain't worried 'cause I won't get no more than five years."

"Stop trying to help the son of a bitch," Jeremiah shouted with hatred enmeshed in his eyes.

"Mr. Ruffin, if you were a first-time offender, you would probably get five years, but you're are a career criminal. Try twenty-five years to life," Mark said.

"I can do the time, I've done time before. You already know this," Ruff replied.

"So you want to do twenty-five years, huh?" Mark asked.

Ruff stared at Mark for a long time before finally speaking. "You know what? I find it hard to believe you agents. You guys say that you'll help me, and then fuck me when I go in front of the judge. How can I be sure that you ain't going to fuck me? If I give you some information, I want the best possible deal I can get, meaning, I don't want to do any time."

"Mr. Ruffin, I don't lie. I'm a Christian first, DEA agent second. My dad is a Baptist minister. If I say that I am going to help you, believe me, I will do what I say."

"I don't give a fuck about you and your Christian shit. Cops lie. You mu'fuckas are just as bad as us."

Mark sighed. He hadn't anticipated Ruff being so hard. He knew it was time to take the conversation somewhere else. "Ruffin, do you remember how tough it was in prison without a woman?"

"What the hell does a woman have to do with anything?"

"We're assuming you are a normal heterosexual male," Mark said.

"I am," Ruff replied.

"You like pussy Ruff?" Jeremiah added.

"Make your point," Ruff said.

Mark walked over to a window and looked out into the city. It was a beautiful day outside as the sun shone brightly. Businesspeople paraded up and down the sidewalk and kids raced on their skateboards. "Come here, Mr. Ruffin, take one last look at the outside world, because I promise you won't get a bond if you don't help us."

"I don't need to look outside. I already know what's out there."

Jeremiah walked over, clutched the back of Ruffin's chair and slid him over to the window. "Think about it Ruff. No more pussy for twenty-five years," Jeremiah said, pointing to two women outside in very short skirts.

Ruff took a deep breath. "What do you want to know?"

"We want to know everything. Let's start by you telling us who the guy is in the white BMW and how long you've been dealing with him."

For the next hour Ruff revealed intricate details about his supplier. He told the agents about Angelo and how they had met in federal prison. He told them about Dawg and Jamal and how they were responsible for distributing drugs for Angelo on the east coast. When he was finished talking, Mark had ten pages of notes.

"Is this Dawg?" Mark held up a picture of Steven Davis.

"Yeah. How did you know?"

"Just call it investigative work."

"Do you think you can help us bust Dawg and Jamal?" Jeremiah asked.

"What are you gonna do for me?" Ruff asked.

"I appreciate what you've told us, and if this information is true, you may not have to spend a day in prison," Mark said.

"Everything I said is true, and I can probably help you bust Dawg, but Jamal is kind of leery about meeting new people. He really didn't want to deal with me. I need to get out of here quick before they learn I got busted. They ain't gonna deal with me if they find out I was picked up. That's just the rules of the street," Ruff said. His voice was low and shaky.

"I wanna infiltrate their little organization. Do you think you can help me?" Mark asked.

"Like I said before, Dawg might go for it, but I'm not too sure about Jamal. He's kind of a strange one, but we can try."

"What's Jamal last name?"

"I believe it's Stewart."

"We're gonna get you out on bond if you promise to help us," Mark said.

Ruff's eyes lit up.

ɱ CHAPTER 6 ɱ

ANGELO HAD CALLED JAMAL and told him he was sending more product for Ruff. He told Jamal that someone had broken into Ruff's house and stolen his safe. According to Ruff, he didn't have any money and he needed consignment. Four days later, Connie and Jennifer had arrived with the product and Jamal met with Ruff soon after.

Ruff smiled broadly when Jamal placed the two brick-like packages on his kitchen table. He took a knife and cut the rubber wrapping from the product and tasted it. "This is definitely some good shit."

"Angelo wouldn't have it any other way," Jamal replied.

"So what happened? I hear someone broke into your house and stole your safe," Dawg said.

Ruff grimaced and avoided eye contact with Dawg. "Yeah. One of these jealous mu'fuckas in the neighborhood probably."

"I think you should move, man. You're making money. Why the fuck do you want to keep staying in the hood? I mean, everybody sees the expensive cars and shit. You know nobody else around here can afford the shit you got."

"I know, man. I should have moved a long time ago, but I got to keep it real and be true to myself and my roots."

"The hell with keeping it real. You're old enough to know that niggas don't want to see you prosper. You need to get the hell away from here."

"Don't worry, I'm gonna be alright. As long as you guys keep me supplied with the good product," Ruff said as he scooped the two packages from the table.

"Well, you ain't got to worry about that," Jamal said, smiling.

"I almost forgot. I got someone I want you guys to meet," Ruff said.

Jamal frowned. "I ain't meeting no new niggas. That's how you go to jail."

"I've known this guy for years. I promise you it ain't gonna be no funny shit. The nigga buys a lot of product. Trust me, he's okay."

"Dawg might want to deal with him but I know I sure as hell don't," Jamal said.

"I'll deal with him if I can make me some money off him," Dawg said.

"Well, Dawg, it looks like it will be me and you," Ruff said, smiling.

* * *

Dawg and Jamal sat on the carpeted floor of Dawg's bedroom playing John Madden's Football on PlayStation 2. Jamal accused Dawg of cheating and slammed his controller down, breaking it. Jamal didn't like losing at anything, and Dawg knew it. Ever since they were kids, playing any kind of game, if Jamal felt like he couldn't win he'd quit before losing. He had to be the best at everything.

"How in the hell can I cheat on a video game? Either you're good or you ain't," Dawg said.

"Fuck it. I don't feel like playing no fuckin' kiddy-ass game anyway."

"Don't get mad at me because you can't play, man. I know it's only a kiddy game because you ain't any good at it."

"I'm good at making money. That's all I need to be good at. Hell, I haven't been out of prison two months yet, and I already have close to a $100,000."

"I hear that."

"But it ain't about what I got. It's about us and the big picture. We're grown-ass men wasting our time playing a kiddy-ass game, while the rich white boys are trying to own football teams. It's about ownership, junior."

"Where did that come from?"

"Just had to vent a little bit, realizing how much time we waste doing nothing. We have to set goals and work toward them, and get away from this lifestyle."

"So what's the goal for you?"

"Five hundred G's and I'll call it quits."

"How long do you think it's gonna take?"

"Between six and nine months. If I ain't got it by then, I'mma still call it quits."

"Then what are you going to do?"

"I'm going to invest in some real estate after I have my house built. What are you going to do with your money?"

"I'mma start my own detail shop."

"Detail shop? You can open one of those now. Shit, nigga, I thought you were going to say something like start your own record label. Your dreams are too small. You gotta start looking at the big picture. A car wash ain't shit."

"It's good for now."

Jamal smiled to himself. "All I need now is a lady."

"What happened to that broad you met down in Miami?"

"I don't know, man. She hasn't called yet, and I've tried to call her several times but she hasn't answered."

"You like her, don't you?"

"Yeah, she's cool," Jamal said, remembering the good times he and Dream had at the beach.

"Didn't you say she was a teacher?" Dawg asked.

Jamal nodded. "Yeah."

"What in the hell do you have in common with someone like her? I thought we were players. You need someone from the hood."

"Listen, junior," Jamal teased, "the one thing I've found to be true, is that every successful man needs a strong woman by his side, preferably someone without a whole bunch of issues. I mean, I don't need the drama, and I definitely ain't trying to be down in no projects taking care of nobody's kids. I need a sense of normalcy, and I think I can get that with a career woman."

"Normalcy? What kind of word is that? You think you a scholar now?" Dawg asked.

"No, I ain't no scholar, but I ain't no dumb mu'fucka either."

"Well, I hope your little teacher girlfriend calls you. I know you blew enough money on her down in Miami. I wouldn't have bought nothing until I hit the skins."

Jamal sat in silence. Dawg had made him feel stupid for splurging on Dream. For the first time since leaving Miami, he felt like he would never see her again.

* * *

It was eleven o'clock when Jamal arrived at his condo. The phone rang as soon as he opened the door. He wondered who in the hell was calling at this time of night. He knew it wasn't any of his workers because he had asked them not to call him after nine o'clock. He would conduct no business at night. "Hello," he answered.

"Is this Jamal?" the voice asked.

"Yeah, who is this?"

"This is Dream. I met you in Miami, remember?"

He smiled. Sure, he remembered. Besides making money, she was all he could think about. She was the woman he wanted to marry. He wanted her to have his children. He remembered everything about her—from her scent to that curvaceous body. However, he wouldn't let her know he was thinking about her. "So what's been up since Miami?" he asked.

"Oh, nothing. Just working as a tutor."

"I didn't think I was going to hear from you again."

"What makes you say that? I thought we had a good time together."

"Yeah, I did as well, but it's been close to two weeks and I hadn't heard from you. I thought you had forgotten about me."

"No. I was kind of busy, but I definitely didn't forget about you. I had a wonderful time."

"So have you been thinking about me?" he asked.

"Absolutely."

He walked into his bedroom with the cordless phone. "What have you been thinking about?"

"The massage you gave me and what a great cuddler you are."

Jamal's mind went back to the hotel room in Miami. He thought about Dream's smooth skin against his. Damn he missed her. He even missed her scent. "Maybe you'll invite me over for more massages," he said as he lay across his bed and rested his hand on his crotch while imagining her lying beside him.

"What are you doing tomorrow?"

"Nothing," he replied.

"Let's get together tomorrow," she said.

* * *

Jamal and Dream decided to meet at Sandford's Urban Bistro, a downtown soul food restaurant. She looked even sexier than he'd remembered. She was wearing a beige pantsuit with heels, and he could tell she had a fresh manicure and pedicure. She paid attention to details and he liked that. He wore a sweat suit and some running shoes. He felt underdressed until she complimented him on his outfit. They had good conversation and white wine by candlelight, and they listened in on a poetry reading—a first for Jamal.

When Jamal looked like he wasn't enjoying himself, Dream asked what he would like to do.

"I just like simple stuff, like renting movies and chillin' out."

"Homebody, huh?"

"I guess you can say that."

"You don't strike me as the homebody type. In Miami, you were wide open."

"Well, in Miami, I was kind of celebrating."

"What were you celebrating?"

"Freedom."

Confused, she asked, "What do you mean, freedom?"

He turned from her gaze. "Dream, you remember when I told you that I use to live in Orlando?"

"Yeah? Were you lying or something?"

He didn't want to tell her about his past, but he didn't want to go into the relationship lying. He had already told her that he got his money from the streets, but this was the real test. "Well, I didn't exactly live in Orlando, but I was incarcerated in Florida at a federal prison."

"I see," she said, and looked away.

"I'm sorry, but I thought I needed to tell you this."

"I appreciate your honesty," she replied.

When they left Sandford's, Jamal walked her to her Jeep and she gave him a small peck on his cheek. "I guess this means we won't be seeing each other again, huh?" Jamal asked.

She smiled. "Now I didn't say that, did I?"

"Am I jumping to conclusions?"

"I think so. I was just thinking that I had a good time, but I could tell you weren't enjoying yourself. Maybe the next time we can go to the movies. I'll bring my girlfriend Keisha along, you can bring your boy along, and we can double date."

"That'll be cool."

* * *

"I don't like that broad," Dawg said of Keisha after Jamal asked him to join him on a double date.

"I didn't say you had to like her. Just do it for me."

Dawg threw his hands up in disgust. "I guess I'll go, but don't expect me to be putting Keisha on a pedestal, because she's just another broad to me."

"That's fine, man, calm down."

"How should I dress?"

"Well, when me and Dream went out I wore a sweat suit and she wore some kind of pantsuit. To tell you the truth, I felt kind of underdressed, but I'm figuring that since we are just going to the movies and dinner, you can come casual."

"Good. I hope you're paying. Don't even look at me when the check comes. I'm letting you know now that I ain't paying for nothing."

"I got it. Don't worry about nothing. I'll pay for everybody," Jamal said, laughing.

* * *

After the movie, the group went to the Cheesecake Factory. After they were seated in a booth in the back of the restaurant, Jamal began to whisper jokes in Dream's ear, and they laughed and flirted.

Keisha looked incredible. She was wearing a black tube dress with heels and her black shiny hair cascaded down her shoulders beautifully. Dawg was actually glad to be sitting next to her until she said, "Will you please get your elbows off the table?"

Dawg frowned. "Who do you think you are, my mother?"

"No. Thank God that I ain't."

Jamal saw that Dawg was becoming angry and nudged him underneath the table.

"What is that suppose to mean?" Dawg asked Keisha.

"Nothing. You just don't have any table manners, that's all."

Dream made eye contact with Keisha. "Be nice, will you?" she whispered.

"I've tried to be nice by coming along on this date. You know I didn't even want to come. For one thing, he is not my type, and he has no class."

"How you gonna say I ain't got no class. You don't even know me. I mean, it ain't all about you," Dawg said.

"It ain't all about you either. At least I know not to sit with my elbows propped up on a table where food is going to be served."

"You are one ignorant bitch," Dawg said.

"Oh, no you didn't just call my friend a bitch," Dream said.

"You heard me," Dawg said.

"Come on, everybody. Calm down," Jamal said.

"Talk to your boy. He is real disrespectful," Dream said.

Jamal pulled Dawg aside. "I know you don't like Keisha, but can you just chill a minute for me?"

"I'm gonna chill, man, but don't you see that these hoochies think they're better than us?"

"Just because she told you not to sit with your elbows on the table?"

"It's the way she said it."

"Just chill until we finish eating."

* * *

Jamal and Dawg got back to the booth but the girls were gone. Jamal quickly tossed a hundred-dollar bill on the table and ran to the parking lot. As Dream was about to pull off, he stopped her. "Can I talk to you?"

Dream glanced over at Keisha who was still huffing. "I need to take Keisha home."

"Go ahead, talk to him," Keisha said.

Dream jumped out of the car and she and Jamal walked around to the rear of the vehicle to talk.

"Listen, I'm sorry about what happened in there. I really don't think we should have double-dated in the first place," Jamal said.

"Well, I know it's easy to say we shouldn't have now, but we did, and your friend Dawg is a real negative person. He didn't have to call Keisha a bitch."

"You gotta understand, me and Dawg are street guys; table manners are not on our list of priorities."

"Is that a reason to call somebody a bitch?"

"No, and I apologize for him."

"I have to take Keisha home."

"Will I see you again? I mean, I don't think our friends should have anything to do with us seeing each other again."

"I'll call you tonight, and we'll talk."

"Promise?"

Dream looked him in the eyes. "I promise."

* * *

After Jamal dropped Dawg off, he went home and showered. After he toweled off, he sat on the sofa thinking about what had happened at the restaurant. He wanted Dream to be in his life badly. He needed someone he could count on. He had Dawg, but their relationship was different. They were like brothers, and though they had love for each other, Jamal needed a woman in his life, especially since he didn't know where his mother was.

As he admired his body in the mirror, he noticed a hint of flab forming around his waist. It was nothing to be concerned about. He knew he would probably lose his toned frame eventually. While in prison he'd had a lot of time to work out. Now that he was free, he had neither the time nor the discipline to work out on a daily basis.

He began to wonder if he had done the right thing by telling Dream he was previously in prison. He figured

Dream must have told Keisha about his past. It seemed to him that Keisha had come on the date with her guard up and she'd expected something to happen. She wasn't the same friendly girl he had met on the flight to Miami. Jamal felt as if he and Dawg were being judged. He remembered when girls thought it was cool to date hustlers. Has this whole idea changed? he wondered. Had he drifted out of his league? After all, Dream was an intelligent career woman who didn't need his money.

He went into his bedroom and pulled a box of belongings from underneath his bed. The box contained letters he'd gotten while in prison and a small picture of him and his mother at an amusement park on his eighth birthday. He stared at the picture. He noticed that his mother and Dream had the same build and that they were the same complexion. He wondered if he had seen his mother in Dream, who was not the type he normally dated. He had dated mostly girls from the street, whose friends didn't know what table manners were. Jamal thought about finding someone else to date, but he wanted Dream.

* * *

Dream had called Jamal the next day, and he apologized again for how Dawg had acted. She accepted his apology but didn't want to talk about what had happened again. She'd given him directions to her apartment, but before arriving, he had stopped at Blockbuster and rented Men of Honor.

Midway through the movie they were all over each other. When Jamal finally attempted to pull Dream's underwear down, she stopped him. "Wait. Let's get in the shower first," she suggested.

While in the shower she washed his back, and she asked him to wash hers. He started, but he was unable to finish once his eyes locked in on her ass. He drove his sex inside her, and when she moaned, her voice was filled with pleasure. The water was hot and refreshing as he grinded slowly and rhythmically. Finally, he turned her towards him. She stuck her tongue in his ear before biting down on his neck. He then picked her up and carried her to the bedroom and finished being the man she knew he was.

The next day Jamal came over with The Brothers and the day after it was Love Jones. On the fourth day he brought Kings of Comedy. She laughed when she opened the door.

"What's so funny?" he asked.

"I see a pattern starting here."

"What are you talking about?"

"I mean, every day this week you've come over, brought a movie, and we've fucked. We have got to start doing something else."

"What else is there to do?"

"How about you and me go have dinner with my parents?"

"That's cool," he quickly responded, though he didn't really want to meet her parents.

m CHAPTER 7 m

JAMAL HATED THE NELSONS immediately. They were too perfect, and they talked too much. The girls he had dealt with in the past had major drama in their families, like infidelity or substance abuse. Never had he imagined sitting at the dinner table with the perfect family, passing potatoes and green beans after saying grace and answering questions about his personal life during the meal.

"So, Jamal, where did you go to school?" Mr. Nelson asked. David Nelson was a dark, slender man with salt-and-pepper hair.

"I went to Garinger High School," Jamal answered.

David Nelson frowned. "Did you attend college?"

"No. Didn't want to go," Jamal said, placing his elbows on the table.

"Why not?" Janice Nelson asked.

"'Cause I was tired of school," he answered. "Besides I'm doing okay for myself."

"What is it that you do?" Janice asked.

"He sells urban clothing. You know it's a lot of money in that," Dream lied, not knowing what else to say. "Could y'all just chill with the questions?"

Mr. Nelson stared at his daughter oddly before buttering his roll. "Well, baby, we're just trying to get to know your friend. Don't get upset."

"It's okay," Jamal said, turning to Dream.

"See, Jamal doesn't mind," Janice said before resuming the questioning. "Who are your parents and where do they work?"

Jamal wished he could say something extraordinary about his parents. He thought about lying but quickly decided not to. He didn't owe these people anything, and he surely didn't have to see them again if he didn't want to. He took a quick sip from his water before he spoke. "I haven't seen my father since I was a kid, and I lost contact with my mother about five years ago," he said softly.

Not knowing what else to say, the Nelsons remained silent for the duration of the meal.

* * *

After Jamal had taken Dream home, he drove around the city reflecting on the evening. He thought about the Nelsons and how they both seemed so phony. He really doubted that any family could be that perfect. The Nelsons made it clear that they would prefer Dream to be involved with someone who had at least attended college. He was not good enough for their daughter. He wondered whether he had made a mistake by telling the Nelsons the truth about his parents. He certainly wasn't proud of the fact that his parents had not been there for him, and he definitely regretted that he had been to prison. But it was the truth.

An hour later, Jamal found himself at Club Champagne, a strip club. He was depressed and he wanted something to drink.

Jamal sat next to the stage and was on his third Heineken. A tall light-skinned woman approached. She had a perfectly toned body and hair down to her waist. The stripper was wearing a black garter belt and G-string. She wore a tiny red football jersey with the number 69 etched in gold glitter and a pair of stilettos.

Her smile revealed beautiful white teeth. "Hello, Sexy. My name is Candy. Would you like a dance?"

Jamal sipped his drink before responding. "I didn't come here for dances. I came here to have a drink."

Candy frowned and sat on Jamal's lap before he could say anything. "Why are you so uptight? Relax, baby. I'm here to make you feel better."

Jamal looked Candy in her slightly slanted eyes and wondered if she part was Asian. "So how can you make me feel better?" he asked.

She blushed. "Well, we can start with a dance, and who knows what can happen next." Candy grabbed Jamal's arm and led him to the VIP section for more privacy.

Eight dances and two Heinekens later, Jamal asked. "How much will it cost for me to take you home?"

She laughed, running her fingers through his braids. "What about your woman?"

"What about her?" he slurred.

"Five hundred dollars and I'll go home with you."

"Are you out of your fuckin' mind?"

"That's my price, take it or leave it." Candy got up from his lap and pulled a large amount of dollar bills from her garter belt. "I know you got the money. You've already spent close to two hundred dollars on dances tonight. Plus, I have to pay the club owner if I leave early."

Jamal contemplated for a few minutes. He had never outright paid for sex before, but he was drunk and horny. "How long will it take you to get dressed?"

"Five minutes."

They stopped at the Waffle House to get some hash browns and eggs. Shortly afterwards, they arrived at Jamal's condo, and he led her to the bedroom where they quickly got undressed.

"Do you have a condom?" she asked.

"No, I don't."

Candy smiled "Don't worry, I've got one." She reached down in her purse and pulled out a small blue-and-white condom packet.

"That ain't gonna work."

Confused, she asked, "What do you mean?"

"I got too much for that little condom."

"Don't flatter yourself," she said, giggling.

"Seriously, those ain't made for brothers."

"I don't know what else to do. I guess you're gonna have to go out and get some condoms."

He stood from the bed, his head spinning. "I don't feel like going to no damn convenience store."

"Well let's get down to business with or without the condom. I need to make this money. After all, I did leave the club with your ass thinking I was gonna get paid."

Jamal pulled the covers back and stared at her coldly. "I'll fuckin' kill you if you give me a disease."

* * *

Mark studied Jamal's file carefully with Jeremiah staring over his shoulder.

"Looks like this guy just got out of prison," Jeremiah said.

"Yeah, not even three months."

"What's his address?" Jeremiah asked.

"According to the Department of Motor Vehicles, he lives on Trade Street, downtown."

"He probably lives in the high-rise where Davis led us."

"That's my guess, too," Mark said.

* * *

Ruff was on a new team now, no longer playing by the code of the streets. Theodore Ruffin, III was officially an informant, and he hated every minute of it, but he couldn't imagine doing twenty-five years in federal prison. He would be close to sixty years old when he got out.

When Dawg arrived with the product, Ruff and Mark were sitting in Ruff's living room watching The Jerry Springer Show. Ruff introduced Mark to Dawg as TJ. He assured Dawg that TJ was cool and could be trusted.

"Anybody who is a friend of Ruff's is a friend of mine," Dawg said as he shook Mark's hand.

"Good, 'cause I expect to be doing a lot of business with you guys. Ruff tells me that you boys have some good shit," Mark said.

"The best in town," Dawg replied.

"I need two kilos ASAP," Mark said.

"How much money you got?"

"I got about $50,000," Mark said.

"I ain't got shit," Ruff said.

"Don't worry, Ruff. We're gonna give you something on your face," Dawg said.

"Can we deal or what?" Mark asked.

"Hold on a second," Dawg said. He left and went outside to his car and came back with three kilos of cocaine. He gave Mark two; the other went to Ruff.

"I see this is going to work out just fine," Dawg said as he counted the money.

"You damn right it is," Mark said as he held the product to the light.

* * *

Two days had passed since Jamal's evening with Dream and her parents.

He had been thinking about his mother every since he'd left the Nelsons'. He needed to find her just to know whether she was alive. He had driven to Dawg's condominium and asked him to take a ride. Jamal shared the questions Dream's parents had asked.

"Maybe this girl ain't for you after all," Dawg said.

Jamal turned and faced him. "What do you mean?"

"I mean, if her parents are all that worried about your mother and what school you went to, it just sounds like they don't think you're good enough for their daughter."

Jamal was silent for a while. Finally he spoke. "I really need to find my mama, though. I need to know if she's alive."

"I understand, man, but you may not want to deal with your mama when you see her."

"What do you mean, man? This is my mama we're talking about."

"I know, but you remember how your mom was out there before you left? I mean, she was like a walking corpse, stealing everything she could get her hands on to buy dope."

What Dawg said had irritated Jamal, and if Dawg had been anybody else, he would have slapped him. "I know, man, but it's my mama, my only living flesh and blood that I know of." His voice full of emotion.

"I feel your pain, man, honestly I do, because you know you're like a brother to me, but some things you have to block out of your mind in order to go on. I mean, if you keep dwelling on shit you have no control over, you will fuckin' go crazy, man. Honestly, you got to let it go. Take my daughter, for instance. I love her to death, but her stupid-ass mother won't let me see her. Some days I want to see her badly, but I know I can't. So rather than fuckin' my whole day up, I have to block it out of my mind or else I will hurt some undeserving stupid mu'fucka who might come out of the mouth wrong."

Jamal had forgotten about Dawg's daughter. She had been born while Jamal was incarcerated.

They rode for the next twenty minutes in silence before Jamal turned onto Albert Street in his old neighborhood. His old house was made of wood, with gray paint peeling from the side. No grass was in the yard, just dirt. The house was abandoned, and the windows were boarded up. Jamal stopped in the driveway, and childhood memories flooded his mind.

Mary Stewart had worked two jobs to support Jamal. She had always made sure he had the best clothes and latest toys. She never missed a day cooking for her only son. Regardless of how tired she was, she always made sure her son was fed properly—until she met Lance. Lance was from D.C. He was a couple of years younger than Mary and a charmer. He introduced her to marijuana, and within a year, Mary started smoking crack and missing work. Eventually she was fired, and with no money coming in, Jamal was left to take care of himself. When he became old enough to work, he started at a legitimate job, but eventually began selling drugs after he met Angelo. There seemed to be such a big demand in the city.

"What's wrong with you, nigga?" Dawg asked, interrupting Jamal's thoughts.

"Ain't nothing wrong with me."

"Why are your eyes all red and puffy?"

Jamal wanted to share his thoughts with Dawg, but he decided not to. Even though he and Dawg were from the same neighborhood, Dawg couldn't possibly understand what he was going through. Dawg was fortunate enough to have his parents. "Let's just leave," Jamal said.

"You're the one driving."

As Jamal was about to drive away, a burgundy Nissan Maxima pulled in front of him, blocking his Expedition. A slender black man with a knotty beard jumped from the car and ran up to the driver's side of the Expedition. "Hey, Jamal?" the man said.

Jamal didn't recognize him. "Who are you?"

Dawg recognized him instantly. "That's that snitch-mu'fucka, Tony. You remember him from back in the day. He used to buy from us before you got locked up. Word on the street is, the nigga got busted and now he's an informant."

Jamal remembered him. "Yeah, what's up?"

"I got some information you might want," Tony said.

"Yeah, you got some information the police might want, too," Dawg said.

"Seriously, I need to talk to you guys," Tony pleaded.

"So talk," Jamal said.

"Hurry up and say what you gotta say," Dawg demanded. "I don't want anybody to see us with you."

Tony looked around before he spoke. "Listen, man, the DEA just got some information about you guys."

"Yeah, right," Jamal said. "I haven't been out of prison two months yet."

"I'm serious, man. They know about you. Some guy named Angelo out in California and everything, man."

Jamal and Dawg looked at each other in disbelief. They knew there was some kind of truth to Tony's story, because Tony had mentioned Angelo. "Where did you get this info from?" Jamal asked.

"It ain't a secret that I work close with some of the agents," Tony said.

"I don't get it. Why are you telling us this information then?" Dawg asked.

"Because I can help."

"How in the hell are you gonna help us?" Jamal asked.

"Because I know one of the agents pretty good, and he's willing to squash the investigation for thirty G's."

A sudden hardness appeared on Dawg's face. "Nigga, you trying to extort us?"

"I ain't trying to extort nobody. I'm simply offering my help."

"How do we know you won't fuck us around?" Jamal asked.

"I tell you what, let's get together tomorrow, and I'll let you talk to the agent on the phone for yourself," Tony said.

"How do you know he's willing to help us?" Dawg asked.

"I've done this before. I ain't new to this," Tony said.

Tony scribbled his cell phone number down on a piece of paper and handed it to Jamal.

"Call me tomorrow around noon," Tony said as he stepped away from the Expedition.

* * *

Jamal didn't know where to find his mother. She'd had one sister who supposedly lived in the Maryland area, but Mary Stewart had severed all ties with her more than twenty years ago. Jamal didn't even bother trying to look her up. He decided it really wasn't worth the hassle. He had tried to locate Lance, his mother's ex, but was unsuccessful. He remembered what Dawg said about trying to block her out of his mind. That had been easy while he was incarcerated, but since he was no longer locked up, it was more difficult. The sheer possibility of being able to find his mother gave Jamal hope. He envisioned the day he could hug her again. He anticipated it.

ɱ CHAPTER 8 ɱ

THE NEXT DAY JAMAL called Tony. They decided to meet at Starbucks coffeehouse on East Boulevard in a predominately white neighborhood. Jamal figured he wouldn't have to worry about someone seeing him in the presence of a known informant. He and Tony sat in the back of the coffeehouse near a group who was singing happy birthday. Jamal and Tony chatted while drinking cappuccino, and after Tony's second cigarette, Jamal asked him to call the agent.

Tony pulled a cell phone from his pocket and began to dial. Seconds later, "Jamal is here, and he wants to speak with you," Tony said and passed the phone to Jamal.

"Hello," the agent said.

Jamal could tell it was a white man by the dialect. "Yeah . . . What's the deal?" Jamal asked.

"You boys are in some serious shit. We've received a lot of information about you and your California connection. It's just a matter of time before we take you down."

Jamal cracked his knuckles before saying, "Tony said something about you being willing to work something out so we can get this matter resolved."

"Yeah, we can resolve this matter one of two ways: You guys can give me a piece of the pie and I'll turn my head, or you can wait and see what happens. I strongly suggest that you don't choose the latter. If my memory serves me correctly, you just got out of prison."

"Is this shit about a payoff or my background? Spit your price and let's get this over," Jamal said.

"Didn't Tony tell you what it was going to cost?"

"I want to hear it from you. Tony might be trying to tax me extra and how can I be sure you're not running game."

"Well, Jamal, that's where you're just going to have to believe me, because at this point you have nothing to lose and everything to gain. My price is $25,000."

Jamal looked at Tony. "You tried to make an extra five grand."

"Do we have a deal?" the agent asked.

"Tony will have the money in ten minutes." Jamal paid for the coffee and walked out to the car with Tony following. He removed five thousand dollars from the black leather bag then gave the bag to Tony. He felt empty when the money left his possession, but he knew it didn't compare to the emptiness of a lonely jail cell.

* * *

It was one o'clock in the afternoon when Dream called Jamal. She missed him terribly and wanted to hear his voice. When he answered the phone she invited him over.

"So you want to see me?"

"What do you think?"

"What do you want to do in the middle of the day?" he asked.

"Come cuddle me," she said.

"I'm not coming over there lying around in the middle of the day."

"Just come over. I'm sure we'll find something to do. We can cuddle later. I just want to see you. Is there a problem with me wanting to see you? I actually miss you."

"I miss you too," Jamal said. "I'll be over in fifteen minutes."

* * *

When Jamal stepped inside Dream's apartment, his eyes were immediately drawn to the picnic basket that rested on her dining room table. "What's in the basket?" he asked.

Dream smiled brightly. "Food that I put together. I figured since the weather was nice we could have a little picnic." She left the room and returned with a Frisbee and a huge blue blanket.

Jamal couldn't remember the last time he'd been on a picnic. He looked at the Frisbee under her arm. The whole idea seemed so innocent to him. "Let's do it," he said.

Thirty minutes later, they pulled into Freedom Park. The sky was clear and the sun looked like a huge orange ball. The temperature was in the mid-eighties. The park was crowded, as usual, with skaters and joggers darting up and down the sidewalk, while others played with dogs and children. Jamal and Dream sat in the grass across from the basketball court.

Dream had prepared macaroni salad, ham sandwiches, and lemonade. After they finished eating, Dream suggested they throw the Frisbee.

"Are you serious?"

"Why do you think I brought it?"

Reluctantly, he stood from the blanket, and she walked across the field with the Frisbee in her hand.

When she had reached the other side, Dream threw him the Frisbee. Jamal caught it and tossed it back. They went back and forth across the field. Surprisingly, he was actually enjoying her dashing across the grass. Her tiny athletic frame was revealed in her fitted gym shorts. After about ten minutes, he yelled, "Let's take a rest."

She approached him. "What's wrong?"

"I just ain't feeling this. Are you trying to make me soft?"

Her eyes narrowed. "Why do you say that?"

"I just feel like I could be doing a lot of other things with my time."

"Oh, am I wasting your time?"

"No, that's not what I'm saying at all."

"What are you trying to say, Jamal?"

"This ain't my thang, that's all."

She put the Frisbee under her arms and placed her hands on her hips. "Correct me if I'm wrong, but didn't you just get out of prison?"

"Yeah, but what does that have to do with anything?"

"You need to try different things, Jamal."

Before he could respond, a white couple with two children walked past. The little girl sat on the man's shoulder while the woman held the hand of the little boy.

"Jamal, that's what life is all about," Dream said, pointing at the couple.

"What? Trying to act white?"

"No, dammit. I am talking about family and children and watching them grow up. There is more to life than going back and forth to jail."

Jamal was silent. He couldn't bring himself to disagree because she was right. He had always wanted children. He felt alone since he didn't know where his mother was. It was obvious that Dream wanted to do more than date. She had clearly thought about a future with him—one that included kids. She offered him a new perspective. He didn't want to argue; he couldn't, she was right. There was more to life than going back and forth to jail and selling drugs, but that was the only life to which he had been exposed.

He tried walking away but she stepped in front of him.

"Where do you think you are going?"

"I was just thinking. You made some good points, but please try to understand that I'm used to having to watch my back and sleep with shanks under my pillow. All this Frisbee and picnic shit is something I'm going to have to get used to."

"I understand, but you're gonna have to talk to me if we are going to be together," she said with serious eyes.

He turned from her glance. "That's another thing I ain't used to, opening up to people."

"Jamal, you can be yourself around me. I know you just got out of prison, and I accept you for you. I know you're kind of hardcore, that's what attracted me to you. But what you have to understand is, you are not in prison anymore. There is nothing sissified about going to the park with your girl."

He stared at the sky. "I understand what you're saying, and you are so right," he said as he turned and faced her. "Let me see the Frisbee."

She handed him the disk and sprinted across the grass. He flung the Frisbee in her direction.

* * *

After the picnic, Dream and Jamal returned to his condo.

"Jamal, whose anklet is this?" Dream picked the gold chain up from the bedroom carpet near the nightstand.

Jamal did not want the peace of the afternoon to end. "I don't know," Jamal replied, realizing Candy must have left it.

Dream's eyebrows rose. "What do you mean, you don't know? This is your apartment, is it not?"

"I let Dawg use the apartment a couple of days ago; he must have had one of his girls here. Honestly, I don't know where the anklet came from."

"Jamal, you don't have to lie to me. I'm grown. Tell me the truth. I can deal with it." Her voice was full of emotion.

Jamal decided very quickly that the truth was something she wasn't about to get out of him. "I don't know where the anklet came from."

Dream's face became serious. "Please don't put my life in danger by sleeping around. I really like you, Jamal."

"It's not what you think, honestly."

* * *

Later that evening, Dawg came over and Dream asked him about the anklet as soon as he walked in the door.

Dawg appeared to be confused and decided to change the subject. "What happened to welcome, how are you doing, Dawg, and all that good stuff?" He smiled.

Jamal made eye contact with Dawg.

"Yeah, I had this chick over here the other night. The anklet must have come off while we were doing our thing," Dawg said, chuckling.

"Why did you bring her over here? Don't you have your own place?"

"Yeah, I got my own spot, but you know, some of these broads I refuse to let them know where I live."

"But you'll bring them over to your boy's house and mess things up for him and his girl?"

"Hell, that's what friends are for," Dawg said, smiling again.

Dream shook her head in disbelief. The story wasn't logical, but there was no way to prove things didn't happen the way Jamal and Dawg said they had.

* * *

"Me and Jamal had our first argument," Dream told Keisha over the telephone.

"What happened?"

"He said that I was trying to make him soft when we were at to the park the other day. We had a picnic and threw the Frisbee." She decided not to mention the bracelet incident.

Keisha sighed and replied, "He's ghetto, that's all. Ain't no other way around it."

"What do you mean? I know he's kind of rough around the edges, but why do you say he's ghetto."

"Ghetto is a state of mind. If you're used to doing something one particular way, and you aren't open for change, that can be looked upon as ghetto."

"I still don't understand."

"Let me give you an example."

"Okay," Dream said, knowing Keisha was going to have something outlandish to say.

"Hmm, let me think," Keisha said. "I have an aunt who pays all her bills in person instead of mailing them, or even paying them online."

"Maybe she just wants to make sure the money doesn't get lost in the mail."

"Okay, good point," Keisha said. "Can you tell me why she cashes all her checks at the local check-cashing business and refuses to use a bank, or why she borrows money from those payday-advance places, giving them ridiculous interest on the money?"

"I don't understand how your aunt relates to Jamal."

"My aunt doesn't know any better. Just like Jamal doesn't know any better for even thinking that hanging out with his girl is making him soft."

"Your analogy is way off base, but I get your point."

"Dream, just because he has money that doesn't mean that he can't be ghetto."

"I know."

"I bet Jamal doesn't have anything invested. I bet his money is under his mattress somewhere, or stuffed in a storage space, or buried in the ground."

"You think so?"

"I know so."

"Why do you say that?"

"He's ghetto. He doesn't know any better."

Dream laughed.

When Dream got off the phone with Keisha, for the first time she wondered how much money Jamal had and whether it was enough to think about investing. She decided to make it her business to find out if Jamal had thought about investing and securing his money. How would she bring it up to him? How will he react to someone asking about his money? she wondered. She didn't want to come across as a gold digger, but in the short time she had been with him, she had grown to like him, and cared about his well-being.

* * *

"Jamal, have you ever thought about investing your money?" she asked, fluffing his sofa pillows.

"Where in the hell did that question come from?"

She walked over and sat beside him on the sofa. "I was just thinking, I don't know how much money you have, and I really don't care. But like I said the other day, you need to change your thought process. I'm sure a lot of guys make money in the streets hustling, but they don't know how to secure it and make it grow."

"Can we talk about this some other time?"

"I want to talk about it now, Jamal."

"You want to talk about my money?"

"I don't want your money. I'm just trying to help."

"You know what, you need to help those kids you teach. I don't need nobody telling me what to do with money."

She looked him in his eyes before turning away. "I'm just thinking about your best interest."

"I don't need your help."

"Remember what we talked about the other day at the park, trying new things?"

"What do you have in mind?" Jamal asked, sighing.

"Basic things, like seeing an investment banker and insuring your property."

"Insuring my property? Hell I don't even have life insurance."

"You're kidding, right?"

Jamal looked her directly in the eyes. "No, I don't need it. Nothing is going to happen to me, and if it does, I can't stop fate. Besides, other than my mother, I don't have any relatives that I'm close to."

Dream didn't respond. What he said hadn't made any sense, but she knew it made perfect sense to him.

* * *

It was eight o'clock in the morning when Mark arrived at work. In the break room he poured himself a cup of coffee, and on the way out he ran into Jeremiah who was dressed in a suit. Mark figured somebody had died, since Jeremiah wasn't known for dressing up.

"Where are you going, looking all spiffy?" Mark asked.

"I got to testify in court today."

"Yeah? What trial are you testifying in?"

"The trial of the Stinson Gang."

Mark took a sip from his coffee. "Are you referring to the Stinson brothers who were operating in Piedmont Courts housing projects?"

"Yeah, those are the idiots." Jeremiah replied.

"Is it a big case?"

"Nineteen people got indicted, and we're trying twelve."

Mark hadn't been assigned to the case but remembered the investigation. The Stinson brothers had a little organization with drug connections in New York. The Feds estimated that the brothers were making close to $50,000 a week with the sales of heroin and cocaine, and they had started to sell ecstasy before they were arrested. "Well, I hope the Piedmont Court neighborhood is safer for the rest of the tenants."

"I doubt very seriously if the neighborhood is safer. Those people live like savages over there. I mean, it stinks and everybody is on crack. They walk around like living zombies."

Mark frowned. "What do you mean by those people, and how can you use an absolute like everybody over there is on crack? I resent that statement." Mark turned and walked away.

Jeremiah ran behind him and tapped his shoulder. "I'm sorry if I offended you, man. I didn't mean anything by it."

Mark faced Jeremiah nose to nose. "You know what? I already felt you were a racist bastard, and you just proved me right."

"Mark, why are we fighting about some no-good dopers, man? I thought you and me were friends. My goal is the same as yours: to get all the dopers off the street."

"Your goal is not like mine. My goal is not only to make sure the addicts get treatment, but also to see that the neighborhood is safe for the children and the elderly. These people are my neighbors, my equals. I was taught to love my neighbor as I love myself, but these are the same people who stink to you, Jeremiah," Mark said.

"Are you trying to say I'm a racist?"

"Already said it."

"You've never heard the N word from me."

"Racism goes beyond the use of the N word. Racism is your thoughts and actions and not standing up when you see something is wrong, and using terms like those people. I wouldn't be surprised if you were talking about me behind my back."

Jeremiah took a step back. "I ain't got nothing but good things to say about you . . . I mean, you are not like the people in the projects."

Mark narrowed his eyes. "You just don't get it, do you?"

ɱ CHAPTER 9 ɱ

THE CHARLOTTE MECKLENBURG school system resumed from summer break during the third week of August. Dream had mixed feelings about returning to work. She had missed the atmosphere and the playfulness of the kids, but she hadn't wanted her summer to end so soon. Spaugh Middle School had undergone some renovations during the summer. The hallways were freshly painted and new lockers had been added. Dream was disappointed when she wasn't assigned to one of the new classrooms. She was a floater; her classes were held in several different classrooms during the course of the day. The first day was somewhat hectic, meeting all the new students and moving from classroom to classroom. After school she was tired. When she got home, she found a letter from DeVon in the mailbox.

August 15, 2002

Dream, baby,

I just wanted to let you know I go up for parole in about three months, and my counselor says more than likely I will make it. I should be out around November. I definitely plan to see you again to prove to you that you and I belong together. I think deep inside your heart you know that we are made for each other. We were the ideal couple and trust me, girl, nobody is going to love you the way that I love you. I hope you find it in your heart to come by and see me. You are still on my visiting list. I don't want to take up too much more of your time.

Love always,
DeVon

DeVon hadn't gotten over Dream, and she saw a potential problem arising upon his release. She felt she needed to pay him a visit to let him know that their relationship was over.

* * *

The correctional officers at White Mountain State Prison stared at Dream strangely when she walked in the door. She was sure they'd remembered the times she had come to see DeVon, but she didn't care because this would be her last visit. She sat up front near the entrance.

It took DeVon about twenty minutes to come after he was called. He came out smiling, obviously surprised to see her. He was sporting a baldhead and had gained some weight. He looked good, but she hadn't come to give compliments. She'd come to end their relationship.

"I'm glad you came," DeVon said, smiling.

"Yeah, I thought it was the least I could do."

He frowned. "The least you could do. What do you mean?"

She took a deep breath. "DeVon, I came to tell you it's over, and don't expect us to get back together when you get out."

"What do you mean, it's over?"

"I've met somebody else."

"That's fucked up!" he yelled.

Dream gathered her thoughts before speaking. "Well, after you threw your little temper tantrum about nothing, and I got a chance to sort my feelings out, that's when Jamal came into my life."

"Are you serious?"

"Yes."

He stood from the table and she expected him to make another scene. "The hell with you." He left and never looked back.

Dream knew she had done the right thing, but she still felt sorry for DeVon; she wanted to call him back and apologize but couldn't bring herself to do it.

* * *

Two days had passed since Mark had last spoken with Jeremiah. He had purposely avoided him. He and Jeremiah were not on the same team as far as he was concerned, though they were both fighting to get drugs off the streets. It seemed to Mark that Jeremiah had a hidden agenda. It was obvious that Jeremiah didn't share the same passion for his work as Mark did. Was Jeremiah wrong for not wanting drug-infested neighborhoods safe? Was he wrong for having an opinion? Mark didn't want to work with Jeremiah any longer. He had to tell somebody about his uneasiness. He decided to go to his supervisor.

Sherman Owens was the Special Agent in Charge at the Charlotte division of the Drug Enforcement Agency. He was responsible for twenty-five agents. He was a very likable guy who had an open-door policy for his staff. Mark was very fond of him and thought of him as a fair man. At eight o'clock on a Wednesday morning, Mark tapped lightly on Sherman's door.

"Come in," Sherman said.

Mark stepped into the office. "Good morning to you, sir."

Sherman smiled. "Good morning, Mark. What brings you in here?"

"I have a problem," Mark said.

Sherman's eyebrows rose. "Please have a seat and let's talk about it."

Mark pulled his chair up to Sherman's desk. "It's Jeremiah Tolliver. I don't know what his angle is. I don't know if you remember or not, but nearly three months ago I was doing surveillance and called in to the office and asked for help. You sent Jeremiah out."

Sherman scratched his head. "Yeah, I think I remember."

"Well, he and I been working on this case together, and I don't think we can be effective working with each other."

"Why not?" Sherman asked. "You both are two of my finest agents."

"I ain't got nothing against his work, it's just that his views are a bit extreme, and I just don't want to deal with them."

"Give me an example," Sherman said.

"I don't really have a specific example. He makes little remarks that I find offensive as a black man. He uses a lot of absolutes and he plays around with the term those people, referring to people in housing projects, and he refers to them as savages."

"I see," Sherman said, nodding. "Aren't you working undercover right now?"

"Yeah, that's right."

"So you guys really don't see that much of each other anyway."

"You're right. It's just something about Jeremiah . . . I can't quite put my finger on it."

"Well, do you think it would help if I talked to him?"

"Only if you can't take him off the case, because I can see major problems down the road." Mark stood and the two men shook hands.

* * *

One day after school, Dream went to her parents' house. Janice Nelson was in the dining room having hot tea when Dream walked in. "Have a seat and I'll fix you a cup of herbal tea, baby. It's mint flavored," Janice said.

Dream turned over a cup that had been neatly placed neatly on a saucer on the table.

Janice poured the tea. "How's school?"

"School's fine. I have some smart kids this year. The only problem I have is that I haven't been assigned a homeroom. I'm a floater, and so I have to walk all day."

Janice sipped her tea. "Why don't you come over to the high school with your father and me? I'm sure he could at least make sure you get a homeroom, and I know he would like that a lot."

Dream knew what her mother said was true. She knew it would be easier to get a homeroom if she taught at the high school where her father was principal, but she didn't want to be there. She wanted to be as independent of her parents as possible. "It's really not that big of a deal. Besides, I like teaching younger children. High school kids are wild."

"Yeah, I know those little boys in high school with the raging hormones would be all over you." Janice laughed.

Dream blew her tea as the steam rose from her cup. "The middle school boys are just as bad."

"Speaking of boys, where is that Jamal boy?" Janice asked.

"He's around."

"I think I liked the jailbird better."

"You mean, DeVon."

"You call him what you want to call him, but I'm going to call him the jailbird," Janice laughed.

* * *

Jamal had stayed the night at Dream's house. They made love and he dozed off. Dream stood over him smiling, examining his body. She liked everything about him—from his braids to his tattoos and scars, to which she was especially attracted. She looked at the scar on the side of his back. It looked like a stab wound and was shaped like a diamond. The tattoos were just as appealing. On his arm was a tombstone with RIP Black written in green ink, and on his back was an image of huge knife with a tag hanging from it that read From a friend. It was evident that both of his tattoos had some kind of meaning. She had been curious about them since the first time they'd made love, and she would finally get around to asking him the story behind the wounds and tattoos.

Two hours later he rose from the bed.

"Jamal, I have a few questions to ask you, and I hope I don't offend you."

He looked at her and wiped the sleep from his eyes. "Whatever you want to know, ask. I don't have any secrets. What else do you want to know?"

She smiled slightly. "I noticed you have a couple of scars on your stomach and side. Did you get shot or something?"

"I've never been shot but I was grazed by a stray bullet when I was twelve." He had pointed to the wound on his stomach first. "Then when I was seventeen, I got stabbed right here by my mama's boyfriend."

"Are you serious?"

"Yeah, the mu'fucka was beating on my mama once when I walked in on them. I had to take it to his ass. When I turned to walk away he pulled out a pocketknife and stabbed me in the side. Opened me up pretty good. I had to get twenty-eight stitches."

"Did he go to prison?"

"Naw, I dropped the charges because he and Ma got back together."

"That's crazy."

"That's dysfunctional, but that was how things went down in my household."

Dream's eyes stretched with surprise. She could only imagine the kind of pain and suffering Jamal must have endured as a child. She wondered if he was capable of having a functional relationship, or whether she was simply fascinated with his imperfections. "What about your tattoos, what do they represent?"

"I got these while I was on the inside; the one on my back is kind of a metaphor. It represents a friend betraying me, stabbing me in the back. After I was locked up, I found out from Dawg that one of my so-called friends had started fucking my ex-girlfriend."

"Are you serious?"

"Dead serious."

"What about this RIP Black etched on the tombstone on your arm?"

"My homey, Black, got shot by some Jamaicans. It was a case of mistaken identity," Jamal said with tears forming in his eyes. "I got the tattoo kind of like honoring the nigga because we was cool. We were the same age, and we did a lot together. He was there when I got my first piece of ass, you know what I mean?"

"Not really, none of my friends have been killed. Not to say that I don't know people who've been killed, just none of my friends."

"Then consider it a blessing then."

Dream walked over and put her arms around Jamal who was silent. "I will," she finally said.

* * *

Jamal and Dream went to San Diego for Labor Day weekend. The California scenery was picturesque. The sky was Carolina blue with huge clouds, and a gentle breeze made the palm trees sway.

Horton Plaza was a huge conglomerate of shops, restaurants, and boutiques. It was like a mall without a roof. Dream and Jamal paraded through all levels of the plaza. After about an hour, Jamal had accumulated several bags, and Dream had turned down all his offers to buy clothing for her until they reached the Dolce & Gabbana store. She saw some hip-hugger jeans that she just had to have. The jeans led to a blouse and a pair of shoes. She came out of the dressing room wearing the whole ensemble. Jamal had the same look on his face that he had when they made love. "Girl, you look good enough to eat," he said when she spun around.

"I'm gonna remember that tonight," she replied. She loved looking sexy for him. She liked feeling desirable.

They left Horton Plaza and headed to Birch Aquarium, a popular tourist spot in San Diego. The aquarium had one of the most extravagant sea-life exhibitions in the country. It contained a huge kelp forest and live sharks.

"I didn't know you were a nature freak," Dream said.

"I'm just a freak," Jamal said, laughing. "Besides, I am taking your advice, I'm trying different things."

m CHAPTER 10 m

It was 6:00 A.M. when Dream woke up. Though she was on the west coast, her brain was on east coast time. She didn't know where Jamal was. She could remember when he kissed her on her forehead before leaving.

She went to the kitchen and cooked some pancakes before turning on the television. The morning news was on. She turned the television set off and decided she would take a morning run when she finished her breakfast.

She slipped into a sports bra and a pair of sweatpants. After searching her bags she discovered that she'd forgotten to pack some sweat socks. She pulled Jamal's suitcase from under the bed and looked through all of his clothes. There were no socks in sight. She discovered a small bag but it contained toiletries. She was about to give up when she noticed a leather bag pushed closer to the head of the bed. She unzipped the bag and money spilled from it. She had never seen so much money in her life. She poured it out, and it covered the entire bed. She knew it had to be at least $200,000.

Dream's heart raced. She knew people who had worked their entire lives and still didn't have this kind of money, but Jamal had it right at his fingertips. She put the money back in the bag as quickly as possible, trying to decide what to do next. She wanted to call Keisha. She wanted to call Jamal's cell phone and ask him what in the hell was going on. She didn't know what to think.

When Jamal got back to the condo, Dream was gone, and he was actually glad because he had business to take care of. Since she wasn't there, she wouldn't know he'd returned. He needed to recount his money, and he knew if she was in the room, he couldn't possibly explain why he had $230,000 with him. Jamal quickly counted the money before leaving to meet with Angelo. They put the girls on the plane and when he came back Dream still hadn't returned. When she finally did get back she looked at him strangely. "What's up, baby?" he asked.

"Hey, honey," she replied dryly.

"Walking the beach, huh?"

"I guess you can say that." She sat on the sofa.

"I already said it. Didn't you hear me?"

"Ha. You got jokes."

"Who pissed in your cornflakes?" he asked.

She stood and walked over to the sliding doors and stared at the cirrus clouds. "Nobody pissed in my cornflakes. I'm just not in the joking mood."

"Something is bothering you. You don't have to tell me, but I know."

She turned toward him. "Jamal, did you bring me out here on some kind of drug deal?"

He was surprised by her question. "Where did that come from?"

"Just answer the question."

His thoughts ran rampant as he wondered what made her ask the question. Then he remembered the bag that he had left with the money in it. He figured she must have seen it.

"Kind of, but it's not what you think."

"What do you think I'm thinking?"

He walked over to the kitchen sink and got a glass of water. "You probably think that we're going to be traveling with drugs on the way back home."

"That's exactly what I think. I can't believe you would put my life in danger."

He put his glass down. "Hell no, baby. I wouldn't do anything like that," he said as he walked over and attempted to put his arm around her. She pushed his chest. "Get off me." She slid through the double doors.

* * *

Dream strolled the beach aimlessly. She took the time to gather her thoughts. She had officially broken it off with DeVon for a man she thought had her best interests in mind. Had her vision become clouded? Had she let material things interfere with her judgment? She thought about her parents and what they would think if they knew Jamal had put her life in danger. "Drug dealers are low-lives," her father would say. Never would she have believed Jamal would put her life in jeopardy. She wasn't so naïve that she didn't know if he were caught with drugs, she would go to jail as well.

When she got back to the condo Jamal was sitting on the sofa watching music videos. "Why, Jamal?" she asked.

"Why what?"

"Why did you put me at risk?"

"Ain't no risk. All I did was bring my girl out here for a good time."

"And a drug deal!" she yelled

He licked his dry lips. "You see, Ms. Dream, I didn't come from a Cosby Show-ass household like you did. My friends didn't go to college; they went to reform schools, penitentiaries, and halfway houses. I don't even know where my parents are."

"Oh, nigga, don't go blaming nobody 'cause you chose to do what you do."

He stepped to her and placed his hand underneath her chin. "Listen, baby, I don't want to argue with you. I would never put your life in danger. Please believe me." Jamal's voice was sincere.

She put her head on his shoulder, and he pecked her jaw.

* * *

On the flight back to Charlotte, the mood was pleasant. Jamal and Dream joked, and though it still bothered Dream that he would bring her to California for a drug deal, she didn't bring it up. Instead she told him how much she enjoyed the trip.

"The next time we go to San Diego, we'll drive up to L.A. and go to Hollywood," Jamal said.

"Only if you don't take me shopping. You're gonna turn me into a shopaholic like you."

"I want to take you to the Mall of America in Minneapolis. It's supposed to be the largest mall in the country."

"Now, I got to take you up on that offer. I have heard so much about that place. I heard it has an amusement park and a wedding chapel in it," she replied.

"I haven't been there in about six years, but it's definitely a landmark."

* * *

After Jamal and Dream loaded their suitcases in his Expedition, he played an India Arie CD. He really wanted to listen to some hip-hop but figured he would put in something somewhat mellow. Dream was grooving to India's sultry voice, and he was happy because the tension was absent. Then his cell phone rang. "Hello," he answered.

"Hello, Jamal," a female's voice blurted out loudly. Dream turned the stereo down and turned her attention to Jamal's conversation.

"Who is this?" Jamal asked.

"This is Candy. We met at Club Champagne."

Jamal glanced at Dream who was looking him directly in the eye. He knew she had heard the loud woman's voice because her expression was no longer pleasant. They were approaching an intersection, and Jamal stopped at a green traffic light. Several cars blew their horns.

"Jamal, the light is green." Dream said.

"Listen, I'll call you back. I gotta go now." He terminated the call and stepped on the gas pedal.

"Who in the hell was that?" Dream asked.

"It's not what you think."

"Somehow I knew you were going to say that. Everything is not what I think. What are you, some kind of magician or something? Nothing is ever as it appears with you."

He frowned. "You know what? I ain't got to explain shit to you. In fact, I ain't gonna explain shit to you."

"That's fine with me," she said as she folded her arms across her chest.

They were silent the rest of the way to her house. When they arrived Jamal didn't offer to help her with her bags, and Dream didn't ask.

* * *

Jamal had made seventy thousand dollars in two weeks. He had traded his Ford Expedition in for a new, white E-Class Mercedes Benz, and had put twenty-inch chrome rims on it. He bought himself a platinum Rolex and some custom suits with matching alligator shoes. He felt it was time for him to start acting like a rich man.

He hadn't spoken with Dream in a couple of weeks and he missed her. He loved going over to her place, watching movies and giving her massages. He wanted to apologize to her, but he just couldn't bring himself to do it. He turned to shopping and alcohol to compensate for his loneliness. He started buying liquor — Hennessy with Coke was his favorite — and he hung out at the strip clubs. He had become a regular at Club Champagne. He often paid to have sex with Candy, and most of the girls in the club knew his name. One day he and Dawg were together and Jamal suggested going to the club.

"You done turned into a booty-club bandit," Dawg said.

"What do you mean?" Jamal asked.

"Hell, you in the strip clubs at least five nights out of the week, man. You need to call your girl back and apologize."

"Apologize for what?"

"For dissing her for one of them trifling hoes from the strip club."

Jamal realized Dawg was right. He had a real woman for the first time in his life, and he didn't appreciate her. All she wanted was some respect. He wanted to apologize, he just didn't know how.

* * *

Mert's Heart and Soul restaurant was located downtown on College Street. It specialized in soul food dishes, with recipes from the low country, a region in the southern part of South Carolina around Charleston. Mert's was an African American-owned restaurant, yet most of the patrons where white. Keisha and Dream decided to get together for dinner since they hadn't seen each other much since school had started. The two women greeted each other with a hug.

The waiter appeared and Dream ordered the blackened pork chops while Keisha had baked chicken with rice. They both requested lemonade.

After the food came they chatted about men — their favorite subject. Keisha told Dream about a partner in her accounting firm who had been pursuing her relentlessly; she said he had sent her roses every day for two weeks and had taken her to lunch for the past couple of days.

"How does he look?" Dream asked.

"Fine as hell."

"Well, what's the problem? Why won't you give the guy a chance?"

"He's married."

"That's too bad," Dream said, shoveling a forkful of pork chop into her mouth.

"Yeah, can you imagine me trusting this man after he shows me that he runs around on his wife?" Keisha asked.

"I know, right?"

Keisha took a quick sip from her glass before speaking. "So, what's been up with you and Jamal?"

"Jamal has some serious issues, and I don't know if I'm going to be able to deal with them."

Keisha sat her glass down. "What kind of issues are you talking about? I mean, I know he hustles, but what else?"

"For one thing, Jamal hasn't seen his mother in years. I haven't talked to him about it, but I can tell it's bothering him. Besides that, he's seeing someone else."

"How do you know this?" Keisha asked curiously.

"When we returned from California, his cell phone rang. When he answered, I heard a woman's voice on the other end saying that she'd met him at Club Champagne. I think she's a stripper."

"Did you ask him about about it?"

"Yeah, and he gave me the typical cheating-nigga answer, it's not what you think, but I know it's exactly what I think because a few months ago, I found a gold anklet at his apartment."

"How did he explain that?"

"Dawg claims to have borrowed the apartment. He went on to say that one of his hoochies left the anklet."

"That actually sounds like something Dawg would do, though. But tell me, why hasn't Jamal seen his mother?"

"I don't know. Jamal is so secretive about his personal life, I didn't bother asking him."

"Well, if you decide you're gonna see him again, I can probably get a private investigator that I know to track his mom down."

"I'll pass the information along if I ever see him again."

* * *

When Dream got home that night she lit several candles in the bathroom and took a long, hot bubble bath. The candles were therapeutic. She sat in the water thinking about Jamal and her past relationships. It seemed as though she always got the ones with the major issues. She didn't regret any of the thugs she had dated in the past. She had a lot of fun with them. But with the fun came the baggage. The babies' mamas, the failure to pay child support, and more recently with DeVon, the prison term. Was all the drama worth it? she asked herself. The water had gotten cold and she added more hot water.

She'd had more fun with Jamal, in such a short time, than with any other boyfriend. She had never met anyone quite as confident as Jamal. He knew how to live, and he made her very happy. Now he was giving someone else back massages and watching movies at someone else's house. She couldn't stand the thought of that.

When she got out of the bathtub, her skin was wrinkled and pale. Dream quickly dried off and applied lotion to her body. Within minutes she was in the bed and under the covers naked. She liked feeling free. She liked the way the covers felt against her skin. She wished Jamal was there lying next to her. She became sad thinking about him, and she felt a tear trickle down her cheek before she decided to dial his cell phone. She blocked her number so he couldn't see it on the Caller ID.

He picked up on the first ring. "Hello."

She didn't say anything; she just wanted to hear his voice.

"Hello. Hello. Hello. Who the hell is playing games?" he said before hanging up.

Her body had begun to shiver. God she missed him. She slowly replaced the receiver and cried herself to sleep.

* * *

"The kingdom of heaven is like a pearl merchant on the lookout for choice pearls. When the merchant discovered a

pearl of great value, he sold everything to buy the pearl,"
Pastor Tommy Stevenson said to his congregation.

Mark sat in the back of the sanctuary looking straight
ahead and focusing on the sermon. He had always enjoyed
sermons about the kingdom of heaven ever since he was a
boy.

Mt. Prospect was a small non-denominational church
with a mixed congregation. The church wasn't anything like
his father's back in Dallas. Where his father's church body
was predominately African-American, Mt. Prospect was
about twenty percent African-American; Caucasians,
Asians, Hispanics, and West Indians also attended. His
father's church collected about a $100,000 in tithes and
offerings a week. Mt. Prospect collected about that much in
a year.

Mark always enjoyed the sermons. Pastor Stevenson was
a short white man in his early forties, with a receding
hairline and a pure heart, and he worked diligently for the
Lord. After service he would always stand at the exit and
shake hands with everyone in the sanctuary.

"The kingdom of heaven is like a treasure that a man
discovered hidden in a field. In his excitement, he hid it
again and then everything he owned and bought it," Pastor
Stevenson said as he paced in front of the pulpit. "How
many of you in here are willing to sell everything you own
to get to heaven? Turn to your neighbor and say that you'll
give up everything you own to go to heaven."

A short, round-faced white woman grabbed Mark by the
arm and repeated the pastor's words verbatim.

"The kingdom of heaven is like a fishing net that is
thrown into the water to gather fish of every kind. When the
net is full, fishermen drag it onto the shore, sit down, sort
the good fish into crates, and throw the bad ones away."
Pastor Stevenson screamed and paced. His face was beet-
red when he finished.

When the service was over, Pastor Stevenson gave Mark a firm handshake. "Pray always," he whispered to Mark.

When Mark got home he took off his church clothes and put on a Nike sweat suit and a pair of running shoes. He reflected on what the pastor had said about the good fish being separated from the bad ones. Mark sometimes felt guilty about having people arrested, especially after working undercover. He would often get close to some of the people he was trying to bring down. He would constantly tell himself he was doing the right thing. He was a good fish and the bad ones had to be separated.

* * *

Later that evening, Mark was watching the Atlanta Falcons play against the San Francisco 49ers when his cell phone rang. "What's up?" Mark said.

"The ship has arrived," Dawg said excitedly.

"Oh yeah?"

"Yeah, man. What are you looking to get this time?"

"Nothing right now. I have a little bit left from the last time," Mark lied. The truth was he hadn't gotten any funds from the agency to buy more product.

"A'ight, playboy, I was just checking on you," Dawg said before hanging up.

Mark had made several purchases from Dawg, and it was just a matter of time before he had him arrested. He wanted to make another purchase to make his grand jury presentation more impressive, but he knew his agency wouldn't allow him to use but so much funds to make drug buys. He decided he would call Dawg the next day and record his conversation for more evidence.

* * *

Mark called Dawg the following day and inquired about some product, but Dawg was smart enough not to say anything over the phone. They decided to meet at Club Champagne.

The girl at the door was a tall, light woman with long hair. She wore fluorescent green spandex and six-inch heels. Her smile was radiant. "Ten dollars please," she said.

Mark pulled out a roll of money and gave her a ten-dollar bill. He placed an extra five dollars in her tip glass before walking in. Black women of all complexions and sizes walked around revealing their half-naked bodies. Loud rap music blared in the background. Mark didn't recognize the artist who was degrading his baby's mother over the drumbeat. He spotted Dawg sitting at a table in the back with an attractive woman who had hazel contacts and a bad weave.

"What's up, TJ?" Dawg said, slapping hands with Mark.

Mark sat directly across the table.

Weavehead stood. "I got to go, baby," she said, and kissed Dawg on his cheek.

"If you see any girls in here you want, just let me know and I'll see to it that they treat you right," Dawg said to Mark.

"I didn't come here for that. I came to talk business," Mark said.

"I can understand," Dawg said as he took a sip from his Corona. "I tell you what, I'm all ears."

"Why don't we take this outside? I have a terrible headache and this music isn't helping," Mark said.

The night air was frigid. Dawg and Mark made their way to Dawg's car and got inside before starting their conversation. "What's up?" Dawg asked.

Mark started the recording device in his pocket. "You said the ship came in yesterday, I just wanted to know what was available."

"Oh, we got plenty, man, and it's the best shit we've had in a long time."

Mark met his gaze. "Good 'cause I should be finished with the last package you sold me soon."

"Well, you know how to get in touch. Is there anything else?"

"No, that's all I wanted to talk about." He stopped the recorder.

When Mark was about to step out of the car Dawg called out to him, "Oh yeah, I forgot to tell you, we got some new connections."

Mark was surprised to hear this. He thought for sure Jamal and Dawg were still getting the product from California. "What, you got a different supplier?"

"Oh no, we got the same supplier. I'm talking about some connections with the Feds."

"What do you mean?"

"I mean, we paying the DEA off now. So if you get in any kind of trouble, just let me know."

Mark wondered what he was talking about. He knew Dawg couldn't possibly be paying the DEA off because he was the agent in charge of the investigation. "I'll make sure I do that," he said as he got out of the car.

m   CHAPTER 11   m

JAMAL HAD GOTTEN TO know Candy. She was twenty-two and had come to Charlotte two years earlier to attend college. When money had gotten tight she began to strip for extra income. During her second year of school she became pregnant and subsequently had to drop out and dance full time to support her child. When money was real tight she offered sexual services to some of her customers. But now she was having sex just to stay ahead. Jamal loved having sex with Candy. There was no limits to their adventures. They had oral sex, positional sex, and they even made videos. Candy had even agreed to a ménage a trois if they could find another girl.

Jamal arrived at Candy's apartment at 7:30, and at 8:00 they were at Red Lobster for dinner. After some jumbo shrimp and red wine, Candy performed oral sex on Jamal while he wheeled his Mercedes. The car swerved and she rose. "Why did you stop?" Jamal asked.

Candy smiled. "Did it feel good?"

"Hell, yeah."

"I know it must have felt good because you were about to kill us both."

Jamal pointed to his stiff penis. "Go ahead, finish the job."

Candy held her hand out. "I need some money."

"What are you, crazy? Why must this always be about money with you and me?"

"Because it's like that. Nigga; I don't love you. I love what you can do for me."

Jamal stopped the car, then reached over Candy's lap and opened the door. "Get out and walk."

"I ain't walking nowhere. You picked me up and you're going to take me home."

Jamal grabbed Candy by the neck and began to squeeze until her face turned red. Then he shoved her and caused her head to hit the passenger window. "Get out before I hurt you."

Candy opened the door and jumped out the car. "Fuck you, Jamal," she said as she walked away.

* * *

Dream was surprised when she opened her door and saw Jamal with a Love and Basketball DVD in his hand.
"Can I come in?" he asked.
"It's a free country."
"But you're in control of your apartment."
She stepped aside as he walked in and seated himself on the ottoman. She sat on her sofa Indian-style, wearing a Carolina Panthers football jersey and some blue gym shorts.
Jamal didn't know what to say. He had never been good at apologies, and he really didn't know where to begin. "So, what's been up?"
Dream shrugged. "Nothing much. Going to work every day and coming back to the house."
Their eyes met before Jamal turned his gaze to some pictures on the end table. He could tell she had been hurt, and this made expressing himself more difficult. "Listen, I don't really know what to say except I'm sorry about the way I acted, and I want you to know it really wasn't what you thought it was . . . I mean, there was a woman on the phone, but it wasn't like I was seeing her or anything. I met her in the club but we did nothing more than talk as she danced."
He had said everything she wanted to hear, and she really did believe him. "Jamal, I really hope you didn't expect to just come to my door with a video and everything would be

as it was before. It doesn't work that way. I mean, I really do miss you. In fact, I miss you so much I cried myself to sleep a couple of times. I just can't let you walk in and out of my life as you please."

He hadn't anticipated her saying this. "Did your ex-boyfriend get out?"

She was confused by what he had asked. "What in the hell does that have to do with anything?" she asked.

"I just want to know why you're treating me like this."

Dream became annoyed. She was the victim, but he was saying she was treating him badly. She stood from the sofa and walked over to the door. "Please leave, Jamal."

He got up from the ottoman and slowly walked past her into the hallway. When she tried to close the door, he grabbed it and stepped back inside and placed his hand behind her neck. She struggled before he forced his lips to meet her wet mouth. "I love you, Dream," he said as he left the apartment.

Ten minutes after he had gone, Dream sat and stared blankly at the Discovery channel. Jamal was the man she loved, but at the same time she hated him. For the rest of the day she tried hard not to think about him. By the end of the evening, she found herself dialing his cell phone number. When he answered, she asked him to come over.

* * *

Dream was awake before dawn, Jamal was still asleep. She smiled as she stared at his muscular body. She was glad he was back with her. Back where he belongs, right back with Mama, she thought. She hadn't realized how much she'd missed him. She had grown to love him in just a short period of time. She loved everything about him—his caress, the anticipation of his sex. She liked his chest against her breasts and the salty taste of his mouth. She smiled again before reaching down and shaking him. "Jamal, wake up. Would you like me to cook you something to eat?"

Jamal rose from the bed. "Naw, that's okay. I don't want you to go out of your way for me."

She leaned to him and kissed him on the forehead. "Nothing is too good for you. You're back where you belong."

"Is that right?"

"That's right."

"What did you see in that stripper in the first place?"

Jamal sighed. "I don't know. I was just passing time at the strip joint relieving frustration."

"I could relieve your frustrations."

"Yeah?"

Dream started dancing teasingly and seductively. She then took off the T-shirt she was wearing, exposing her perfect breasts. "Hell, if you pay me, I'll fulfill all your fantasies."

"Really?" Jamal asked.

"If the price is right," she teased.

Jamal's eyebrow's rose. "What about a threesome?"

"A threesome?"

"Yeah, me and you and another woman."

"Hell, no!" Dream frowned. "What do you think I am, some floozy?"

"Well, you're the one that said if the price was right."

Dream folded her arms across her chest. "Jamal, I was only joking. I guess I ain't enough woman for you."

Jamal pulled her closer. "Baby, you know it ain't even like that. I don't need to have a threesome. It's just a fantasy."

"Believe me, we won't go there," she said adamantly.

* * *

In early October, maple leaves in beautiful shades of orange, yellow, and red decorated the neighborhood lawns.

Dream loved the fall. It was her favorite season. She liked teaching during the fall because of all the activities that went on at the school, especially the football games and dances. The feeling she got was nostalgic, and it made her reminisce about her high school days, which was another reason she liked teaching.

Dream pushed a cart containing an overhead projector and several workbooks. She had just left her third-period World history class, and she was headed to her U.S. history class, which was located on the third floor of the school. She got in the crowded elevator and as the door was closing the intercom sounded. "Dream Nelson please report to the office."

A short, burly white boy with red hair reiterated what the intercom had just said. "Ms. Nelson, they called for you to come to the office."

"I heard. Thank you very much."

He smiled. "I sure hope you ain't in no trouble, 'cause whenever they call me to the office, I'm always in some kind of trouble," he said.

"I think I'll be okay. I appreciate your concern," Dream said before pulling the cart off the elevator and moving in the direction of the office.

When she got there, the school secretary presented Dream with some balloons and twelve yellow roses. The card read: THANKS FOR BEING YOU. LOVE, JAMAL.

"Looks like someone cares a whole lot about you," the secretary said.

"Yeah, I'm fortunate to have a good boyfriend." Dream smiled.

"Those are high-dollar roses," the secretary said in a very country accent. "I sure wish my husband would send me something every now and then to let me know he appreciates me."

Dream didn't respond. She just inhaled the scent of the roses and relished the moment.

* * *

When the school day was over, Dream called Jamal and immediately thanked him.

"Listen, I'm tired of you thanking me for everything. You're my woman, and I'm supposed to do little things like that for you."

"Yeah, but sometimes I feel like you go too far."

"Since when can't a man buy his woman some flowers?"

"Silly, you know what I mean. What do you have planned for today?"

"Actually I'm supposed to meet this Nigerian attorney today, and he's supposed to show me this loft that he has for rent."

"Can I come along?"

"I was going to ask you to."

* * *

The Arlington was the tallest high-rise complex in downtown Charlotte. It housed about five hundred tenants. Guests were required to check in with security before seeing a resident.

When Jamal and Dream arrived at the security desk, they paged Nigel Ojukwu and he invited them up.

"I'm Jamal, and this is my girlfriend, Dream," Jamal said after they entered the apartment.

Nigel was a tall man with a very dark complexion and a large head. He was wearing a gray, pinstriped Armani suit and a crisp white shirt. Jamal shook his hand, and Nigel showed them around the loft. The bedrooms were spacious, and the view was even better than the one Jamal had at the place Dawg had rented for him. It had two full bathrooms, and everything was in excellent condition.

"I love this place," Dream said as she looked onto the huge terrace.

"It's nice, except I don't really like the brown carpet," Jamal said.

"It's one of the best, if not the best high-rise building in the city," Nigel said.

"How much are you asking?" Jamal asked.

"I just want the mortgage, three thousand a month."

"What about some new carpet?" Jamal asked.

"I'll have some put in if you get the apartment. Now what was it you said you did for a living?" Nigel asked curiously.

"I'm a concert promoter," Jamal answered quickly.

Nigel looked at Jamal then glanced over at Dream. "I just got one main rule: No drugs in my apartment."

Jamal's face became curious. He wondered whether he had a look on his face that said he was a drug dealer. He knew the guy was a lawyer, and he wondered if Nigel had done a background check on him. "Mr. Ojukwu, why did you put so much emphasis on that statement?"

"Oh, no reason, I just know how some of you concert promoters are, having those wild parties with the stars and all." Nigel placed his arm around Jamal's shoulder. "It's a joke, man. Don't be so uptight." He laughed.

Jamal smiled weakly while looking at Nigel suspiciously.

* * *

Rain fell lightly when Jamal and Dream stepped out of the lobby of the building.

"Did you really like it?" Jamal asked Dream after they were in the car.

"I loved it, but I don't really see the logic in paying that much money for something that's never gonna be yours. Have you ever thought about buying a house?"

He opened the glove compartment, pulled out some papers, and passed them to her before firing up the ignition. "This is gonna be our future home."

The papers were the house plans Dawg had sent him during the five years of his incarceration. The plan showed a two-story, two-bedroom home with a huge children's activity room and a formal dining room; a three-car garage, a home theater, and his-and-her bathrooms attached to the master bedroom.

"I like it. When are you gonna have it built?"

Jamal pulled his Mercedes through the exit gates. "I don't know. Right now, it's gonna be hard to put it in my name because I don't have a job, which is one reason I rent."

"Jamal, have you ever thought about taking some of the money you make and going legitimate?"

He glanced over before wheeling the Benz carefully onto the slick street. "I have, but honestly, I don't know what to do. I've been dealing so long."

Dream felt sorry for him. She knew he was smart. She knew if he applied himself to something legitimate, it could very well work out for him. But what could he do? she wondered. He had no marketable skills.

* * *

It was 5:00 A.M. when Jamal received a call from Angelo. When he saw the number on the Caller ID, Jamal immediately answered the phone. He knew it had to be important for Angelo to call so early. "I got bad news," Angelo said.

"What happened?" Jamal asked as he sat up in his bed.

"The girls got busted."

"How did this happen?"

"Connie called me about an hour ago. She said the DEA agents bum-rushed them as soon as they checked their luggage last night."

"Can't nothing good come out of that," Jamal said as he stood and began to pace with the cordless telephone to his ear.

"Make sure you tell Ruff. Connie said she ain't told the cops shit, but she don't know about Jennifer. As soon as they took them to the jail they separated them."

"Well, what do you think she'll say?" Jamal asked.

"To be honest with you, Jamal, I don't know," Angelo said.

Jamal appreciated Angelo's honesty, but that wasn't what he wanted to hear. "Well, if you hear anything else, give me a call," Jamal said before hanging up.

* * *

Mark arrived at his office shortly before eight o'clock. He had three messages on his phone—two from his father urging him to call home because he hadn't heard from him in a while and one from Agent Don Gonzales of San Diego.

He had waited until noon before calling Gonzales back.

"Don Gonzales speaking."

"Good morning to you, sir. My name is Mark Pratt, a DEA agent with the Charlotte, North Carolina Division. I received a message from you stating that you had some info that might be helpful to me."

"Yeah. We made a bust at the airport yesterday. Two young, African-American women headed in your direction. They had four kilos of cocaine on them. One of them cooperated immediately. She said she was heading to Charlotte to meet a guy by the name of Jamal Stewart. When I called, I initially got another agent who said you were investigating this Stewart fella."

"Yeah, that's right; I've been watching him and his little organization for a few months now. In fact I infiltrated, and I'm now hanging out with Jamal's right-hand man."

"Well, this girl says she is willing to do anything to save her skin. If you'd like, I can have two agents fly both of them out to you to see if you can get some statements from them."

"I would like that very much."

m CHAPTER 12 m

JENNIFER PHILLIPS WAS A very pretty girl with light skin and delicate features; she looked to be in her early twenties. She was kind of shy and reserved at first, and she kept biting her fingernails in the interrogation room. She just looked at the floor while Mark, Jeremiah, and U.S. Attorney David Ricardo asked her questions.

David Ricardo's friends considered him a nice man, but he was well known for his bulldog questioning tactics. "When did you first start coming to Charlotte?" David asked.

"I started coming around the second week of June," she answered without looking at him.

"How much cocaine did you bring on your first trip?"

"I brought two kilos and Connie brought two."

"Do you know this man?" David asked as he held up a picture.

"No." She shook her head and looked up briefly at David.

"What about this man?" Mark asked.

"Yeah, that's Dawg,"

"What about this man?" David asked.

"Jamal," she said.

Mark smiled at David. They were definitely onto something. They questioned Jennifer for the next two hours, and she told them everything she could think of about Jamal, Dawg, and Angelo. When they were finished questioning her, Jennifer looked Mark in the eye for the first time. "Am I gonna get out to see my babies?"

Mark was caught off guard by the question. This was the part of his job he didn't like. He hated seeing people separated from their children, especially young women. Looking at her, Mark didn't expect her to have babies, but he should have known. Usually the women with the children were the first to cooperate. "I don't know, but I certainly will make a recommendation that you receive a bond since you have been helpful to us."

"I see," she said, dropping her head again.

* * *

When Connie entered the interrogation room, she seemed to be a lot more relaxed than Jennifer. Mark saw experience in her eyes. She even asked Jeremiah for one of his cigarettes.

"You didn't come in here to smoke, you came to answer questions," Jeremiah said.

Connie nodded. "What do you want to know?"

David held up a picture of Dawg. "Do you know this guy?"

She shook her head. "No."

Next he held up a picture of Jamal. "What about this man?"

"No," she answered.

"How is it that your friend knows these guys and you don't?" Mark asked.

"She got her people that she deals with and I got my people," she answered.

David looked her in the eye. "Well, do you want to tell us about your people?"

"So what are you going to do for me?" Connie asked.

"It all depends on the information you have. If you give us something helpful, we can definitely get you a lighter sentence, or perhaps let you go."

"Really," she said, nodding.

"Tolliver give her a cigarette," David ordered.

Jeremiah pulled one of his Camel Lights from his pocket, lit it, gave it to her, and placed a small paper cup on the table to be used as an ashtray.

"Let's talk now," David said. "Do you wanna help yourself or not?"

Connie took a drag from the cigarette. "I want to help."

Jeremiah sat beside her. He held a yellow legal pad. "Tell us about your people. Who are they?"

For an hour and a half Connie filled them in about a man named Tyrone Anderson, who she said lived on Seventh Street. She said that she had brought multiple kilos of cocaine to him over a six-month period. According to Connie, she had made more than sixteen deliveries.

"Can you get him on the phone?" Mark asked.

Connie stared at him avoiding his eyes. "Probably not . . . I mean, he knows I've been busted now."

"What's his address?" David asked.

"It's 2892 Seventh Street."

Mark looked at her suspiciously. "Are you sure?"

Connie flicked ashes in the small cup. "I'm certain."

"What about Angelo?" Mark said.

"What about him?" Connie replied.

"Is he your connection?"

Connie rolled her eyes and took another drag from her cigarette. "Did I say he was my connection?"

Mark looked her straight in her eyes. "Why are you being difficult?"

"I've told you my story. Can I go now?"

After the Marshals transported Connie to the county jail, Mark, David and Jeremiah accessed the information. Mark and Jeremiah both came to the conclusion that Jennifer had valid information and that Connie was lying. David was adamant about seeing if there was any substance to Connie's story. "We've got to check out all information received. I'm going to the federal magistrate to get a search warrant to check out this Tyrone Anderson guy on Seventh Street.

* * *

At eight o'clock the next morning. Mark, Jeremiah, and ten other DEA agents kicked in the door at 2892 Seventh Street.

"What the hell is going on here?" a lady asked, looking at the DEA officers in her living room.

"We got a search warrant for this residence. Does a Mr. Tyrone Anderson live here?"

"Yeah, he lives here," the woman replied before a husky, full-bearded black man appeared. "I'm Tyrone, What do you want?"

"We've received word that you are involved in the drug trafficking and we have a search warrant for this house," Mark said.

Jeremiah cuffed Tyrone and ordered him to sit on the sofa. "I ain't no drug dealer. I'm a hotel manager at the Days Inn."

"My husband might be a lot of things, but he is definitely not a drug dealer," the woman said.

"This is procedure. We have to search, but if we don't find any evidence of wrongdoings we'll leave," Mark said.

They searched the house for more than an hour, finding no evidence of drugs or drug paraphernalia. Finally, in the bedroom closet, Jeremiah found a matchbook with Connie's name and a phone number written on it. He quickly presented it to Tyrone. "How do you know this lady?"

Tyrone looked at the matchbook and trembled. "I met her at the hotel."

"Why did you get her number, and how did she know where you lived?" Jeremiah asked.

Tyrone looked at Jeremiah then turned to his wife who was looking on curiously.

"Answer the man," she said.

"I ain't a drug dealer. I done told you I work hard every day to provide for my family. You guys should have checked my criminal record before you came busting up in my house. I ain't never even had a jaywalking ticket in my life," Tyrone screamed, in tears.

"Give us an answer. At this point we don't have anything to hold you for, but we can detain you until we find further information," Mark lied.

Tyrone turned from his wife. "Like I said, I know her but it's not what you think. I just met her. She and her friend come to the hotel every week from California; I believe that's where she said she was from. I met her at the hotel bar one night and we kind of hit it off. She's a real nice girl," Tyrone felt foolish as his wife looked on coldly.

"How did she know where you lived?" Mark asked.

Tyrone closed his eyes and took a deep breath. "I brought her here while my wife was at choir rehearsal one night."

Total silence permeated the room as Tyrone's wife stared him down with furious eyes.

"Take the cuffs off of him," Mark said. He felt Tyrone was telling the truth. Tyrone had escaped the grips of the Feds but still had to face an interrogation from his fuming wife.

* * *

David was less than thrilled about the hoax Connie had perpetrated. He showed his gratitude by having a nice little indictment delivered to her cell. The charges included conspiracy as well as drug trafficking.

That afternoon when Mark got home, he thought about Jennifer and the way she was staring down at the floor. Though she had agreed to work as a drug runner for the dealers, she was a victim herself. He was thinking about her being separated from her children. After he hung his coat up, he got a Coke from the refrigerator and called his dad.

Pastor Fred Pratt picked up the phone on the second ring. "Praise the Lord," he said.

"Dad, this is your boy," Mark replied.

"Well it's about time you called. I've been trying to reach you for a couple of weeks now. Me and your mama had started worrying, but I prayed about it and just left the situation in the Lord's hands."

Mark took a quick sip from the Coke. "I've been kind of busy with this big case."

"So what's on your mind, son?" Pastor Pratt asked.

Mark felt very fortunate to have a father to call when he was troubled. His father had always been there for him, and Mark could always count on getting good advice. "I've been feeling kind of bad today because we've been trying to bust these drug traffickers. In the process we arrested two girls used as mules, and one of them began to cooperate right away. We debriefed her yesterday and I'm sure she was being truthful with the information she gave. After giving her statements, she asked me if she was gonna get out to see her babies again. For some reason this troubled me. I don't know why, because I arrest criminals with kids all the time."

"Mule? What do you mean by mule?"

"A mule is a drug runner or a person used to haul drugs from one point to the next. They're usually young women, but they don't have to be," Mark said. He had a bad habit of assuming people knew the street terms and lingo of the underground drug culture.

"Alright," Pastor Pratt replied. "So what did you tell her?"

"I told her I would put in a good word to the prosecutor and recommend she get bond."

"Son, I don't know much about the bond process, but I say if you feel that the woman is going to be there for her kids, see if you can get her out. If you feel that she is going to traffic more drugs into the community, do not make a recommendation. Everyone has to be held accountable for his or her actions. Let the spirit lead you."

Mark finished the rest of his Coke. What his father said made perfect sense.

* * *

"Put down the gun, Jamal, and come out with your hands up," the white cop yelled through the bullhorn.

"Fuck you," Jamal yelled from his terrace and fired a shot from his 9mm.

"Come on. Use your head, man. You don't want to go out like this, do you?" the cop yelled.

"No, but I don't want to spend the rest of my life in prison giving you mu'fuckas the satisfaction of putting me away," Jamal replied. More police arrived and barricaded the building. When Jamal stepped back on the terrace, he heard a loud, thunderous sound and turned to see law enforcement officers in his living room. He closed his eyes and fired.

When he awakened, he was sweating and his heart was beating fast. He was glad it was only a dream.

He hadn't been out of prison five months yet, and he didn't want to go back to jail. He had vowed that he would never go back. He would hold court in the streets, he had told other inmates before he got out. This was a saying he had heard while growing up. All his idols—gangsters and big drug dealers—had said the same thing. He had never known any of his friends to actually shoot it out with the cops, but he knew he had the heart to do it. That's how much he hated prison. Ever since Angelo had called, Jamal had been worried that Connie and Jennifer would give the Feds information about him. It had been three weeks since he had received the call, and yet he still worried about going to prison. He knew all the guys he had left behind would be thrilled to see him come back and spend the rest of his life in prison, but he would rather be in the hereafter than locked up. He would never be caught without his gun and he wasn't going to let another cop get the satisfaction of caging him.

* * *

That night when he got to Dream's house, she had cooked his favorite—spaghetti and garlic bread—and they had Chardonnay by candlelight. She had gone out of her way to make sure the mood was special.

"What's wrong, baby?" she asked as she gave him a quick peck on the cheek.

"Nothing. What makes you ask something like that?"

"I don't know, it's just that you haven't touched your food and you ain't talking much." She had been around him long enough to know something was bothering him.

"I got some bad news a few weeks ago."

"What's up?"

"You remember Angelo, don't you?"

"Yeah, your friend in Cali."

"A couple of his girls got busted with drugs."

"What does that have to do with you?"

He took a quick sip from his wine. "They might be talking to the police or the Feds."

"So as a result you might get picked up?" Dream said.

"That's right," he said, his voice barely audible.

"Don't you think it may be time for you to reevaluate your life?"

He hesitated before speaking, "You might be right," he finally said.

m CHAPTER 13 m

JESSICA IRVING SAT ON the front row of Dream's World History class. She was a very pretty girl with a golden complexion and reddish-brown hair. She was generally a very quiet student who never caused any problems. Jessica hadn't turned her homework in for the past three days, and Dream had asked her to stay after class.

"Jessica, why haven't you turned in your homework?"

"I just didn't," Jessica answered without looking at Dream.

"Well, I hope you know you have a zero as your homework grade for today."

"I know, Ms. Nelson," Jessica answered, still staring at the floor.

"Jessica, look at me," Dream said. "What's wrong?"

Jessica raised her head and met Dream's eyes. "I don't want to talk about it."

Dream pulled Jessica into her bosom. "I want you to tell me what's bothering you."

"It's Mama. She needs help," Jessica said.

"What's wrong with your mother?" Dream asked.

"She's on drugs, and Daddy has been trying to get some help, but she don't want none. She says she can help herself."

"Is your daddy at home? I would like to speak with him, because I can't have you neglecting your assignments. You have to do your homework or else I'll have to fail you."

"Daddy is at work. He gets off around three o'clock."

Dream looked Jessica directly in her eyes. "How about meeting me in front of the office after school and I'll take you home today. It's urgent that I let your daddy know what's going on."

Jessica met Dream in front of the office at 3:10. They made one stop at a gas station then pulled up to Jessica's home fifteen minutes later. It was a plain, white, vinyl-siding home with a large porch and a wooden fence. Jessica led Dream into her home and showed off her bedroom. It was small and neatly decorated with stuffed animals covering the bed.

* * *

Charlie Irving arrived home at four o'clock. He was a caramel-colored man with black hair that was graying at the temples. He looked to be in his late thirties.

"Daddy, this is Ms. Nelson, my history teacher," Jessica said.

They shook hands. "Pleased to meet you," Charlie said.

"Mr. Irving, I won't take up too much of your time. I just wanted to let you know that we have a problem."

Charlie's face grew serious. "What type of problem?"

Jessica hasn't been doing her homework lately and this concerns me very much."

Charlie lit a cigarette and took a seat on the sofa beside Dream. "I guess you can say I'm partly at fault for her not doing her homework."

"Jessica told me a little bit about your family issues. Please realize that she has to do her assignments if she wants to pass my course."

"Then I guess she must have told you about her mama."

"Yes. She told me a little bit of what's going on."

Charlie turned to Jessica. "Go to your room and let me and Ms. Nelson have some privacy."

After Jessica's door was closed he began to speak again. "Ms. Nelson, my wife is on crack cocaine and she just miscarried a baby because of her addiction."

"Jessica told me about her addiction. I didn't realize that she had lost a child."

Charlie turned away from Dream. "Yeah, we have all been under a lot of pressure since the miscarriage."

"I can imagine," Dream said softly.

"Can you really imagine?" He turned toward her. "That's not the half of it. The doctors found she had been using drugs while pregnant, so now they're trying to get her to sign up for this program that pays addicted women two hundred dollars to take permanent birth control."

"Well, that's a plus," Dream replied.

Charlie became angry. "How can you say that's a plus?"

"Because at least she won't have a crack baby."

"You see, that's exactly the kind of thinking the system wants us to have. The program is targeting blacks. They want to eliminate us for two hundred dollars. They want to make us sterile for life. This is nothing but modern-day genocide if you look at the big picture. I'm just a regular guy, a machinist making eleven dollars an hour, but I got common sense."

"You know, I hadn't thought about it like that." Dream was intrigued by what Charlie had said about genocide.

He smiled weakly while examining Dream. "Ms. Nelson, I hope I don't offend you, but I have a question."

"Go right ahead."

"You're not from the 'hood, are you?"

"No, I'm not, but that doesn't mean that I don't identify with you."

"Have you ever seen a crack baby?"

She hesitated before speaking. "I've seen them on TV." She felt foolish with her answer.

"So your answer is no, you haven't seen an underweight baby with nervous conditions, shaking and trembling at no fault of its own?"

Dream became sad. "Listen, I sympathize with you, I really do, but we need to do something to make sure Jessica gets back on the right track."

"I'll have a talk with her, and I'll start watching her more closely."

Dream stood from the sofa and extended her hand. "Good talking with you."

"Same here," he said.

* * *

Charlie Irving's speech was on Dream's mind for the rest of the evening. She knew she lived in a world that was very different from the one in which he lived, but she did know what a crack baby was, though she hadn't seen one. She knew if she had seen one it would be hard for her to look at it without crying.

Jessica's father had definitely brought up some good points that she hadn't thought about. She had never looked at permanent birth control as modern-day genocide. She had always felt birth control was a good idea, especially for drug addicts. Now she wondered why it was being offered mostly in minority neighborhoods. She began to think about Jessica, who was a victim of her circumstances. At fourteen the girl had a lot to deal with, and Dream felt Jessica was a lot tougher than she could have been under the same circumstances.

Dream went to her computer, got on the Internet, and typed in the words crack baby. At least a thousand different entries came up. She scanned them carefully, clicking on the ones that got her attention. She double-clicked on one entry for pictures of crack babies. The site contained five photos. All of the babies were underweight and they were little bundles of flesh hooked up to respirators and life support systems, fighting for a chance at life.

She clicked on an entry that read: GET PAID NOT TO HAVE A CRACK BABY.

The story was about a white lady in California starting a program for addicted women to get paid for permanent sterilization. Opponents of the program said that it targeted minorities, while no treatment was offered to the drug-addicted woman. The women would still be addicts, but unable to have children.

The last entry she clicked on was titled: MYTHS ABOUT CRACK BABIES PROVEN WRONG. A study conducted at the University of Syracuse found that children born to crack-addicted mothers were just as competent as children born to non-addicted mothers; at the kindergarten level, some of the crack-addicted children scored even higher on some of the cognitive tests.

Dream turned the computer off and stared at the blank screen. She thought about what Charlie Irving said about a mass genocide being perpetrated, and realized her man was a contributor.

* * *

For the next two weeks Dream avoided Jamal. He tried calling her but she didn't want to talk. He even came to the school but she refused to see him. He sent her more flowers but she didn't respond.

Jamal decided he would pay Keisha a visit to find out what was going on. He remembered Dream mentioning the name of Keisha's apartment complex, Vanity's Way. Jamal drove up to the rental office. A fat white woman with a nametag reading Pam sat at a desk devouring a bag of Cheetos.

"Excuse me, can you tell me what building Keisha Ferguson lives in?" Jamal asked.

"I'm sorry, I cannot give you this information," she said, placing the bag of Cheetos on her desk.

Jamal frowned. "I ain't no serial killer or rapist. I'm a friend."

"If you're a friend, why don't you know where she lives?" she asked.

Jamal was getting upset. Pam had made a valid point,one that he hadn't thought about.

"Listen, I'm not here to start trouble." He smiled, remembering that it always helped to smile and pretend to be polite when dealing with white people. He knew from experience that an angry black man could easily be labeled as a troublemaker. "Can you perhaps call Keisha and ask her if she wants to see me?"

"I'll give her a call, but if she doesn't want to see you, I'm going to have to ask you to leave the premises."

"I'll leave, but I don't think that's going to happen." Jamal said

Pam wiped her orange-colored fingertips on her pants before picking up the phone. In less than ten seconds, she had Keisha on the line. "Yeah, I have a young man here wants to know where you live."

"Tell her I'm Jamal."

"Says his name is Jamal," Pam said, sucking cheese powder from her finger, "Okay I'll give him your apartment number."

Jamal wanted to say, Bitch, I told you so, but he didn't need to play one-upmanship with Pam. She was nothing to him, and he figured her life was miserable enough just being her size.

* * *

Keisha came to the door wearing a pair of cut-off jean shorts and a T-shirt revealing her stomach. Her hair was down and she wore a hint of lip-gloss. Jamal's eyes were immediately drawn to her thighs.

"Come in, have a seat," Keisha offered.

Jamal sat on the sofa and Keisha sat in a chair across from him. Again Jamal found himself staring at her legs. He finally caught himself and made eye contact with Keisha.

"What is going on with Dream?," Jamal asked.

"What are you talking about?"

"She doesn't want to see me, and she hasn't answered any of my phone calls," Jamal said.

"Jamal, I haven't spoken with Dream in a couple of days. I thought everything was still cool with you two."

"She's mad at me about something, and the real fucked-up part is that I don't know what is going on. She won't have shit to do with me . . . I mean, I've been cut off overnight," Jamal said as he threw up his hands in disgust.

"I can give her a call if you want me to," Keisha said as she stood and strolled to the other side of the room picking up the cordless telephone.

Jamal stared at Keisha's ass and noticed how shapely she was. He hadn't remembered her body looking so well proportioned. For a brief instant he imagined having sex with her. "No, Keisha, you ain't got to do that. I think I have a better idea now," Jamal said as he stood and made his way to the door.

Keisha walked over, and smiled innocently, before saying good-bye. Jamal took one quick look at her legs again before leaving.

* * *

It was seven o'clock when Jamal arrived at Dream's apartment complex. She wasn't there so he sat back in his Mercedes, prepared to wait.

Dream arrived at nine o'clock. When she stepped out of her white jeep he was right in her face, nose to nose. She was wearing Beautiful by Estee Lauder. He knew that smell because she would often leave the scent on his pillow.

"Can we talk?" he asked.

"I'm not in the mood. Would you mind getting out of my way?"

"Not before we talk."

She attempted to walk around him but he stopped her. "Look, you're making a scene. Please leave," she said.

"Can I come in?"

"You can do whatever you want."

"I know that, but I just don't want to barge in your house."

"You barge in on people's lives, I don't see why you can't barge in people's houses. What's the difference?"

"What's that's suppose to mean?"

"Let's just take the conversation in the house," she said.

Once they were inside he asked, "What's up with the little comment you made about me barging in on people's lives?"

She met his gaze. "Think about it. You do have a brain, don't you?"

"The last time I checked it was still there. I may not be as educated as you, but, yeah, I do have a brain," he said.

"Well, do me a favor, please use it!" she shouted.

"Where did that come from?"

"Jamal, you have a lot of potential. Don't ruin your life, and please don't ruin the lives of others."

"I guess you must be talking about my drug dealing."

"You do have a brain," she announced sarcastically.

Jamal stared at her coldly. Who was she to be telling him what he was doing to his life and the lives of others? She didn't know what he had been through. She wasn't a black man in this country, and she definitely had her family for support. "So I guess you would be happy if I got a real job?"

"That would be a start," she said, her eyes were blazing.

Jamal paced the floor wearily. He felt like he was on trial. "Hell, you don't know what it's like to be a black man with no education and being a convicted felon," he said.

"You're right, Jamal. I wasn't born a man, and I didn't choose to be a convicted felon. I do know you need to quit blaming people for the decisions you made."

"Baby, I'm not blaming anyone. I'm just simply saying it's hard out here," he said.

"Well, welcome to the real world. You want to know what hard is? Try being fourteen with a mother on crack and trying to get to school every day."

Jamal turned from her gaze. He began to think about his mother, whom he hadn't seen in years. He remembered the last day he had seen her. The once healthy, beautiful, strong black woman was thin and sickly. Her teeth had rotted from years of drug use. "Now that's where you're wrong. I do know what it feels like to have a mother on crack. You, on the other hand, don't know what the fuck you're talking about."

"Well, Jamal, if you know the feeling, why do you keep poisoning the community? Don't you see all those fancy cars and condos and Sean John outfits ain't worth it? I don't think you want to go back to jail."

Jamal dropped his head. He knew she wanted him to feel guilty about what he was doing, and he knew that he probably should feel guilty, but the fact of the matter was, he didn't. He walked over and embraced her, then stroked her hair. "I know I can't go on like this if I want to keep you."

She lifted her head from his shoulders and kissed him. Dream was thankful for her parents. She was glad they had instilled morals and values in her. Above all she was glad they had given her the confidence she needed to do anything she desired. This was a confidence Jamal obviously didn't possess. He seemed to think that drug dealing was all he knew, and he was quick to point and blame society for his problems.

ɱ CHAPTER 14 ɱ

DREAM FELT IT WAS her duty as a teacher and a human being to encourage Jessica and give her the confidence she to needed to transcend her situation. She kept Jessica late to bring her up to date on her assignments. One day after school they were on their way to Jessica's house when Dream stopped by her apartment to get her overnight bag to stay at Jamal's for the night.

"Ms. Nelson, you have a very nice apartment," Jessica said.

"Thank you," Dream said, smiling as she disappeared into the bedroom. She came back and found Jessica staring at her degree and her National Honor Society plaques.

"Ms. Nelson, you must have been really smart in school."

"No, Jessica, I consider myself average. I just have a good work ethic."

"Are those your parents?" Jessica asked, pointing to a picture of Dream and her parents on her college graduation day.

"Yes. Don't I look like them?"

"Yeah, especially your mom. You are very blessed to have such wonderful parents."

"Jessica, you are blessed as well," Dream said.

"Really?" Jessica's eyes looked innocent and confused.

"You have a wonderful father, and you have me. See, when you lack in one area, God will send someone to help you pick up the slack."

She smiled. "Ms. Nelson, I am blessed, too, huh?"

"Please believe it."

Dream had become Jessica's mentor. She helped her with her homework and they hung out together. They talked about college and Jessica's career goals. Jessica told her she wanted to go to Howard University and become a doctor.

Dream was surprised at Jessica's aspirations at only fourteen years old. She encouraged Jessica to look beyond her circumstances and to try not to worry about the things she had no control over. She even discussed women's health issues, and on one occasion they even got into a discussion about sex. Jessica proclaimed to Dream that she was a virgin still, but she had a boyfriend whom she talked with over the phone.

"A boyfriend?" Dream asked, surprised.

Jessica blushed.

"You're too young for a boyfriend."

"I'm fourteen. I'm old enough."

"Do I know him?"

Jessica shrugged. "I don't know."

"Does he go to school at Spaugh?"

"Yeah."

"Who is he?" Dream asked.

"I can't tell you," Jessica said, avoiding Dream's eyes.

"Why not?"

"He's white and you might tell my daddy. I don't think he likes white people too much."

"How do you feel about white people?"

"I don't have anything against them. I know there are differences between the races but I know there is only one race, the human race. God created us all."

Dream smiled. She was impressed with Jessica's answer. The child clearly had her own opinions and views. "Jessica, I want you to feel free to tell me anything. Whatever you tell me, I'll keep between us."

Jessica met Dream's eyes. "His name is Ian Pilcher."

"Yeah, I know Ian. I taught him last year."

Jessica smiled. "He always wants to kiss but I don't want to kiss him, though."

"Why not?"

"My lips are bigger than his."

Dream burst out laughing.

* * *

The next day, after school, Dream drove her jeep up to Jessica's house to drop her off. Charlie Irving sprinted to the car, beads of sweat covering his face, and his eyes were red as if he had been crying. "Jessica, go in the house. Let me talk to Ms. Nelson," he said.

Jessica jumped out of the jeep and quickly and ran in the house.

Charlie met Dream's eyes. "Ms. Nelson, I have a problem, and I need your help."

"What can I do to help you?" Dream asked.

"My wife came here today and stole my car; I need you to take me to look for her if you have time. I have to find her before she sells it to one of the local crack dealers."

"How do you know she stole the car?"

"She has a set of keys, and she's stolen it before, loaning it out for crack."

Dream contemplated. She really didn't have time to take him to look for his car, and she knew this was dangerous. She didn't know how Charlie Irving would react if he saw his wife or some drug dealer in his car. "Come on, but I can't spend too much time looking for her, I have some papers to grade tonight."

Charlie ran back inside and grabbed a thin blue and gray nylon jacket. He rushed out and jumped in on the passenger side of the truck. "I need you to drive to the west side of town."

Once they arrived, Charlie directed Dream to Woodview Drive, a long winding road that consisted primarily of old, wooden, dilapidated homes. Most were crack houses. Drug dealers sat on the porches dealing. Young teenage boys paraded up and down the street with walkie-talkies and binoculars. Curiously, Dream turned to Charlie. "What is going on with these guys walking around like they're in the army?"

"They look out for the drug dealers."

"Really."

"Yeah. One guy runs this whole neighborhood."

Dream sat in silence. She was afraid, and she wondered what Charlie planned to do if he saw someone driving his car. She certainly didn't want any trouble. Finally she asked, "Do you know this guy who runs the neighborhood?"

"Yeah, I had it out with him the last time I had to go find the car."

She glanced over at Charlie who was biting his nails. "Are you sure it's okay?"

"Yeah, it's cool. Just drive to the end of the street then pull in the driveway of the last house on the right."

When Dream reached the house, two men approached the passenger side of the vehicle. "What are you looking for?" one of the men asked.

Charlie let down his window. "We ain't come here to buy no dope. I came here to try to find my wife. Is Rico around here?"

"Rico don't want to see nobody," one of the men said.

"Rico knows me," Charlie said.

"Who the hell are you?"

"Listen man, I didn't come here to get in no altercation with you. Is Rico here or not?"

The man pulled a walkie-talkie from his belt. "I still need to know your name so I can tell him who's looking for him."

"Tell him Charlie is looking for him."

The man had summoned Rico by radio. Five minutes later Rico drove up in a white Infiniti Q-45. He was a short, stocky, dark man with flashy platinum jewelry and teeth.

"Wait here for a minute, I'll be right back," Charlie said as he left the car.

Dream scanned the area. She could feel the danger lurking. Inadvertently she made eye contact with one of the walkie-talkie boys who was licking his lips suggestively.

She quickly turned away. As Charlie and Rico made conversation, she rolled down the window to eavesdrop.

"I just want to know where in the hell is my car?"

"I done told your punk-ass, I don't know nuthin' about yo' damn car," Rico replied.

"You had it the last time. In fact, you were the one who was driving it."

"I had your car the last time because your crack-head wife gave me the car, remember? I ain't steal shit. I ain't got to steal," Rico said, pulling out a wad of money.

"This ain't about whether or not you have to steal. I just want to know where my car is."

"I don't know where your car is, and I don't need your car. My rims cost more than that cheap-ass Ford Focus." Rico chuckled, pointing to his Infiniti. "Your best bet is to get the hell away from here before you get hurt."

"I'm gonna find my car if it means searching this entire street. I know it's over here."

Rico pulled a huge pistol from his side. "You're going to get the hell away from here is what you're gonna do. Now get out of my face."

Charlie turned and hurried back to Dream's jeep, which she already had running. "Let's go," he said.

Before she pulled off, Rico fired two shots in the air and she and Charlie slid down in their seats. Dream shook nervously as she slouched. She had never been so close to a real gunshot before. She was certain after she heard the gunshot she was going to die.

Rico and the walkie-talkie boys roared with laughter. Charlie sat up in his seat and looked at Rico and his workers still laughing. "It's okay, Ms. Nelson. Those clowns were just trying to get a laugh."

Her heart pounded, and chills traveled her spine as she held her ears, which were still ringing from the gunshots. Finally she got herself together and drove away.

***

When they reached Charlie's house, Dream noticed he looked more depressed than earlier. She felt sorry for him. "Mr. Irving, if you'd like, I can take you to the police department so you can report your car stolen."

He looked at Dream, avoiding her eyes. "I would like that, but I don't know how to give the police a report when I know my wife has the car. How do you turn your own wife in to the police?"

Dream sat in silence. She had nothing to say, and she definitely didn't know how to answer his question.

"Ms. Nelson, the sad part about the whole thing is that I love my wife very much. I wish you could see her. She is really a beautiful woman when she ain't using dope." Charlie was in tears.

Dream wanted to say something to ease Charlie's heartache. She felt she needed to say something, but she just couldn't seem to find the right words.

***

Dream arrived home at eight o'clock after a late workout at the gym. Her gym clothes were soiled and she smelled dreadful. She never took showers at the gym because of a few lesbian members, some of whom made her uncomfortable. The water in the shower was a bit cold, but quite refreshing. After she dried off she put on some shorts and an Atlanta Falcons football jersey. Hunger pains cramped her stomach. She was preparing herself a baked potato and a small salad when the phone rang. She glanced at the Caller ID and saw it was a number she did not recognize. She hesitated before picking up the phone. "Hello."

"Dream, baby, what's up?"

She knew the voice immediately. Is he out? she wondered. She hadn't heard the little prison recording that usually preceded his calls. "Hey, DeVon. What are you doing calling here?"

"I got out this morning. Just thought I would hit you up to see what you were up to."

"I'm chillin'. I'm really glad to hear your voice."

"Are you?" he asked.

"Yes, I am."

"Listen, I was wondering if I can come over to see you." She contemplated before speaking. "I don't think that would be a good idea."

"You still seeing that guy, Jamal, huh?"

"Yes."

"Well, I ain't going to try to come between you two, but I was wondering if we can get together for lunch tomorrow."

"I would like that. I can probably get away from the school around one o'clock. I don't have a fifth-period class, so we can meet downtown at Mert's on College Street."

"Cool," DeVon said.

* * *

By 1:15 P.M. the following day, the lunch crowd at Mert's had thinned. Dream arrived at one o'clock and there were only four tables occupied. She took a seat near the front. When DeVon arrived his smile covered his entire face when he saw her. Instantly she realized how much she actually missed him. She stood and they embraced.

"I'm glad you decided to meet me," he said.

"Yeah, and I'm glad I came. You look very nice," she said, admiring DeVon's bulging biceps and massive chest. His black fitted sweater looked as though it was shellacked on him.

He grinned. "Yeah, you still look good as hell. How's your family?"

"Everybody's good. Thank you."

"So what's good here to eat?"

"My personal favorite is the blackened pork chops."

When the waitress appeared, they both ordered the blackened pork chops with yellow rice, gravy, and macaroni. They caught up on old times until the food came. DeVon made it perfectly clear that he didn't want to go back to jail, and somehow she believed him. After all, he hadn't actually intended to commit a crime. He'd had an accident and as a result, someone lost a life. He filled her in on rehabilitation and vocational classes that he had taken while incarcerated.

She took a sip from her iced tea. "What kind of classes did you take?"

"Basic electrical ones. Hopefully I can get a job as an electrician."

She nodded, impressed. It definitely seemed as though he had a plan. At least he had used his prison time wisely. She realistically knew it would be hard for a black ex-con to succeed in today's job market. She remembered that DeVon smoked marijuana religiously, and the day of his car accident the investigating officer said DeVon reeked of it. Later, after being examined by the doctor, marijuana was found in DeVon's bloodstream, and as a result, vehicular manslaughter charges were filed against him. "So can you pass a drug test?"

He chuckled. "Are you interviewing me?"

"No, I just want to know because that's going to be essential if you really want to make it out here. Almost everybody is drug testing."

"For your information, I can pass a drug test. As a matter of fact, I haven't smoked any weed in more than six months. I have a job lined up already. I appreciate your concern."

She stared at him briefly before turning away. Dream's mind drifted to the last time she had made love to DeVon.

He had come over the day before court. She hadn't wanted him to be alone, because she knew he was nervous about his court appearance. When he arrived, it was dark, and she had candles lit. The dimly-lit apartment was very romantic. She'd met him at the door wearing a robe, and nothing underneath. Laying eyes on her, he scooped her up and rushed to the sofa before they made their way to the bed. Their sexual appetites were ignited, and DeVon pounded her head against the headboard during intercourse. Before it was all over, they were outside on the back deck. It was 2:00 A.M. when they finally finished.

"Sounds like you've gotten yourself together."

"I have. I mean, this whole prison thing has taught me that I ain't no real thug. I thought I was until I met some serious brothers in there. Rapists, cold-blooded killers, and big-time drug dealers—real criminals who showed me I wasn't shit. If not using drugs means I'll stay out, then I won't use again."

"So why did you want to see me so bad?" she asked, bored with all the prison talk.

He hesitated before speaking, then he reached across the table and grabbed her hand. "I missed you, and I think we made a real good couple. I want us to get back together."

Dream turned away briefly before resuming eye contact. "You know I'm involved with somebody."

"But I need you," DeVon pleaded.

She pulled her hand back, stood, flagged the waitress, and asked for the check. "I've got to go now, DeVon."

He pulled a ten-dollar bill from his pocket and looked up at her. "Want to go dutch?"

"Save your money. This one is on me."

He winked at her. "You know you still love me."

"Find yourself a woman. I have to go now."

* * *

Two days later, Dream was in the faculty parking lot loading her things in the back of her jeep when she felt a tap on the shoulder. She turned and was face to face with DeVon. "What do you want?"

"I just need to talk to you."

"How did you get here?"

"I walked. I needed to see you."

She took a deep breath. "Get in. We'll ride and talk."

As they pulled out of the school parking lot, she glanced over at him. She noticed he was casually dressed, wearing loafers, jeans, and a gray blazer. It was only three o'clock, wasn't he supposed to be at work? Though she didn't know much about electrical work, she figured he should at least be wearing work boots. "So were you off today?"

"That's what I wanted to talk to you about."

"Is there something wrong?"

"Yeah, I didn't get the job."

"Why not?"

"I need money for tools."

"How much are tools?" she asked naively, because she really didn't have the faintest idea. She didn't even own a screwdriver.

"I mean, I can probably get all the tools I need from the pawn shop."

She turned and looked at him. He looked very sad and she wanted to help him but wondered why. He had cursed her out while visiting him in prison. Why did she feel so gullible? Why did she want to help someone who didn't appreciate her? "How much do you think you'll need to get the tools from the pawn shop?" she asked.

"One hundred and fifty dollars."

Dream pulled into a convenience store, jumped out, went to the ATM, and retrieved two hundred dollars. "Get the tools you need," she said, handing him the money.

"I can't take your money," he said, leaving her hand dangling in mid-air.

She frowned. "Take the money. I want you to have it to get what you need."

He quickly grabbed the bills and put them in his pocket. "I'll pay you back when I get my first paycheck."

"If you do, fine. If you don't, fine," she said, looking straight ahead.

He turned her face toward him and they stared at each other for what seemed a long time. "I really appreciate it, okay?"

m CHAPTER 15 m

AFTER THE DEA BUSTED Angelo's girls, Jamal and Angelo figured they needed to come up with a different method of getting the drugs back to North Carolina.—at least until they felt better about going through the airports again. Angelo found a couple who was in desperate need of money. The husband-and-wife team had fallen on some hard times and needed to make some money to stop foreclosure on their home and to help their daughter with tuition. They agreed to drive the product across the country but said they would stop delivering product as soon as they were caught up on their bills. Angelo paid them two-thousand dollars each trip and they made at least two trips in a month. Everything seemed to be going well for Jamal until he received a call from Tony the informant who said it was very necessary that they meet.

"I'm beginning to think this shit is a game." Dawg's face became hardened.

"Why do you say that?" Jamal asked.

"I don't know, it just seems like something ain't right about this whole situation."

"Well, Tony called me this morning saying that the Feds had some new info about us, and he wanted to meet with me again."

"Are you sure this mu'fucka ain't telling the cops about us?"

"How? He's not around us enough to find out anything."

"Well, I want to go with you this time when you meet him."

* * *

It was 7:00 P.M. when Dawg and Jamal reached the Starbucks. They took a seat next to the fireplace.

Twenty minutes later, Tony showed up biting his chapped lips and rubbing his ashy hands together as if he was trying to keep warm. "What's up, guys?"

Dawg stared at him. "What's up with you?"

Tony pulled out a pack of Newports and looked around. Nobody else was smoking. "Is this the smoking section?"

"Who gives a fuck? Tell us what's going on," Dawg demanded.

Tony lit his cigarette before starting. "Okay. Two girls from San Diego got busted and they called your names."

"How do you know this?" Dawg asked.

"I have connections with the DEA. Must we go through this again?"

"Okay, so what do we have to do now?" Jamal asked.

"Well, again, they're trying to gather enough evidence to go to the grand jury to get you guys indicted."

"What are you getting at?" Dawg asked.

"We need more money."

"I thought your man said the $25,000 would take care of us," Jamal said.

Tony took a puff from his cigarette before flicking the ashes on the shiny hardwood floors.

"He did say that, but that was before the new evidence was introduced. Now the agent has to get in the files and dispose of the new shit."

Dawg stared at Tony again. "This shit sounds kind of funny to me."

"Jamal spoke to the agent the last time. Everything I say is legit. How else would I know so much about what's going on with you guys?" Tony asked.

"So, how much do you need now?" Dawg asked.

"Twenty thousand, and we'll clear everything up, I swear to you."

"When do you need it?" Dawg asked.

"I need it now. We need to do this fast before it's too late."

Dawg looked around the coffeehouse. Everybody was busy minding his or her own business. He then reached across the table and gripped Tony by the collar and yanked him halfway across the table. "If I find out that you're fuckin' us around, I will kill your ass. Know what I mean?"

"Y-yeah, man, I understand."

Dawg then shoved him backward. Tony straightened out his rumpled shirt while looking at Dawg.

"Okay, Tony, this is the deal. I'm going to meet you back here in an hour," Jamal said.

"Cool, I'll be waiting on you in the parking lot."

Jamal and Dawg headed to the car. Twenty thousand dollars more, Jamal thought. He definitely didn't want to pay Tony the money, but he needed the protection. It was quite obvious that Tony had connections. He had names and specific incidents about a drug bust directly connected to Jamal and Dawg.

"I still say we don't give the mu'fucka shit," Dawg said.

"He knows something. How else would he know about the girls who got busted?"

"My whole thing is, whatever is gonna happen is gonna happen anyway."

"You're right, but I don't want nothing to happen to us that can be avoided. You know the man is a snitch working closely with the Feds, and you know he's probably friends with some of them agents. Besides, I talked to one of those redneck bastards on the phone. I believe Tony can help us out."

Jamal quickly pulled in through the underground parking deck of the Arlington Condominiums. He hopped out of the car and got on the elevator. Once he was in his bedroom, he opened his safe and gathered twenty thousand dollars—all hundreds—and put them in a small, brown paper bag.

It took them twenty minutes to get back to Starbucks. Tony was in the parking lot behind the wheel of a black Buick.

"Give me the money. I want to emphasize the fact that I will fuckin' kill him if he fucks us," Dawg demanded.

Jamal passed Dawg the small brown bag. He knew that Dawg would be better at getting the point across to Tony. Jamal didn't want to pay for the protection, but it seemed as though Tony had the key to his freedom.

* * *

The third week in November, Dream invited Jamal to a black-tie affair, honoring her father for thirty years of service in the school system. Her parents sat at the reserved table along with the superintendent and a couple of other principals from local high schools. Janice Nelson looked on in disapproval when Jamal approached the table in a full-length mink coat, wearing a diamond-encrusted pinky ring. She nudged Dream who was sitting beside her. "Why is Jamal making a spectacle of himself?" Janice whispered.

"What do you mean?" Dream asked.

"Look at what he's wearing. Didn't he know that this is your father's day? He's embarrassing us. He looks like a pimp."

Prime rib was served, and shortly after everyone finished eating, a series of long-winded speeches about David Nelson's dedication to service and his advocacy for higher learning followed. At the end of the evening, Harry Stevens, the district superintendent, approached the Nelsons with a glass of champagne in his hand. "Again, I want to commend you for your service," he said to David Nelson. "Hello Dream. Are you still teaching at Spaugh?"

"Yes," she nodded.

Harry turned to Jamal. "I don't believe we've met?"

"That's my boyfriend, Jamal Stewart," Dream said.

"Well, I know you can't be a teacher wearing a coat like that. That thing must have cost a fortune," Harry said.

"No, I'm not a teacher," Jamal said.

Harry sipped champagne and adjusted his crooked bowtie. "What do you do for a living, Jamal?"

Jamal became embarrassed. The Nelsons became silent. They, too, seemed a bit rattled by Harry's question. Finally Jamal said. "That's none of your business."

Harry's face reddened immediately. "Jamal, you are absolutely right." He extended his hand. "One last question for you."

Jamal sighed. "What is it?"

"Who is your furrier? I must get my wife a coat like that for Christmas," Harry said sarcastically, and chuckled as he walked away.

When Jamal and Dream left for the evening they met up at Dream's apartment. Dream figured Harry's comments must have upset Jamal. She could only imagine how he felt. Once they were inside her apartment, she turned the TV to David Letterman.

"Can you turn that, please? I've had enough of white, corny-ass humor."

"I guess you're mad at the little comment Harry made."

He grabbed the remote control from the coffee table and changed the channel to ESPN. "You are so smart."

"Oh, it's okay for you to be sarcastic but nobody else can, right?"

Jamal looked at Dream briefly but remained silent.

Dream walked over to the sofa where Jamal was seated and sat beside him. "Listen, baby, I'm sorry you felt uncomfortable at the dinner."

"I just don't fit in with your family and friends," Jamal said.

Dream rubbed his leg. "As long as we like each other, nothing else should matter, okay?"

"That's easy to say, but it does matter."

"Jamal, I don't know what you want me to say. I mean, I will admit that the way we think is different, but I see that as the good part of the relationship. I like the fact that you ain't this straight-laced nigga who don't know shit about the streets."

He smiled boyishly, turned, and kissed her. "So you like thugs?"

"Basically."

"Did I embarrass you by what I wore to dinner?"

She turned from his gaze. "Honestly, Jamal, you could have saved the fur coat and the diamond pinky ring for the player's ball."

* * *

Dawg had told Mark that he and Jamal were taking a break from the business for a while because they thought the Feds were watching. Though it meant that he wouldn't be hanging out with Dawg, Mark still kept him under surveillance.

Mark and Jeremiah were working together again. Jeremiah had apologized for offending him, and Mark had accepted the apology. Two days later, Mark overheard Jeremiah celebrating a trial victory of the Stinson brothers. Jeremiah was laughing about sending the boys' seventy-one-year-old grandmother to prison for ten years. She was found guilty of conspiracy in allowing the boys to hide drugs in her house. The case was a real travesty, Mark thought. How could anyone delight in an elderly person's misfortune?

Mark decided not to confront Jeremiah and figured it would be of no use complaining to the supervisor. He decided he would try to forget what he'd overheard. But he

146 • K. Elliott

couldn't forget. When he got home he quickly turned on the six o'clock news. He didn't see the news anchor. Instead, he pictured Jeremiah's laughing face, and it made him literally sick. Mark's head was pounding, and sharp pains pierced his brain. Whenever he got headaches he knew he was stressed.

How had he allowed Jeremiah to get to him? Why was he thinking about the misfortune of the Stinson grandmother? During his nine years with the agency, he had witnessed whole families become confined. He had seen a disproportionate number of blacks get locked up for drugs, more than any other race, and yet he had not been affected. Maybe it was Jeremiah's attitude, he thought. It seemed Jeremiah enjoyed locking up blacks.

It was seven o'clock when the news went off, and Mark hadn't the slightest idea of what the headlines had been about. He pulled himself up from the sofa and went to the bathroom. In the mirror he saw that his eyes were bloodshot. He was neither looking good nor feeling well. For the first time in nine years with the agency, he wasn't having fun. At that moment Mark no longer knew if he still wanted to be a DEA agent. It seemed as though his work was in vain. His life had become a paradox. Was he the only agent with a conscience? Was he the only person in his department who didn't delight in an elderly lady's confinement? Were there other agents going through the same thing? There had to be. Maybe he needed counseling.

Mark quickly dismissed the thought. Counseling was for crazy people. He wasn't crazy; he needed someone to talk to. He thought about going to the agency's chaplain, whom was Lutheran. Mark had only spoken to him once, and they didn't know each other. Mark didn't have anything against a Lutheran minister, but he knew there was nothing like the good old-fashioned, southern Baptist, fire-and-brimstone minister to tell it like it is. He needed the truth. He needed to know if he was wrong for having a heart. Was he wrong for disliking Jeremiah? He didn't know how long he could go on without talking to someone.

Maybe it was time for him to call it quits or time to find something else to do. He was thirty-four now, and he needed to start a family soon. He wanted children of his own. He wanted a wife, but every time he met a woman, she couldn't understand his obsession with his job. It consumed him. Whenever he worked on a case, he gave one hundred percent. He took the job home with him and would often integrate it in his conversation. This sometimes annoyed women.

Once, at thirty-one, he'd almost gotten married. Kendra was a twenty-nine-year-old psychologist he had met at a church picnic. She was everything he wanted in a woman—tall, attractive, intelligent, and spiritual. Two months after meeting, they were inseparable, and within six months, Kendra proposed. He had accepted. The wedding was to take place one year after their engagement. His parents were absolutely delighted because they loved Kendra, too.

Mark remembered his father telling him, "Boy, you got yourself a virtuous one."

Mark was very happy until the agency sent him to Miami as a Panamanian to work undercover in an operation, targeting some big-time Columbian drug lords. He was then barely seeing Kendra, and his absence put a strain on the relationship. Finally she gave him an ultimatum: either he leave the agency or she'd walk. He had begged for her understanding, but she stuck by the ultimatum. When they split, he was in tears. The agency had cost him a lot.

At nine o'clock Mark called his father but got no answer. His father and his brother had gone to a pastor's conference in Memphis. At 10:30 Mark found himself taking in the cold night air while warming his hands with his breath on the doorsteps of Pastor Tommy Stevens.

Pastor Steven's smiled broadly. "Come right in, Mark."

Mark eased in the door, and Pastor Stevens took his coat.

Pastor Stevens' home was modest with antique furniture. On his living room wall was a huge mural of Christ nailed to the cross. A family Bible sat on the coffee table. "Can I get you anything to drink?"

"No, I'm fine," Mark said.

The two men sat down. "So what brings you here?" the pastor asked.

"I'm troubled a little by my work."

The pastor's eyebrows rose. "Have you prayed about what it is that's bothering you?"

"Yeah, I have, but I thought I needed to talk to someone about it."

"Well, I'm glad you decided to come, because if you can't bring your problems before the church, then who can you turn to?"

"I don't want to take up too much of your time. You know that I work for the DEA, right?"

"Yeah, I think you told me this. I commend you on making a difference."

Mark took a deep breath and stared up at the ceiling. "My career and my beliefs are in direct conflict, and sometimes I find it hard to deal with."

"How are they conflicting?"

"I have a conscious, unlike some of my coworkers. I love my work, don't get me wrong, it's just that . . . I became a DEA officer to help the community keep the kids safe."

"So you feel your coworkers are not working to help the community?"

Mark looked at the pastor with serious eyes. "I had one of my coworkers revel in the fact that he locked up an elderly lady."

The pastor looked surprised. "What in the world did she do to get locked up?"

Mark waited a few seconds before speaking. "It wasn't my case, but I think she may have had knowledge that her grandsons were drug dealers."

"And for that she got locked up?"

"Yeah. It's called conspiracy, meaning if you assist with any aspect of the crime, you're just as guilty, no matter how small your role is."

"Wow, I didn't know they could do that." The pastor placed his hands behind his head. "I can see why you're having a difficult time doing your job. Mark, I really don't know what to tell you except to keep doing your job and know that there are more good people out there than bad."

Mark nodded. He was glad he had talked with someone about his problem. He had actually known officers to go to therapy sessions for job-related stress, but being a man of God, Mark felt he could only get his counseling from above. Pastor Stevens hadn't been much help to him, but his soul was soothed.

The pastor picked a Bible up from the table and showed Mark a scripture. Luke 48:

Much is required from those to whom much is given, and much more is required from those to whom much more is given.

Mark was familiar with the scripture. He knew that the Lord would not place a burden on him that he could not handle. A lot was required of him. Most of the time he welcomed new challenges, but lately he hadn't been up to the day-to-day confrontations that came along with being a black DEA officer. It had become hard to distinguish the good guys from the bad. Some of the bad guys were working right alongside him, and some of the so-called street thugs weren't that bad underneath. He had to admit that his visit with Pastor Stevens had been a good one, and the scripture he had read was refreshing. He stood and the pastor retrieved his coat. They hugged before he left.

ꟽ CHAPTER 16 ꟽ

IT WAS NOW THE end of November. At 6:00 A.M. the alarm clock sounded. Dream promptly hit the snooze button and dozed for five more minutes before jumping up and heading to the shower. Breakfast consisted of bacon and pancakes. After she was through eating she finished grading the tests that she had started the previous night. At 7:15 her doorbell rang. She looked through the peephole and DeVon was standing outside with a white hard hat in his hand. She quickly opened the door.

"What are you doing here?" she asked, surprised.

"I just came to give you your money back for the tools you bought."

"Come in."

"Okay, but I can't stay long; I have to be at work at eight. I got to catch the bus, unless you want to take me."

"Where do you work?"

"Downtown."

"I can drop you off. I see no harm in that."

DeVon pulled a brown leather pouch from his pocket and took out two wrinkled hundred-dollar bills. "I'm sorry the money is so worn."

"Are you sure you're able to pay me?"

"Yeah. I can stand it. I'm expecting a big paycheck Friday. I've worked at least three hours overtime each day since I started. Take the money. You don't know how much I appreciate what you did for me. I want to take you out to show you a good time."

Dream walked over to the dining room table, picked up her test papers, and packed them in a small white book bag. "Listen, DeVon, I don't think that's a good idea. I mean, you know I have a boyfriend. This can't happen. I can't go out with you. I can't believe you haven't met any women working downtown."

"Those women downtown are too damn stuck-up. They see a brother with a tool belt on and he gets no play. They want those white-collar mu'fuckas."

Dream knew exactly what he was talking about. She had known many women who refused to go out with a plumber or an electrician. Doctors and engineers were in, not a man in a tool belt. She gathered her things and they left.

They chatted while listening to the Russ Parr morning show. DeVon told Dream how much he was enjoying his job and that his boss was thinking about sending him to school. Devon said he planned to be a licensed electrician by the following year.

"Good for you," she said.

He didn't say anything; he just nodded and glanced over his shoulder.

"I hope you stick with it; I know electricians make decent money."

"Yeah, they do all right I guess." He looked back again. "What kind of car does your boy, Jamal, drive?"

"Why?"

"Because someone is following us in a white BMW."

Dream looked over her shoulder quickly before refocusing on the road. She knew the car immediately. It was Dawg, and he was talking on his cell phone. She drove a half a mile farther and pulled into a service station.

"Who the hell is that, and why are you pulling into the gas station?" DeVon asked.

"Don't worry. Relax. Everything is going to be okay."

DeVon looked frightened. He was jittery and kept jerking his leg. "Is that your boyfriend?"

"No."

"Who is he?"

"Nobody," Dream hopped out of the jeep and walked to Dawg's BMW.

He rolled his window down. "Jamal is on his way."

"For what?" she asked.

"He's probably gonna want to know who that mu'fucka is you're riding with this early in the morning."

"You know what? You are a stupid motherfucker, Dawg. It's not what you think," Dream shouted.

"No, you are the stupid mu'fucka. You're the one with the nigga in the jeep," Dawg said, laughing.

"What did you tell Jamal?"

"You'll find out. He'll be here in about five minutes."

DeVon walked over and stood beside Dream. "What's going on?"

"Playboy, I think you about to have a bad day," Dawg said

"What the hell is he talking about?" DeVon asked Dream.

"Don't pay him any mind."

"I don't like the fact that this mu'fucka just threatened me," Devon said.

"I didn't threaten you. I just promised you an ass whoopin'," Dawg said.

"Get out of the car, and I will fuck you up," DeVon shouted.

Dawg turned his car engine off and bounced from the seat. He was met with a hard right across his nose. He quickly nursed his nose and held one arm to protect his face. DeVon charged him swiftly, his head pounding Dawg's stomach hard before they landed on the pavement.

"Stop it, dammit!" Dream demanded.

"I'm gonna fuck you up," Dawg yelled from the ground.

Dream tried to pull DeVon off Dawg, but he was too strong for her. She finally yelled for someone to break up the fight but nobody cared.

Jamal's Mercedes arrived. Dream ran to his car quickly. "Jamal, please break it up."

Jamal got out of his car and shoved Dream out of his way as DeVon pounded Dawg's face violently. When he reached the fight he grabbed DeVon's neck, forcing him backward until Dawg was up on his feet. It was now two against one. DeVon made a futile attempt to cover his face. Jamal and Dawg pounded and kicked DeVon for three minutes.

Finally, Dream went inside the store and returned with the manager, a thin Indian man. "I am going to call the police if you don't get off the property," the manager said.

"You need to call the ambulance," Dawg said. "This mu'fucka needs some medical attention. Look at him, bleeding like a bitch," Dawg said, pointing at DeVon, who was lying unconscious with blood oozing from his mouth and nose.

Jamal pulled Dream aside. "Who the hell is this nigga and why were you with him?"

"No, the question is, who in the hell do you think you are?"

"So you've been playing me, right?"

She looked at him then turned toward DeVon who was still on the pavement. "It's not even what you think. You are so fucking stupid. You didn't ask me what was going on; you just reacted."

"Look at me," Jamal turned her face toward him. "What in the hell am I suppose to think when my girlfriend is riding with a nigga this early in the morning?"

The shrill sounds of police and paramedic sirens rang out. Dawg walked over, wedging his way between Jamal and Dream. "Jamal we need to get the hell out of here."

Jamal and Dream stared at each other for a few seconds before Dawg pulled Jamal away, ordering him to get in his car and drive away.

The police arrived, and the manager told the police that Dream had seen the whole altercation and was engaged in conversation with one of the perpetrators.

"Ma'am, you want to tell us what you saw?" the officer asked.

Dream gathered her thoughts. She knew the police wanted to know who assaulted DeVon. She was caught in the middle. The right thing would be to tell the police what had happened and to give the officer some names. She then looked over toward DeVon who remained unconscious, with the paramedics tending him. Finally he was carried away on the stretcher.

She looked the officer directly in the eye. "It started over an argument."

"What were they arguing about?" the officer asked.

Dream looked at her watch. "Listen, can I talk to you later? I'm a middle school teacher and I'm already late. Do you have a card? Maybe I can call you later."

The officer stared at her oddly. "Now the store manager said you saw the whole thing and that you were talking to one of the assailants. Do you want to help us out or not? You're not under arrest, but you do have a moral obligation, and I should hope you would want to do the right thing since you are a teacher."

Dream stared at the pavement. "I don't want to talk right now."

* * *

Dream didn't even bother going to work. She couldn't after the fight. She knew she wouldn't be in any mood to concentrate until she heard something from DeVon. At three o'clock that evening, she had called several hospitals before locating DeVon at the Carolina's Medical Center in Room 338. Upon arrival the receptionist said only family was allowed, and Dream quickly lied, saying she was his sister. Inside DeVon's room, Dream found him conscious, sitting up in the bed wearing a light blue hospital gown with thick white bandages wrapped around his head and several tubes inserted in his mouth. The nurse had told her that his jaw had been broken and his ribs fractured. He had also suffered a minor concussion.

Dream approached to the side of his bed and grabbed his hand. He jerked it back as he looked at her intently.

"DeVon, I know you're mad and you have a right to be. I'm really sorry this happened to you."

He turned his back toward her.

"So you're going to turn your back on me?" she asked.

He then turned and faced her again. He pointed to a small pad and pencil on the table beside his bed. She handed him the items, and he jotted some words down and gave it back to her.

The paper read, Did you tell the police who did this to me?

She looked down at him. Finally she shook her head and he asked for the paper and pencil.

He jotted more words on the paper again and handed it back to her.

You are the one who turned your back on me. He looked sad, and his eyes were full of disappointment. She looked at him for long time. He was right. She had betrayed him. There was no denying it. She had been in a very compromising position, and she hated to betray anyone, she really did. Suddenly a tear trickled down her cheek.

DeVon pressed a button on the side of his bed and a nurse appeared and he indicated he wanted Dream to leave.

* * *

An hour before dark, Keisha and Dream, draped in thick sweat suits, walked through Dream's neighborhood, absorbing brisk air and the dying sunlight. They walked swiftly facing traffic. Walking was Keisha's favorite exercise, simply because she could talk and burn calories at the same time. Dream had contemplated telling Keisha about the fight. Finally, on the last mile, she decided to confide in her.

Keisha stopped in her tracks. "They were fighting?"

Dream stopped. "Yes."

Keisha smiled. "It must be nice to have three men fighting over you."

"DeVon is in the hospital," Dream said.

"Are you serious?"

Dream didn't answer, instead she started to walk again and Keisha followed.

"Are you serious?" Keisha repeated.

"Yes. Dawg and Jamal jumped him and the nurse said a couple of DeVon's ribs are fractured, and his jaw is broken."

"Why were they fighting in the first place?"

Dream faced Keisha. The wind was blowing and Dream's lips had become chapped. "A few weeks ago, DeVon was released and I decided to meet him downtown for a harmless little lunch. A couple of days afterward, he came by the school and told me he had a job as an electrician, but he needed money to buy tools. I went to the ATM and got the money out and loaned it to him. This morning he showed up at my apartment to pay me back. I accepted the money and offered him a ride to work. While riding he noticed a white BMW following us, so I drove to a gas station and found out it was Dawg, who then gets on the phone and calls Jamal. Dawg and DeVon got into a fight, and when Jamal arrived he jumped in. He and Dawg beat DeVon up so badly that the paramedics had to come and get him."

Keisha became serious. "That's real fucked up."

"I know," Dream said.

"So did the police come?"

"Yes."

"You told them what happened, right?"

Dream looked away. "No, I didn't."

"Why not?"

"I know that would have been the right thing to do, but somehow I just couldn't bring myself to do it."

"I know you and DeVon aren't seeing each other anymore but you owe him that much. You should at least tell the police who was involved or what happened," Keisha said, glaring at Dream from the corner of her eye.

Dream didn't say anything. She turned from her friend and faced the oncoming traffic.

"Dream, you're protecting Jamal. He has hurt someone. You can't go on protecting him."

"I know," Dream said, still avoiding Keisha's eyes.

"You aren't going to the police though, are you?"

Again Dream was quiet. She didn't have to answer.

* * *

Dawg looked in the mirror examining his swollen eye. It was practically closed, and he had been wearing sunglasses for the past two days. His eye looked worse than it did on the day of the fight. He had tried heat pads and ice packs but, nothing seemed to bring the swelling down. He picked and nursed it for about five minutes before stepping out into the living room where Jamal sat.

"Nigga, you look like you got beat with a baseball bat," Jamal teased.

"Fuck you. If your girl hadn't been so trifling, I wouldn't be suffering now."

"You suffering 'cause that nigga was whooping your ass until I came."

"Forget you."

"Put your damn glasses on," Jamal said, chuckling.

"So, have you heard from your girl?"

"Naw. I haven't called her."

"Do you think she told the cops what happened?"

Jamal shrugged. "I don't know. That's a good question." He pulled out his cell phone and dialed Dream's number.

"Hello."

"This is Jamal."

"Yeah. What do you want?"

"I just wanna know if you told the cops who me and Dawg were."

"No, but I know I should have. You had no right jumping DeVon like that."

Jamal felt a sudden numbness in his stomach. Had he heard her right? "Did you say DeVon?"

"Yes, I did, but it ain't what you think. I was trying to explain to your stupid-ass friend before he decided to take matters into his own hands."

"My question is, what were you doing with him?" Jamal asked.

"I was taking him to work, as if I have to explain anything to you."

"You ain't got to explain shit to me."

"You know what, Jamal? I ain't gotta listen to this," she said sighing. "I didn't tell the police on you. That's all you really wanted to know anyhow," Dream said before slamming the phone down.

* * *

It was Friday night and Club Champagne was crowded as usual. The crowd was a mixture of hustlers and professional athletes. Jamal took a seat in the corner, next to the pool tables and asked for Candy. One of the other girls in the club said she wasn't working.

He drank straight Hennessy. After three shots he was drunk and horny. Later that night, a short, busty Dominican girl led him to VIP. After two dances Jamal pulled his penis out and tried to penetrate the young woman, but she jumped off his lap and ran downstairs and informed the bouncers. When they arrived they found Jamal zipping up his pants.

"I'm going to have to ask you to leave, buddy," one of the bouncers said.

"Why?" Jamal asked.

"I've seen you in here before, which means you know that you can't be pulling your dick out in here," the man said.

"Come on, man. I was just playing with the girl."

"I need you to leave," the man replied.

"You can't put me out, man. I'll buy this fucking club," Jamal said as he flashed a wad of money, offering it to the bouncer. "Go ahead, man, get you a couple hundred dollars, or take it all," Jamal slurred.

The bouncer took the money, stuffed it back in Jamal's pocket, and grabbed him by the arm.

Jamal turned toward the huge man and shoved him. Another bouncer then grabbed Jamal's other arm. They led him to the front door of the club and tossed him out head first onto the gravel-filled parking lot. Jamal got up from the ground, brushed himself off, and staggered into his car. It was 1:00 A.M. and he was horny. He wanted to have sex with somebody. But who? Dream wasn't speaking to him, and he couldn't find Candy. He suddenly remembered Keisha and the day he had visited her when she was wearing those sexy little shorts. Fifteen minutes later he was at her apartment.

Keisha opened the door wearing a black form-fitting silk robe. "Jamal, what's wrong?" she asked with a concerned look on her face.

"Nothing's wrong," Jamal said as he eased his way into the apartment. "I was in your neighborhood and I thought I would stop by and say hi."

Keisha closed the door and glanced at her watch. "It's 1:30 in the morning."

"I'm sorry. I didn't realize it was so late."

"Hey, listen, if you come back tomorrow, I promise I'll talk to Dream for you and ask her to give your sorry ass another chance."

"I didnt come to talk about Dream."

"What are you talking about?"

"You know what I'm talking about."

Jamal then placed his arm around Keisha's shoulder and massaged lightly.

"Stop it, Jamal," Keisha said as she pulled away from him.

Jamal put his hands around her waist then leaned into her and forced a kiss on her lips.

Keisha tried to get away from his grip, but he was too strong for her. He kissed her again and again. Finally she stopped resisting. As soon as he unzipped his pants she scurried off to her bedroom. She returned with a huge sword-like knife. "Get the hell out of here before I kill your sorry-ass." Keisha said.

Jamal chuckled. "Put that damn thing up."

"Jamal, I'm not playing with you. I want you to leave now!"

Jamal saw the seriousness in Keisha's eyes. "I'm going to leave, but can you do me a favor? Please don't tell Dream this happened. I swear to you, Keisha, this will never happen again. I had too much to drink."

"Just leave, Jamal," Keisha said, pointing at the door.

m   CHAPTER 17   m

IT WAS ELEVEN O'CLOCK Monday morning when Mark marched into the United States Attorney's office. The gold lettering on the door read: ASSISTANT U.S. ATTORNEY, DAVID RICARDO. Mark knocked lightly on the door and a voice called out for him to come right on in.

While on the phone, David spun around in a black, leather swivel chair nursing a cup of coffee. He managed to point to the chair across from his desk. "It'll be a minute," David managed to say.

"Take your time," Mark said, looking around the office at David's various academic degrees and a picture of him shaking Attorney General John Ashcroft's hand with the U.S. flag in the background.

Finally David hung the phone up and smiled. After pleasantries were exchanged, "What can I do for you?" David asked.

"There's something that I've been meaning to talk to you about which totally slipped my mind."

"What is it?"

"You know that I've been undercover for a few months now working on the Stewart case, and have since gotten close to his right-hand man."

"So you're making progress, right?"

"I think so."

"What's the problem?"

"Dawg, also known as Steven Davis, said something very peculiar to me . . . " Mark paused before resuming. "One night while we were out, he said he had connections with the agency. Someone inside is taking bribes, promising to disrupt our investigation."

David's eyebrows rose. "How did you let something like this slip your mind?"

"I don't know. I don't think I took him seriously."

"Can it be confirmed?"

"I don't think so. I'm in charge of the case and I know damn well I haven't been accepting any money from him."

"Jeremiah Tolliver has been helping you out, hasn't he?"

"Yeah."

"Do you think he's been involved in anything like that?"

Mark hadn't considered the possibility. Though he'd made it clear that he disliked Jeremiah, he never thought Jeremiah would be involved in the extortion of drug dealers. "No, sir, I don't."

"Mark, I don't want you to discuss this with anybody else until we find out more information. Is that clear?"

"Yes, sir," Mark said.

* * *

Peering through the peephole of her apartment door, Dream saw DeVon. It had been two weeks since she'd visited him in the hospital. He looked much better. An inflated purple lip was the only visible scar. She opened her door slowly.

"Can I come in?" he asked.

"Yeah, come on in."

She led him through the kitchen, and they sat at the dining room table. Dream felt awkward in his presence. "Would you like something to drink, lemonade or water?"

"No," he replied, mouth still wired shut, speaking through clenched teeth.

His stare made her nervous, and she didn't know what to do. Finally she said, "I'm glad you're doing okay."

"Wiff my mouf wired shut, I can't pronounce da T-H sound."

"DeVon, I know what happened was kind of messed up, and I want you to know I'm really sorry for what happened."

He leaned forward and placed his forearms on the solid oak table. "I don't believe you."

She stood and began pacing. "I don't know what you want me to do to prove myself."

"Dream, you don't owe me anyting. You had your chance to tell da police who beat my ass, and you didn't. I just wanted to let you know dat you really let me down; I just can't believe you're involved wiff drug dealers. I would have never imagined you would do dat."

"How do you know he's involved with drugs? Do you know him?"

"It don't take a genius to figure out doze niggas are up to no good. One of dem was driving a Beamer and da udda was in a Benz. Bofe cars had rims, and it was just something about da skinny mu'fucka in da Beamer. His whole attitude was like it was all about him."

She nodded but didn't respond.

"Lowered your standards, huh?" DeVon asked.

Dream glanced in his direction avoiding, his face, particularly his swollen lip. "What are you talking about? You've sold drugs before," she said defensively, remembering that when she first met him he peddled dime bags of marijuana.

"Yeah, I was small-time, probably smoking more weed dan I sold, but doze niggas are big-time."

"Whatever."

He stood and walked over to her. "Do your mom and dad know what's going on wit you and dis man of yours?"

"Nothing is going on. I haven't seen Jamal since the day of the fight."

DeVon stared at her without saying a word. "Leave dem guys alone before it's too late. I don't want anyting to happen to you. I came over here out of concern for you. When you visited me in da hospital a couple of weeks ago, I really had made up my mind dat I didn't want to see yo' ass again, but someting in my heart just won't let me walk away from you like dat. I know you really need help, and I want you to promise me dat you won't see dis Jamal character again."

"I already told you that I ain't seeing him anymore."

"I know what you told me, but I want you to promise me dat you ain't gonna see him again."

Dream was silent for a moment before raising her head to look DeVon in his eyes. She could tell he was concerned, and she knew that he wasn't about to leave until she promised to stop seeing Jamal. Though she hadn't considered her relationship with Jamal officially over, she knew it probably was. The last time she had spoken with him, he hadn't bothered to apologize for his behavior.

"Baby, don't you see dat I care about you?" DeVon said.

"You sure as hell didn't seem to care a whole lot about me when you were in jail."

He grabbed her hand and gazed into her eyes. "Promise me you won't see him again."

Impulsively she hugged him but he quickly pulled away.

"My ribs are sore as hell. Remember your mobster-ass boyfriend kicked my ass," he said, laughing.

She frowned and replied, "Lift your shirt up and let me see."

He pulled up his shirt, and Dream examined the white bandages that clung to his torso. "Dey fucked me up pretty bad."

"Did the doctor give you any painkillers or anything?"

He pulled a small white tube of cream from his pants pocket. "Dis is all I have. Da doctor told me to apply dis twice a day, and it's suppose to help da soreness, but I can't stand to touch my ribs; dey hurt so fuckin' much."

"A woman's touch is what you need."

"Is dat right?" He forced a painful smile.

She took his hand and led him to the bedroom. "Lift up your shirt again and lie across the bed on your back."

He quickly pulled the black nylon shirt over his head and tossed it on the floor.

Dream unwrapped the bandages and took the cream, squeezing it into the palm of her hand. She applied it, smoothing it out in a circular motion. "How does it feel?"

"Ah, dis feels so good," he responded, staring at the ceiling.

"Turn over on your stomach."

"It'll hurt."

Dream grabbed the fluffy white pillows from the head of the bed. "Here use these, silly boy."

DeVon's Hershey-colored backside glistened as she applied the cream.

After several minutes, "I can't take much more of dis."

"What are you talking about?"

"I'm horny."

She smiled. "You're hurt, remember?"

Without a word he leaned toward her and their lips met briefly.

"We shouldn't do this."

"Why? You just said a few minutes ago dat you ain't seeing Jamal anymore."

She had become aroused as well. The sight of the rippling muscles in DeVon's back had caused droplets of moisture to roll down her leg. Though she hadn't seen Jamal in two weeks, she felt kind of guilty.

DeVon placed his hand behind her neck and pulled her toward him for another quick kiss. Then he unbuttoned her blouse. Her small brown breasts sat upright, and he smiled seductively before running his finger across an erect nipple.

She looked at him and attempted to fasten the buttons on her blouse before he leaned into her and grazed her neck. Her body tingled, and her hand fell from her shirt. Part of her wanted to fight the temptation, but another part of her wanted DeVon badly. He kissed her breast, and this put her in the mood. Finally he stood and dropped his pants, revealing an erection.

She took off her clothes and got a condom from her dresser drawer, tossed it to him and smiled.

* * *

Jamal sat quietly in Dream's parking lot in an inconspicuous car. He had observed Dream and DeVon coming and going for the past three days. He had followed them to restaurants, the cinema, and a park. He had become sick of the sight of them kissing and hugging and seemingly having a good time. Today will be different, he vowed. Today he would end all the laughter and the good times. His nine-millimeter rested at his waist with a loaded magazine clip.

It isn't fair, he told himself. How could he lose the love of his life so quickly? How could she betray him? He had money and DeVon had none. How could Dream leave him for a broke man? A damned nobody. This was not the way the relationship was supposed to end. It can't end like this, he thought, as he pulled his gun out and stared down the barrel. He smiled, thinking of DeVon begging for his life.

Jamal had watched DeVon come over at 6:00 P.M. for the past three days. Each day Dream would open the door and greet him with a warm hug, obviously glad to see him, and this made Jamal angrier. He couldn't remember her ever being that excited to see him. At 7:00, Dream and DeVon left her house and went to a little restaurant downtown. He followed them. Inside the restaurant, he took a seat on the other side, occasionally gazing in their direction. They didn't see him because they were too busy laughing and smiling. He fumed inside.

Keisha arrived with a date midway through the meal. It was officially a double date, and the fun was much more apparent. The laughter grew louder, and the kissing and flirting was sickening. At one point they had gotten so loud that the manager came from the back to calm them down.

After dinner, the happy group went to a comedy show, which Jamal chose not to attend. He was in no mood for laughter. He figured, with his luck, one of those stupid-ass comedians would call him out and reveal him. He drove back to Dream's parking lot and waited for her to arrive.

* * *

Dream and DeVon showed up around 11:00. Jamal had it all planned out. Whenever DeVon decided to leave, Jamal would follow, abduct him at gunpoint, take him to a remote location, and kill him. Take the body to a nearby river and dump it there. At 11:45 Jamal saw Dream giving DeVon a good-night kiss. DeVon left walking as usual. He apparently preferred walking, and Jamal thought he must live nearby.

In the pitch-black dark, DeVon walked quickly along the highway. Jamal pulled alongside DeVon and slowed the vehicle. The two men made eye contact.

"Yeah, what do you want?" DeVon asked.

Obviously, DeVon didn't recognize Jamal. He stared intensely and Jamal could only see the whites of his eyes. DeVon was shaken and visibly afraid. Jamal placed his finger on the trigger of the handgun. Just one shot to his chest would rip through his lungs or stop his heart. Go ahead, don't think, just fire. But Jamal couldn't bring himself to fire. It would be senseless to kill DeVon. Jamal glanced over his shoulder once again. There was no traffic on the dark road. He could kill DeVon, and nobody would ever know. But why kill someone who had done absolutely nothing to him directly. Why take the risk of being charged with murder? He didn't want to end up back in prison where there would be no money to be made and no women. He placed the gun between his legs, and pushed the gas pedal to the floor.

He drove back to Dream's apartment and dialed her number.

"Hello," she answered.

"Hello, this is Jamal."

"And?"

"I want to see you."

"Why?"

"Because I haven't seen you in a while."

"Listen, Jamal, I have to go to work in the morning. I'm a grown woman, and I don't have a whole lot of patience for your childish games."

"So you're back with DeVon, huh?"

"I'm not with anybody."

"You gonna tell me that you haven't been with DeVon tonight?"

"I ain't telling you nothing. In fact, I don't feel that I have to tell you anything. Good night."

m CHAPTER 18 m

CHRISTMAS DAY. It was very cold, and a thin layer of ice covered the ground. Dream and DeVon were dating steadily but hadn't officially given themselves a title. Whenever someone would ask whether they were a couple, they would both reply that they were just hanging.

It was around six o'clock and Dream had just returned from her parent's home where she had gone to pick up her gifts. Her phone rang an hour after returning.

"Hello."

"Before you hang up, look out the window," Jamal said.

"Why?"

"I bought you a Christmas gift."

"Bye, Jamal."

"Well, it'll be outside whenever you decide to check it out."

She hung up then looked out of the window. A black 320 E-class Mercedes, with red and white bows wrapped around it, sat in the parking lot. She anxiously rushed outside.

It was beautiful, and her name had been sprayed across the windshield with whipped cream. She examined the charcoal-colored leather seats and the wood-grained dash. A Christmas card lay on the seat.

Just wanted to say I'm sorry, and I hope we can work out our differences. Jamal.

Dream immediately called Keisha; she arrived at Dream's apartment fifteen minutes later. "Do you think I should keep the car or return it? I don't know what to do."

Keisha opened the door of the Benz and got behind the wheel. "I can't tell you what to do, but I can tell you what I would do."

"What would you do?" Dream asked with serious eyes.

"I would keep it."

"Keep it?"

"Don't you want to keep it?"

Dream hesitated before speaking. "Well, yeah of course I do."

"Well then that settles it. Keep it."

Dream didn't reply, instead she walked around to the passenger side and sat down.

Keisha turned toward Dream. "You're worried about what DeVon is going to think, huh?"

"Yeah."

"Is he your boyfriend?"

"No."

Keisha turned the key, firing up the ignition. "Well, keep the damn car. Are you crazy?"

"Correct me if I'm wrong here, but weren't you the one who said that I should have told the police who Jamal and Dawg were?" Dream asked.

"You didn't though, so that's irrelevant. Don't you know this is a fifty-thousand-dollar car?"

"Let's take it for a spin!" Dream said.

* * *

Later that night, Dream was sitting cozily by the fireplace in her pajamas, sipping eggnog. The Christmas tree lights blinked splendidly as the Temptations sang the classic Silent Night. DeVon arrived with a gift, and she invited him inside and hugged him.

"Merry Christmas," she said.

"Merry Christmas to you," he replied and passed her the gift along with his coat.

She grabbed his hand, led him to the fireplace and poured him a glass of eggnog, She then opened his present. "You shouldn't have," Dream said, examining a black Coach handbag.

"I had to. You have been so good to a brother," he replied, no longer speaking through clenched teeth.

"I got you a present as well," she said, disappearing into her bedroom and returning with a green box with a beautiful red bow. "Here you go."

He smiled and tore into the package. It was a sweater from Banana Republic.

"Do you like it?"

"I love it," he said as he picked her up and spun her around.

She smiled innocently then became saddened. "There's something I have to tell you."

He looked her directly in the eyes. "Good or bad news?"

"It depends on how you take it."

"I don't like the sound of it already."

She looked at him then poured another glass of eggnog.

"What is it, Dream?" he demanded.

"Jamal gave me a present."

He smiled. "Oh, that's cool. I mean since we are not officially a couple, and we're just chillin'. Is that what you were afraid to tell me?"

"Yeah. Don't you want to know what he gave me?"

"Not really, but you can tell me if you like."

"He bought me a car."

DeVon's bottom lipped dropped. "A car? What kind?"

"A Benz."

"Well, you didn't take it, did you?"

"Yeah, of course I did. Why wouldn't I?"

"Because the mu'fucka is gonna think he owns you now. I think you should give it back."

"Seriously?"

"I am serious," he said, staring at Dream with intense eyes.

She sipped her eggnog slowly without responding.

"Give it back," he demanded.

"Me and you ain't together. You can't tell me what to do."

DeVon stood, went to the hall closet, retrieved his coat, threw it over his arm, and headed for the door. "When are you going to get it? That nigga ain't no good. Okay, he has money, but is money everything?"

Their eyes met and held but neither said anything. Finally DeVon opened the door and left.

Later that night Jamal called Dream.

"Hello," she said.

"How did you like the gift I got for you?"

"The car is really nice. Are you sure you want to give me something that expensive?"

"Don't worry about the cost. I can afford it, or else I wouldn't have bought it, believe me. The question is, what is your little boyfriend gonna say once he sees the car?"

"You mean DeVon?"

"Who else?"

"He already knows about the car. He stormed out of here after he learned that you gave it to me."

"Good, now I won't feel guilty about asking you can I come over."

"Come on over, I'll be waiting on you."

* * *

The evening of Valentine's Day, Jamal took Dream to T-Bones on the lake, a cozy little steakhouse located in Lake Wylie, a subdivision just south of Charlotte. The food was mediocre. But Jamal really liked it. He could have dinner overlooking the water. For February the weather was kind of warm but breezy. Jamal and Dream looked wonderful together. She was wearing a long wrap skirt with black leather riding boots and a gray turtleneck sweater with a black leather jacket. He wore a black leather jacket, black jeans with a black headband, and a huge diamond in his left ear.

When the waitress appeared, Dream ordered a flounder and shrimp dinner and Jamal a rib-eye steak, medium well. While they waited on their food, they talked about everything from politics to music. Finally, Dream felt the moment was right and pulled a small Valentine's Day card from her purse and passed it to him. Inside the card was a gift certificate to Dillard's department store. It was the only thing she could think to get him, since he was such a shopper.

He smiled. "Dream, I love you," he said, gazing into her eyes. He then dug inside his jacket pocket and pulled out a small box. When she opened it, a beautiful smile emerged as she pulled a four-carat diamond ring in a platinum setting from the box. Jamal placed it on her ring finger.

"Will you marry me?" he asked.

She turned from his gaze, looking out on the lake at the water rippling in the moonlight. "I don't know. I have to think about it."

He looked sad. "Listen, Dream, I know you can't picture yourself marrying someone like me, but I'm about to go legit, baby. I'm going to stop dealing in a couple of months."

She looked him in the eyes. He seemed serious and his voice sounded sincere. Despite their differences, Dream did love him more than she had loved any of her previous boyfriends. "I need you to stop if we're going to have any kind of future together."

"So I take that as a yes."

She met his eyes and smiled. "I'll marry you, Jamal."

"Yes! Yes! She said she'll marry me," Jamal told the waitress who had appeared with the food.

The waitress sat their food down and announced their engagement to the entire restaurant. The patrons went wild, shouting and cheering. Dream held up her ring and Jamal just looked on, sipping his iced tea.

* * *

"You're gonna get married?" Keisha asked, surprised.

"Yeah," Dream answered, showing off engagement ring.

"Do your parents know?"

"No. I haven't told them yet."

"Are you sure you want to marry this guy? I mean, after all, you were saying just a few months ago that he had issues and you didn't know if you wanted to deal with him."

"I know what I said, but he promised me he was going to stop dealing."

Keisha looked at Dream oddly before saying enthusiastically, "Congratulations. When is the wedding?"

Dream beamed with excitement. "We haven't set a date yet."

"Well has Jamal found his mother yet?"

"No, and you know what? I totally forgot to tell him you said your private investigator could probably find her."

"Yeah, I'm sure he can locate her. All he needs is her name, date of birth, and birthplace. I know Jamal would probably like to find her now, especially since there's going to be a wedding."

"I'll get him to give me the information, and I'll call you with it."

Keisha didn't respond. Her attention seemed to be somewhere else.

"Did you hear me, Keisha?"

Keisha took a deep breath. "I have to tell you something before you get married."

"What's wrong?"

Keisha turned away from Dream briefly. "Do you remember the last time you and Jamal had broken up, after Jamal and Dawg had the fight with DeVon?"

"Yeah."

"One night, Jamal came over to my apartment after he had been drinking, and he tried to go there with me."

Dream hesitated. "Why are you just now telling me this shit?"

"I didn't know how you would respond. I knew you cared about him a lot, and I knew this would hurt you."

Dream's eyes became bloodshot. "You damn right it hurts. If you were anybody else, I wouldn't have believed you, but I know it's the truth because you're my girl." Dream began crying.

"Like I said, he was drunk. And since that night, it hasn't happened again."

"I don't think I can marry him now."

"Dream, it is not that serious. If you love the man, marry him," Keisha said as she grabbed Dream's hand. "Girl, look at this ring. If this ain't love, I don't know what is."

"I still need to hear what Jamal has to say about the whole situation."

* * *

Jamal blew his horn and Dawg came running to the car with a small nylon bag in hand. Inside the car, he unzipped the bag and showed Jamal what he had traded for product. "Check it out, man. It's a baby .380," Dawg said, rubbing the small chrome handgun.

Jamal looked at the gun briefly before screeching out of the parking lot. He wasn't in the mood to comment about a handgun. Actually, he felt Dawg should have left it inside. They rode a few minutes before Dawg asked where they were going.

"Nowhere specific. Just needed to talk to you about some things."

Dawg put the gun back in the bag and tucked it under his jacket. "What you want to talk about?"

Jamal looked at Dawg for a second then shifted his attention to the oncoming traffic. "I proposed to Dream."

"You did what, nigga?"

"I'm going to get married."

"You making a big mistake."

"I love this woman, and I think I'm doing the right thing by tying the knot."

"What about your goal to make $500,000?"

"What about it?"

"So I guess making money is no longer your focus, huh?"

Jamal looked away briefly before resuming eye contact, "Of course it is; I just think this is the right thing for me to do. You should be happy for me, man."

"She's going to change you. Her mama and daddy already think she's too good for you, remember?"

"I ain't marrying her mama and daddy; I'm marrying her."

Dawg looked out the window. "Don't do it, Jamal. The next thing you know, she's going to have you talking about getting a job."

"I plan on looking for one real soon," Jamal said.

"There goes the goal out the window."

* * *

"I feel like I'm losing my best friend," Dawg said to Mark.

"What do you mean?" the agent asked, admiring Dawg's apartment.

Dawg looked at him intently as if he were contemplating the disclosure of a deep secret. "Jamal, my boy, is about to get married. I mean, I know I should be happy for him, but I really think the woman is going to change him. He's already talking about getting a job and retiring from the game. That's the reason I haven't been able to supply you lately."

Mark took a deep breath. "This must be one helluva lady to make a man think about giving up the kind of money that comes along with the game." Mark had not gotten any closer to Jamal over the months. For this reason, he had not yet sought an indictment against Dawg.

"She's okay, I guess. She's a teacher. She comes from a family that thinks she is too good for my boy."

"So what about you, Dawg? I don't ever hear you talking about no women in your life."

Dawg pulled a picture from his wallet and presented it to Mark. It was a photo of a little girl in a leotard and ballet shoes.

"Is this your daughter?"

"Yes, that's my angel."

"Where is she?"

"In New Jersey with her mother."

"Do you get to see her often?"

Dawg yawned. "I haven't seen her in three years. Her mother won't allow me."

Mark passed the picture back to Dawg. He didn't want to ask too many questions about Dawg's personal life, because he didn't want to become attached to him. Dawg was a criminal and Mark knew he had to keep that in mind.

"So what about you? Do you have a woman?" Dawg asked.

"No, I don't have one."

"Kids?"

"No."

"Why not, man? You have got to be at least thirty."

Mark smirked. "Yeah, I guess you can say I'm an old man now, but to be truthful with you, I've just been concentrating on making money. I guess one day I'll find a woman. She's gonna have to be strong, though."

Dawg turned and faced him again. "You know what? You sound a lot like Jamal. I wish you could meet him, man. You two guys are a lot alike."

Mark longed for the day he could meet Jamal as well, but he knew it wouldn't be under pleasant circumstances. He was nothing like Jamal. As far as he could tell they were opposites. Jamal was pushing the poison, and he was trying to stop it from coming into the community.

m CHAPTER 19 m

THE HUGE SMILE ON Jamal's face revealed that he was glad to see Dream as he entered her apartment. He kissed her on the forehead and noticed she was frowning.

"What's wrong baby?"

Dream placed her hands on her hips. "Jamal, do you want to tell me about the night you visited Keisha's apartment and tried to get with her?"

"Ah, shit," Jamal said as he threw his hands up in disgust. "Do you know how long that's been?"

"Answer the question, Jamal," Dream demanded.

"I was drunk, okay? I was drunk and horny. If I hadn't been drunk, I would have never tried her."

"Why didn't you tell me about it, Jamal?"

"It happened during the time we weren't speaking, about a week after we kicked DeVon's ass?"

"Why did you have to try my best friend?"

Jamal approached Dream, placed his hand under her chin, and kissed her lips gently. "Baby, I made a mistake. Nothing happened, I promise you. What did Keisha say happened?"

"She said nothing happened."

"Okay, there you have it. Why are you still tripping?"

Dream became sad. "Because I don't know if I can trust the man that I'm about to marry."

Jamal entered the living room and took a seat on the sofa. He rested his chin in the palm of his hand then glanced at Dream. "I guess that stupid-ass Keisha is trying to mess things up for us now. Since she doesn't have a man she probably doesn't want you to be happy either, huh?"

"No, that ain't even the case, Jamal. Believe it or not, she actually thinks I should go ahead and marry you."

"And what do you think?"

"Jamal, you already know that I love you but—"

"But what?" Jamal interrupted.

Dream took a deep breath then ran her fingers through her hair. "I don't want to get hurt. Marriages are meant to last forever."

"And we'll be together forever." Jamal responded.

"I don't know if I can live with the fact that my man has tried to have sex with my best friend. You know, if we get married both of you will be part of my life forever. How will I get over thoughts that you may be looking at her sexually? You may be attracted to her more than you are to me." Her voice cracked as if she were about to cry.

Jamal stood and hugged Dream. "Baby, I know I'm not perfect. Lord knows I've made many mistakes. I swear to you, you're the only woman I've ever loved."

Dream pushed Jamal away. "Jamal, I love you, too, but many changes have to be made if we want this relationship to work."

"I promise you, I'll change," Jamal said softly.

* * *

The third day of spring, U.S. Attorney David Ricardo convinced a federal grand jury to indict Dawg, superceding Connie and Jennifer's indictment. The grand jury had refused to indict Jamal and Angelo. The evidence simply wasn't there. Jeremiah was pleased, though, because he thought Dawg would cooperate to bring down Jamal and Angelo. Mark had pleaded for more time to get closer to Jamal. He knew there was no longer a chance to connect with Jamal.

It was 6:00 A.M. when the task force comprised of local policemen, U.S. Marshals, and DEA agents used a battering ram to knock Dawg's door down. When he looked up there were three Marshals pointing automatic weapons at his head.

"Put your damn hands up where I can see them!" one of them shouted.

Dawg slowly held his hands up and was yanked off the bed. He was handcuffed, and the gun inside the nightstand was confiscated. "Will somebody tell me what in the hell is going on?" he asked.

"We have a warrant for your arrest, Steven," Mark said before he ordered the other agents to search the house.

Dawg's eyes met Mark's, and then he started to laugh. "This is a joke, right, TJ?"

Mark pulled his DEA badge from his pocket and showed it to Dawg. "I'm afraid not. This is serious business. You've been indicted by the federal government."

"For what?"

"Cocaine conspiracy," Mark replied.

"So you're really working for the fucking cops, huh?"

"I guess you can say that," Mark said. "Take Mr. Davis downtown. We'll search the apartment."

Two local cops picked Dawg up from the floor and forced him toward the front door of the apartment. He stopped and turned to face Mark. "You know, I would have never thought you were a fucking sellout, low-down-ass cop."

"I know, which is why you're in deep shit"

The search yielded cell phone records, rental car receipts, and $120,000 in cash, all of which would be used in court. Mark was hoping they would find some product but was satisfied with the evidence that was gathered.

* * *

"Yo, man, I'm locked up," Dawg said over the phone.

Jamal sat up in the bed and wiped his eyes. He glanced at his clock. It was ten in the morning and he was still half asleep. "I told you to pay that child support. How can you be so stupid?"

"I'm not locked up for child support, man. The Feds came and got me this morning."

After a long pause, Jamal finally spoke. "What do you mean the Feds?"

"The DEA came and arrested me for drug conspiracy."

Jamal stood and paced nervously. "Are they looking for me?"

"Naw, man. You wasn't on the indictment, just me and those two chicks from Cali. It was a superceding indictment. They had already indicted the chicks months ago."

"Are you sure?"

"I'm positive. What I need you to do is to get me a lawyer so I can find out what in the hell is going on. I go to court in the morning for arraignment."

"You got that. I'll make sure you have one of the best," Jamal said before hanging up.

* * *

Dawg was arraigned and denied bond. Hours later, two Marshals brought him to an interrogation room for questioning. Mark, Jeremiah, and U.S. Attorney David Ricardo were present. "Good morning, Mr. Davis," Mark said.

Dawg leaned his head back, avoided eye contact with Mark, and stared at the ceiling. "I don't know what make brothers get with the white man and bring other brothers down."

"Don't give me that white man shit!" David shouted. "The bottom line is, everyone in the room is from different backgrounds. We all had the same choices to make. It just so happened you made the wrong choices."

"I can't believe this shit," Dawg said.

"Well, believe it, and also believe that you're facing a life sentence," David said.

"I'm going to go to trial on these charges. I ain't accepting no plea, and I definitely ain't helping ya'll mu'fuckas bring other people down," Dawg replied.

Mark pulled a small black device from a manila envelope. He turned the device on and a recording of Dawg's voice suddenly filled the room. "Oh, we got plenty, man. It's the best shit we've had in a long time."

"How do you think a jury would react to hearing you brag about how good your shit is?" Mark asked.

"That wasn't me," Dawg replied.

"Sure sounds like you to me," David said, smiling.

Dawg met David's eyes with a hard stare and then placed his feet on the conference table. "I don't give a fuck what it sounds like. You won't get me to admit to shit."

"Davis, I've seen you with drugs; you've sold me drugs. Don't you see you cannot win?" Mark pleaded.

"I ain't admitting to shit."

"And you are definitely going to get life," David said.

"Why am I here talking to you guys in the first place?" Dawg asked as he turned toward Mark.

Mark paced the floor. "Well, Dawg, it's like this: Despite the fact that I feel you're a low-life, I want to help you."

"Well, if you want me to turn into an informant, you have the wrong man."

"So I guess you don't want to help yourself," David said.

"Take me back to the county jail," Dawg said.

* * *

The inmate visitation room at the county jail held a long line of phones on a Plexiglas partition, separating the inmate from the visitor. Jamal sat in a chair nervously awaiting Dawg's arrival. When Dawg finally appeared, the two men smiled at each other before picking up the phones. "What's up?" Jamal asked.

"A whole bunch of shit is going on."

"Like what?"

"I don't really trust these phones," Dawg said.

"Keep it clean."

Dawg looked over his shoulder at a deputy who was a few feet away reading the sports section of the newspaper. "The guy that Ruff introduced me to, TJ, turned out to be a DEA agent."

Jamal's jaw dropped. "So what's up with Ruff? Has he been indicted?"

"I don't think so. I think he's informing, though."

This made sense to Jamal since Ruff was the guy who had introduced TJ, and he had not been indicted. "Has anybody said anything about me?"

"They brought me in to interrogate me, but I didn't cooperate with them. I didn't give them a chance to ask me nothing."

Jamal nodded. "Is there anything you want me to do for you?"

"I just need you to get me an attorney, man. I really ain't got no money since the Feds took my stash."

"Okay, you have my word, I'll get you the best attorney."

"What about the girls? How do they come into the picture?"

Dawg shrugged. "I really don't know. All I know is that their names were on the indictment. The Feds must have linked them to me or something."

"Time's up, guys," the deputy said.

Dawg stood and smiled at Jamal once again. "I'm going to be a'ight, man. Don't worry about me."

"I know you're going to be a'ight," Jamal said before turning and walking out of the door. He really wanted to believe everything was going to be okay, but somehow he couldn't.

* * *

Jamal didn't know where to turn. His childhood friend was now in custody, and he knew it would be a matter of time before the Feds came after him—if they weren't already looking for him. He needed someone to talk to, someone who could probably make some kind of sense of this whole situation. He knew Dream wouldn't understand, and he knew he shouldn't call Angelo because he didn't want to say too much over the telephone since there was a strong possibility that his phone was tapped. After serious contemplation, he called Tony. For some reason, Jamal felt he would have some answers. They decided to meet at Starbucks again.

Jamal and Tony sat outside as a huge crimson sun beamed brightly. Tony was surprised to learn about Dawg's detention.

"What in the hell did I pay you for?" Jamal asked.

"For protection from the DEA."

"That's what I thought," Jamal replied.

Tony sipped his cappuccino slowly. "Well, you didn't get indicted, did you?"

Jamal tapped the table nervously. "No, not yet. But who's to say that it isn't going to happen."

"You're right. It very well might happen. You boys should have stopped dealing when I told you about the investigation. I know you didn't think the protection was going to last forever."

"Listen, man, I don't want to hear about what we should have done. The bottom line is, we chose to keep going. What I need for you to do is ask the agent if they're still trying to indict my black ass, and if so, can I pay my way out." Jamal's eyes were intense.

Tony placed the Styrofoam coffee cup on the table. "I'll call you tonight."

* * *

Later that night Tony called Jamal. "I have some good news for you," Tony sighed. "Dawg ain't informing on you."

"I already knew that. What else can you tell me?"

At this point, there is nothing we can do to help him. He is more than likely going to prison for a long time. It seems like Dawg has been selling to an agent and his case is pretty much open and shut."

A brief silence subdued them. Jamal thought about his friend who had been jailed a few times in the past but had never actually done any prison time. Prison was a dreadful experience that Jamal didn't wish on his worst enemy. "So can I pay your man some more money like I did the last time to get them to ease off me?" Jamal asked.

"No. There is nothing I can do about it now. You guys should have stopped when I warned you the last time."

"I didn't know Dawg was dealing with the DEA."

" Jamal, my advice to you is just lay low. If your boy don't go running off at his mouth, you may have a chance, but you need to stop dealing."

m CHAPTER 20 m

DREAM'S LONG LEGS CLUTCHED his waist. Jamal breathed heavily as entered her. He kissed her passionately as her wet tongue whirled around in his ear. He loved when she did that; it made him harder. He also liked the fact that she was open and willing to try new things.

Twenty minutes and three positions later, they stopped, and a tear rolled down her cheek. The sex was so good. He lit a Black and Mild cigar and sat up on the edge of the bed.

"Since when did you start smoking cigars?" she asked.

"In case you hadn't noticed, I've been stressing lately," he said as he exhaled.

She stared at him. His eyes were heavy, and he looked as though he had gained a few pounds around the midsection. "What's wrong now?"

"The Feds locked Dawg up on drug charges."

She looked him in the eye. "When did this happen?"

"About two weeks ago."

"So what does this mean for you?"

He stood and put his boxer shorts on before answering. "Nothing, I hope."

"But you don't know whether you're going to jail or not, do you?"

"No, I really don't." He sat back on the bed and dropped his head.

"Well that's just fuckin' wonderful. The man I am about to marry is going to prison. Let me tell you something, Jamal, I am not going to be spending my weekends visiting nobody at no damn prison."

Jamal was dizzy from the cigar. He put it out in a Mountain Dew can that was on the floor. "I ain't going to jail."

"I guess this means you're going to stop," she said.

"No, this means that if the police, FBI, DEA, or anybody else comes to get me, they better be ready to die, because I will die before I go back to jail."

Dream stood and slipped on some gray gym shorts that were lying on the dresser. "I can't believe you're talking like this. What are you, stupid or something? I mean, first these two girls get locked up, then your boy goes to jail. You might be next, but you don't want to stop? Instead you are making preparations to shoot it out with the police. Jamal, you're going to have to stop if we're going to get married."

Jamal avoided Dream's eyes. "I already told you I was going to stop, but right now I need to make some money just in case the bastards are lucky enough to catch me with my guards down. I won't be broke doing time. Plus, I'm gonna have to get Dawg a lawyer and retain one for myself."

She suddenly remembered what Keisha had said about finding his mother. "I almost forgot to tell you that Keisha knows a private investigator who can probably find your mother if she can get a birth date and birthplace."

"She was born November 17, 1954, in Orangeburg, South Carolina."

Dream walked to the kitchen, opened the junk drawer, retrieved a pen, and quickly jotted the information down. She could tell by Jamal's response that he really wanted some kind of closure in his search for his mother.

* * *

Jamal paid fifty-thousand dollars for Dawg's legal defense. After he had left Dawg's attorney's office, Jamal and Dream visited Jamal's old defense counsel for consultation. Thomas Henry was a board-certified criminal defense lawyer who specialized in drug cases. Thomas was a short, plump, white man with a receding hairline. He wore his hair in a ponytail. He drove a blue convertible Jaguar with ACQUIT on the license plate.

Thomas had represented Jamal on his last case. Initially Jamal was sentenced to twenty years, but Thomas had argued on a sentencing issue and got it reduced to five years on appeal. It had cost Jamal $75,000, but he felt he couldn't put a price on his freedom.

Thomas and Jamal shook hands as soon as they saw each other. "Hey, buddy. It's been a long time," Thomas said. He turned to Dream and smiled.

"Yeah, almost six years," Jamal said.

"Have a seat," Thomas pointed to the two plush burgundy leather chairs that were in front of his desk. "What you got for me?"

"How much will you charge me for a retainer?"

"Is it a state or federal case?"

"Federal,"

"Usually it's thirty thousand for a federal case, but for you, I'll work something out since we go back," Thomas said, smiling.

"I need to retain you now. I got a feeling I'm about to have a case real soon," Jamal said as Dream looked on, concerned.

"Why do you say that?" Thomas asked.

Jamal turned from his gaze and Dream grabbed his hand. "Let's just say a few people I know have been indicted for a drug conspiracy."

"How do you know these people?" Thomas asked as he placed his elbows on the desk and rested his chin in the palm of his hands.

"I just know them from hanging out."

Thomas looked at him suspiciously. "Now, Jamal, you know I know the game and besides, I'm on your side. Now if you want me to help, you must tell me what's going on. I am not authorized to repeat anything that you say. Everything that goes on in this office is confidential."

For the next twenty-five minutes Jamal disclosed all his dealings to Thomas. He told him about the California trips, his relationship with Tony, and the knowledge that Tony had given him about the DEA seeking an indictment. Thomas didn't say anything; he just nodded and scribbled on a legal pad.

Dream was amazed at the whole story. It's better than watching the Sopranos, she thought. She had known about most of Jamal's involvement, but today was the first time she had heard about Tony and his involvement with the DEA.

"Do you think you can help me?" Jamal asked.

"Technically, Jamal, since you are not indicted, there's nothing I can really do. I've got a few sources downtown in the U.S. Attorney's office; I'll keep my ear to the ground and see what I can find out for you."

"Now, how much should I expect for you to charge me for the retainer?"

Thomas leaned back in his chair and began to run his fingers through his oily ponytail before saying, "Since you don't actually have a case yet, I'll say fifteen thousand dollars. I'm going to need an additional $45,000 before I can represent you in a trial."

"I understand. Do you still take cash?"

"I'm not supposed to, but since it's you, I'll do it."

Jamal smiled. "You know I've always been a cash-money type of guy."

Thomas stood and walked over to the oak double doors and turned the gold lock. "Do you have the money on you now?"

"Yeah," Jamal said before opening a black leather bag. The money was in thousand- dollar stacks. Jamal counted fifteen stacks.

Dream couldn't believe what she had witnessed. In less than an hour she had seen Jamal spend $65,000 in cash for attorney's fees for him and Dawg. It was no secret that Jamal and Dawg had been up to no good, but the attorneys were bigger crooks than the dealers were. The sad part was that they were robbing people, legitimately, with outrageous fees.

When they left the attorney's office Dream noticed Jamal looked sad and he wasn't saying much in the car. "What's wrong, baby?" she asked.

"I feel like a goddamn fool. I only have eighty grand left. The fucking lawyers are breaking my ass. I need to make some money."

She didn't know what to say. She didn't want him to feel this way, and she certainly didn't want him to think that he needed to have a whole bunch of money to have her affection. "I can sell my ring and the Mercedes. Those things aren't important. The only thing that's important is the way that I feel about you," she said as she placed her hand on his ear.

What she said made him feel better. He had never met anyone who loved him unconditionally. He liked the feeling. They stopped at a downtown traffic light. "Baby, ain't nobody selling shit. You're keeping everything I bought for you. That's the bottom line," he said.

"I know you want me to keep the ring, but I don't want you to feel like you have to do something desperate."

He glanced over at her before the light turned green. "I don't want to be broke and in jail. Eighty grand won't last long. The lawyer will want forty-five grand of that." He thought about the ring, the vehicles, the new apartment, the vacations and trips. He might have reached his goal of $500,000 and gotten out of the game if he hadn't been so foolish with money.

"Baby, honestly, I don't think you're going to jail. I don't see how," she said naively.

"Well, I've been dealing with the system for a while, and I've got a better idea about how it works. The Feds are after me, and I need to go to Cali to see Angelo so I can make some money."

"Well I'm going with you. I don't want anything to happen to you."

Jamal hadn't anticipated this. He grabbed her hand and held it tight.

* * *

Mark was sitting at his desk reading a Sports Illustrated article when his phone rang.

"DEA, Mark Pratt speaking."

"Listen, man, I got some information you might want," a voice said.

"First of all who is this?" Mark asked.

"My name is Eric Culpepper."

"Would you speak up? I can barely hear you."

"I can't really talk too loud. I'm in the county jail, and the other inmates might hear me."

"How did you get through without calling collect?"

"My baby's mama called on the three-way."

Mark assumed this guy had overheard somebody talking about some relevant information and decided to call the DEA. He knew more than likely the guy was facing some kind of charges himself that he was trying to get out of. In all his years of law enforcement Mark had never had anyone call from jail with information unless they were trying to get out. "You say you are in the county jail, huh?"

"Yeah,"

"I'm coming to see you tomorrow."

* * *

Mark wore a black Kenneth Cole suit and a gray shirt. With a yellow legal pad in hand, he looked like a lawyer when he entered the room. The room was a large, cafeteria-style area with long white tables and mismatched chairs.

The inmate was a huge bronze-colored man with cornrows. He reeked of generic cigarettes.

"I'm Agent Mark Pratt."

"I'm Eric. My friends call me Psycho." The men shook hands before seating themselves.

"First of all, let me ask you, what are you in here for?" Mark asked.

"I'm awaiting trial for accused rape."

The answer caught Mark totally off guard. Mark could never understand why a man would force himself on a woman. He suddenly disliked Psycho. "So what did you hear?"

"Before I give you my information, I'm going to have to know what you're gonna do for me."

Mark took a deep breath before speaking. "I can't promise you anything, especially with the type of case you have. With a rape case, you either did it or you didn't."

"Listen, man, I did it," Psycho said, wiping sweat from his brow. "I know I'm going to prison, but I don't want to go for twenty years, which is the plea the D.A. is offering since I'm a habitual offender. I have two priors."

Mark fumbled with his class ring as he listened carefully to Psycho. Now he really didn't want to help a career criminal. "If your information is relevant, I'll recommend that the D.A. give you ten years. Please understand that I cannot guarantee you anything."

Ten years was still a very long time to be incarcerated, but Mark figured a veteran of the judicial system like Psycho could serve the time with no problems as long as there were weights, poker games and generic cigarettes. Psycho certainly didn't appear to be the type that people would miss once he was away from the streets.

"A guy name Dawg is in my cell block and he shared a lot of information with me about his dealings."

"Steven Davis?"

"That's my man," Psycho replied.

"What did he tell you?"

"He told me about trips he and his boy Jamal made to California and the girls who got busted bringing drugs from Cali. He told me about you and how some cat named Ruff introduced you to him."

Mark didn't bother writing the information down since there was nothing he didn't already know. "This information you have is very general, but I still may need you to testify about what he told you. Would you have a problem with that?"

"No. I wanna do everything possible to help myself."

Mark grimmaced at the sight of Psycho. He was indeed a real low-life. He was a rapist who would do anything to save his skin, but Mark thought he would be needed if Jamal was arrested. "I'll be in touch with you a week before trial if we decide we need your testimony."

Psycho frowned as he stood. "If you don't decide to use me to testify, will you still be able to help me get a lower plea agreement?"

"I'm afraid not."

"That's fucked up."

"That's life," Mark said.

m CHAPTER 21 m

MAY 29, 2003. Dream somehow believed she could protect Jamal. She felt that if she wasn't with him, something would happen to him. She didn't agree with what he was doing, but she knew she had to be there.

Angelo picked Jamal and Dream up from the San Diego National Airport. This was the first time Jamal had seen Angelo since Dawg had been arrested. Jamal filled him in on all the details.

"Your boy Ruff turned out to be an informant."

"Jamal, I don't know what to say. I'm sorry, man."

"You say you're sorry, but my best friend is in jail now because of your sorriness."

Angelo's face became serious. "Hey, man, did you come out here to do business, or to jump all over my ass? Me and you are the last men standing."

"I came to do business; I need money," Jamal replied.

"Okay, that's what I wanna hear. How much money do you have?"

"Enough for two kilos."

"How are you gonna get the product back to the other side?"

Dream listened to their conversation, though she vaguely knew what was going on. She remembered Jamal telling her that the mules, Connie and Jennifer, had gotten locked up.

"I'll take my own shit back. That ain't my biggest concern," Jamal answered.

Dream looked at Jamal. She never expected him to say that he would travel with drugs on him. "Honey, I don't mean to butt in, but I don't think that would be a good idea, especially since you feel that you're being watched."

"What in the hell am I suppose to do?"

Dream didn't know what to say. She knew he was determined to make some money any way he could. She didn't want him to take any unnecessary chances. She envisioned herself going through the airport with the drugs on her. Nobody would ever suspect her, she thought. "I'll take it back this one time if you keep your promise that you're going to stop dealing, Jamal."

"She'll probably have a better chance of getting it back than you," Angelo said.

Jamal was surprised. He knew that she could probably go through the airport undetected, but he wanted to make sure that she understood what she was getting herself into. "Can I have a minute alone with her?" Jamal asked Angelo.

After Angelo had excused himself, Jamal said, "I don't want you to think you have to do this, baby. I mean, I don't want you to get in any trouble. You know if you get caught you're going to jail."

She looked straight in his eyes. "I know the risk, but I want to do it. I know nothing is going to happen to me. Look at me; do you honestly think anybody would suspect me?"

She was innocent and naïve. He knew she was right. "I think it will work as long as you're alone," he said.

"It will. Trust me," she said. He pulled her close and they held each other.

"So what are we gonna do?" Angelo entered the room again.

"Get the dope, man. We're ready to get out of here," Jamal replied.

Jamal explained to Dream that the drug game was serious business and that she was expected to act accordingly. He made sure that she was dressed conservatively for the flight. She wore khaki pants and a white button-down shirt. Her hair was up in a bun, and she wore glasses and carried a San Diego State book bag. The drugs were stuffed in a girdle underneath her blouse. At the airport, she passed through the metal detectors and returned to North Carolina with no problem.

* * *

Two weeks later, Dream and Jamal returned to San Diego, but this time they weren't able to score. In the California airport on the way back to Charlotte they were rushed by the DEA just as they stepped away from the ticket counter.

"Let me see your IDs," a heavyset black man demanded, flashing a shiny DEA badge.

Jamal and Dream showed the man their IDs. "Okay, we're going to have to conduct a strip search," the man said before walking up to the attendant at the ticket counter and asking her to retrieve their bags. They would be searched as well.

"Why do you want to strip search us, man? What's your reason?" Jamal said.

The big man grabbed Jamal's arm and escorted him away.

Two female officers, one white and one Mexican, led Dream to a small office. "Okay, honey, I'm gonna need for you to get undressed," the Mexican said.

Dream shook nervously. She knew she didn't have any drugs on her but she had never experienced anything like this in her life. She felt violated. "You want me to do what?" she asked.

"Strip. Take everything off, ma'am."

Dream was confused. "Can you tell me what's going on?"

"We have reason to believe you are traveling with narcotics," the white agent said.

"That's ridiculous," Dream shouted angrily.

"Just strip down, ma'am. If you're clean you can go on about your business. If it turns out to be true then you are going to have to go with us."

Reluctantly Dream peeled off her pants and shirt. "See, I ain't carrying no drugs."

"I'm gonna need for you to take everything off, ma'am."

198 • K. Elliott

Dream looked at the white agent coldly. Is this lady some kind of lesbian? she wondered. She couldn't believe they were going to infringe on her privacy. The last time she had been exposed was for her gynecologist for her yearly pap smear. She finally pulled down her panties and the agent asked her to bend over and cough.

Dream was absolutely embarrassed.

"Okay, Ms. Nelson, everything seems to be fine. You are free to go. But let me warn you: Be careful who you hang out with," the white agent said.

"What's that suppose to mean?" Dream asked as she pulled up her pants.

"Means your boyfriend, Jamal, is a known drug dealer, and it's just a matter of time before we get him. I suggest you stay away from him, because he is the subject of a federal investigation."

"I'll keep that in mind," Dream said sarcastically as she stepped out of the stall.

Jamal was nowhere to be found when she left the bathroom. Dream assumed he was still being searched. Hesitantly, she went to the gate where they were supposed to board, then took a seat. When Jamal showed up she was shaking, and he could tell she had been crying. He kissed her forehead. "Baby, I'm sorry this happened to you."

She stood and they hugged. Her heart raced. He knew she had never experienced anything like this. He didn't know what else to say to comfort her. Travelers scurried to different concourses. Announcements of flight departures and arrivals filled the airport, but Dream and Jamal were oblivious to their surroundings; all that mattered was that they were together and safe.

* * *

Dawg smiled broadly as he entered the visitation room and saw his best friend. He picked up the phone.

"What's up, nigga?" Jamal asked.

"Not much. In here it's the same old shit. Just trying to make it. You know how this shit can be."

"I know."

"So what's been up with you?" Dawg asked.

"Just paying them lawyers up and trying to stay free, man, 'cause if both of us are locked up, we can't help each other."

"Well, you ain't gotta worry about me. I mean, you know I ain't gonna tell them shit. I'll swallow a life sentence before I go out like that."

Jamal stared at his friend through the Plexiglas partition. He suddenly remembered when he was on the other side awaiting trial a few years earlier when Dawg had come to see him. Now the whole scenario had reversed. Life was strange. "So what is your attorney saying?" Jamal asked.

"He's says it's not looking too good. He wants me to take a plea."

"What kind of plea?"

"Ten at eighty-five percent, meaning I'll have to do about eight and a half. If I take the plea, I'll be thirty-six when I get out."

"So what are they saying about me?"

"I don't know, man. They took me to the interrogation room. Since I told them I ain't have shit to say, and they brought me back here, I ain't heard from the bastards."

"How is your mom taking it?" Jamal asked.

"Ma is taking it alright. She's gonna be at my trial."

Jamal hated to think about Ms. Davis in the courtroom during Dawg's trial. He knew the prosecution would make

Dawg look like a madman. Prosecutors had to make the jury
think that all dealers were a menace to society. The sad part
about the whole thing was that the jurors almost always
sided with the prosecution. Jamal knew the Feds had a
ninety-five percent conviction rate. It was almost inevitable
that his friend was going to prison. Jamal stared at Dawg.
His hair had grown out wildly and the orange Mecklenburg
county jumpsuit swallowed his thin frame. Dawg had lost
about ten pounds. Many people lost weight in jail because
of worrying and not being properly fed. "So when is trial?"
Jamal asked.

"In three weeks," Dawg said.

A deputy burst into the visiting room and held his arm
up, looking at a watch. "Time's up."

"You know that I can't be at your trial, right?" Jamal said.
He didn't particularly like hanging out in courtrooms. Plus
he was afraid that he would be recognized by one of the
DEA agents or the prosecuting attorneys.

"I know, man. Don't worry about coming. Hell if I were
you, I wouldn't come either," Dawg said as he stood and
placed his hand flat on the glass. "One love."

Jamal held up his hand, and they high-fived through the
glass. "I'm wit' you, nigga," he said.

***

When Dream walked into Keisha's office, she knew
something was wrong because Keisha avoided eye contact.
"Bad news, huh?"

"I'm afraid so," Keisha said as she looked Dream in the
eye for the first time.

"What's wrong?" Dream asked.

"The private investigator couldn't find Jamal's mother."

"Oh, I know he'll probably be disappointed, but he'll
live."

"That's not all the bad news," Keisha said as she glanced through the window of her office.

Dream narrowed her eyes. "What do you have to tell me?"

Keisha handed Dream a copy of a newspaper article dated February 8, 1999.

The headline read NORTH CHARLOTTE BAGLADY BURNED: Dream read the article.

The eerie smell of charcoaled human flesh hung in the air as firefighters retrieved what is believed to be Mary Stewart. The burns were so severe she couldn't be positively identified. Court documents with her name were discovered outside the abandoned house where her body was found. For the last four months, people of the North Charlotte neighborhood saw Stewart pushing a grocery cart up and down the streets or standing at the corner of Davidson and the Plaza with a cardboard sign that read: PLEASE HELP ME EAT TODAY. The cart contained her belongings: a couple of sweaters; a huge black nylon purse; two pairs of socks, one of which she had used as mittens; and a huge blanket.

Who was Mary Stewart and why was she so down on her luck? People of the neighborhood, who asked to remain anonymous, said Stewart was a crack addict who stole and conned to get her hands on money to support her habit. Police records indicate that she had been picked up three times within the past year for petty larceny and other misdemeanor charges, often released on her own recognizance. When she got out of jail she had nowhere to go, and she often slept in abandoned houses along with other addicts.

February 6 was the coldest day of this winter, with temperatures below freezing. Before nightfall Stewart is believed to have made her way into one of the houses to start a fire for warmth. Shortly after that, it is believed that she dozed off, and the fire burned out of control, trapping the victim inside. She is survived by a son whose whereabouts are unknown.

Dream couldn't believe what she had just read. She sat looking ahead without saying a word. She immediately thought about Jamal and how he would react to the news. Why hadn't somebody told him? she wondered. With all the things Jamal was going through, she didn't know if now would be a good time to break the bad news to him. She looked at Keisha who was still staring out of the window not saying a word. "Keisha, what should I do?"

"I don't know. This is one of the saddest stories I have ever read in my life."

"I know. How did your private eye find it?"

"He searched the Internet and found the article. After reading it he went down to county records and found the death certificate. He's good, isn't he?"

"Too damn good," Dream said, still staring at the article.

"You got your hands full, baby girl, "Keisha sighed. "I suggest that you don't tell him."

Dream placed her hand underneath her chin and shook her head sadly. "I can't tell him. Now is definitely not the time with all that is going on."

"What's going on?" Keisha asked curiously.

"Nothing to concern yourself with."

"I gotta be concerned if my girl is concerned."

Dream knew Keisha would keep prying for information. It was her nature. Dream could never hide anything from her. In college, Dream had briefly dated Chris Watson, a guy from White Plains, New York. One night after a basketball game, she and Chris had started arguing in front of the sophomore dormitory. Chris got upset and slapped Dream, leaving her with a black eye. Keisha found out, but Dream denied that it had happened. Keisha confronted Chris, and when he admitted to assaulting Dream, Keisha had several guys on the football team rough him up.

Dream didn't really want to go into detail about what was going on with Jamal, but she felt she had to tell her friend something. "Jamal is being watched," Dream said in a barely audible voice.

"Watched? What do you mean? Who is he being watched by?"

"I think the Feds are watching him."

Keisha's face grew serious. "What makes you say that?"

Dream knew she had just opened the door for a barrage of questions. She knew Keisha would start telling her what she should and shouldn't do, and she wasn't in the mood to hear her best friend acting like a mother. "His boy, Dawg got, locked up."

"That nigga ain't involved you in his bullshit, has he?"

Dream and Keisha's eyes met briefly before Dream turned away. She thought about the trips to California. There was no way she could let Keisha know that she and Jamal had been approached by the DEA. Though she had volunteered to bring drugs back, she knew she couldn't tell Keisha, because she would assume Jamal had forced her to do something she didn't want to do. "Of course not," she lied.

"Good. You remember what happened to Kyla Stevens, don't you?"

Kyla Stevens, a beautiful, light-skinned girl with long, wavy hair, had attended high school with Dream and Keisha. After high school, when Dream and Keisha headed to North Carolina Central University, Kyla went to Clark Atlanta University and got involved with a big drug dealer. After Kyla's freshman year, she came back to Charlotte driving a Mercedes CLK. A lot of girls were jealous of her—until she was indicted as part of a drug ring. Ten months after her arrest, she was sentenced to twenty-five years in federal prison.

"I remember what happened, but believe me, her situation is nothing like mine," Dream replied.

"I want you to leave Jamal alone. If you don't, I'm going to tell your parents what he's into," Keisha said, her voice full of emotion.

"Don't you dare," Dream said. She thought about the possibility of her parents learning that Jamal was selling drugs. She would never hear the end of it. She could imagine the disappointment on her father's face. She knew her parents would be hurt, especially if she was ever charged with anything. She knew God had been on her side in San Diego. If she had gotten arrested, she would have embarrassed her parents, and that was something she would never want to do.

"You need to stop seeing him or else I swear to you, I'm going to tell your parents."

"Keisha, don't test me. It's not that easy, especially since we planned to get married. I mean I am human. I just can't cut somebody out of my life and say the hell with them."

Keisha walked up and placed her arm on Dream's shoulder. "I know, but please understand, I don't want to see anything happen to you."

"Nothing is gonna happen," Dream said. But she wasn't so sure.

ꭑ CHAPTER 22 ꭑ

AT 8:00A.M. JAMAL rolled out of bed, showered, and was putting some frozen blueberry waffles in the toaster when the phone rang.

"Jamal?"

"Yeah," he answered.

"Thomas Henry here. Just calling to touch bases with you."

The toaster bell sounded. Jamal spread some strawberry jam on his waffles and added maple syrup. "Did you find out anything?"

"Yeah. One of my ex-law partners works in the U.S. Attorney's office says you are definitely being watched closely. He said something about you being affiliated with Steven Davis."

"Yeah, that's my friend, the guy I was telling you about," Jamal said as he put his plate down and walked to the living room with the cordless phone.

"As of right now, you are in the clear, but it seems like one of those agents down there has a wild hair in his ass. He wants you bad and is asking every new arrestee if they have any information about you."

Jamal paced nervously and peered through the huge bay window. He was glad Thomas Henry had looked into the investigation, but he wasn't thrilled with the information that had been relayed. He suddenly lost his appetite. Prison time looked very possible. He thought about Dawg and how he looked in jail with his orange jumpsuit. He thought about not being able to do simple things again such as: chewing gum, driving cars, and dating a woman. He knew he would lose Dream if he went to jail. He sat on the sofa and took a deep breath.

"Actually there is nothing you can do, except hope everything blows over after your friend goes to trial."

"And if it doesn't blow over?"

"Just come to my office in the morning."

* * *

The following morning, Jamal was restless and jittery as he sat in the lobby of Thomas Henry's law firm. He bit his fingernails while looking at a People magazine. The lobby brought back many unpleasant memories. He remembered his first visit. He was nineteen the first time he had gotten into trouble. He had gotten locked up for the unlawful possession of a handgun, and the arresting officer had promised that he would go to jail. Jamal was a kid then, and the possibility of being locked up was scary. He had known older guys in the neighborhood who had gone to prison and lost their minds. Some even turned gay. Others became dangerous predators, like child molesters and rapists. He was so afraid of going to jail at nineteen, when he first met Thomas he had told him he would take any amount of probation; he just didn't want to go to prison. That case was ultimately dismissed. Here it was almost ten years later, and he was a now veteran of the judicial system. The possibility of prison time was still just as unappealing.

The receptionist called and led him to Thomas's office.

"What's up?" Jamal said. He took a seat in the chair across from Thomas's desk.

"Jamal, I'm gonna be honest with you. Like I said on the phone, it seems as though they don't have anything on you as of yet, but if your friend is convicted and it doesn't blow over, they are going to try to get you and put you away for a long time," Thomas said as he adjusted his tie and avoided eye contact with Jamal.

Jamal was silent.

Thomas met his gaze. "If you are indicted and the trial blows, yeah there's a pretty good chance you'll go back to prison."

Jamal turned from Thomas. "Fuck that. I'm leaving this place now. I ain't sticking around to go to jail for some bullshit."

"Where are you going?"

Jamal stood and turned toward the door. "I ain't telling you shit. I don't trust nobody."

Thomas hesitated before speaking. "I was just going to tell you that if you needed a passport I can get you one, but you've got to pay. I don't suggest you go anywhere until after your friend goes to trial."

"I'll keep that in mind," Jamal said.

* * *

The first week in June, it had rained for three days straight. Rain was common during this time. Dream sat on her living room floor looking at pictures of wedding dresses as the thunder roared and crackled outside.

It had been four months since Jamal had proposed, and they still hadn't made any plans and hadn't set a wedding date. Jamal admitted to her that he was waiting on the outcome of Dawg's trial. Dream knew that if Dawg was sent to prison, they weren't going to get married.

The trial was two days away. Dream would be glad when it was all over, regardless of the outcome. She dozed off, lying on the floor, and dreamed of her wedding day. She dreamed of a huge wedding with more than five hundred guests: two pianists, and two soloists, ten bridesmaids and three flower girls. All her friends from school were there, and Keisha was her maid of honor. Jamal wore a black tuxedo with a lavender vest and tie. Everybody stood as she walked down the aisle. Her parents were there, looking proud.

Something was missing from her dream. As she strolled down the aisle, she noticed that there weren't any family or friends on Jamal's side of the church, not even a best man. She woke up in a cold sweat and said a quick prayer for Dawg before dozing again.

* * *

The morning of Dawg's trial, Jamal didn't eat breakfast. He didn't have an appetite. All he kept thinking about was his friend and what he was in for. Jamal felt kind of guilty that all of this had happened to Dawg. He knew it was going to take a miracle for his friend to win this trial. Jamal had known only one guy to beat a federal drug case, and just before leaving the courtroom, that same guy had a new indictment from another district by fax.

It was ten o'clock when Jamal finally got out of bed. The trial was set, and he knew, regardless of the outcome, his life would never be the same. If Dawg was convicted, Jamal would have to get out of town. If he was acquitted, Jamal knew he had to find something else to do besides drugs, because the Feds would pursue him relentlessly.

Jamal wanted a normal life with a house, a wife, and a dog. He wanted to find a good job and settle down with Dream. She was a good woman, and he knew he was very fortunate to find someone like her. She wanted him to stop selling drugs. She had asked him a long time ago, and he really wanted to stop. He had initially planned on making a half-million dollars, and they had hoped to make it quickly, get out of the business, and stay legitimate. Having set aside all lawyer fees, he now had nearly $100,000. But how long would he have it? he wondered. How long could he run with such a relatively small amount? He needed to make preparations for the worst—and fast. He needed a new identity.

* * *

Cedric Patterson was a tall, slender, clean-cut man with honey-colored skin and perfect teeth. He had a fetish for designer clothing. He and Jamal had met at a federal prison in Butner, North Carolina. Cedric had been sentenced to twenty-four months for credit card fraud. He had six other co-defendants who were placed on probation, but he was sentenced to prison since he was the mastermind of the little credit-card scheme. Cedric was a fairly intelligent guy who had worked at American Community Financial Company as a loan officer. For six years he took profile information from consumers and stole identities. He would then pass the information on to members of his ring who would get credit cards and loans under the assumed identities. Some even got cars that they would later sell to a chop shop in Pennsylvania, along with fictitious titles that Cedric made on his home computer.

Two months earlier, Jamal had run into Cedric in a local nightclub. Cedric told him he could get him a new identity for four hundred dollars.

Cedric had several identities Jamal could choose from. The first was Jeremy Collins, who was born in 1970 in Indiana. He had excellent credit and only a few minor brushes with the law, according to the criminal record Cedric pulled from the Internet. Jamal liked his profile— except for the fact that he was white. Because of this, Cedric warned that it might raise a red flag if Jamal was ever to get a job, or even use it for credit purposes.

The next identity was Rashaun Ingram. Rashaun was a twenty-six-year-old black man with poor credit, and he was wanted for child support. It didn't take long for Jamal to decide he didn't want any part of that guy. The last and final identity was for Andre Michael Von, from Tampa, Florida. He was a thirty-one-year-old black man with a decent credit history and a simple possession-of-marijuana charge. After reviewing his identity, Jamal decided Andre would have to work. "What information do you have on this guy?" Jamal said.

"I've got his birth certificate, and I can make you a Social security card. You can either take it down to the Department of Motor Vehicles and get you an ID, or I can make you one of those, too."

"What do you suggest?"

"I would probably get the one from the DMV, because the one that I make really ain't the best quality. A veteran cop can tell that it's fake."

Jamal was silent for a moment. He didn't want to use a low-quality ID. He would probably have to get a passport through his lawyer and leave the country soon. Jamal pulled four crisp, one-hundred-dollar bills from his wallet and gave them to Cedric.

Cedric smiled and gave Jamal the necessary paperwork. "Let me know if you meet anybody who needs their credit straightened out. I can do that for five hundred dollars," Cedric said.

Jamal put the documents in his pocket and nodded. He couldn't believe it had been three years since he and Cedric were at Butner together. They had both gotten out and gone back to the same things that had put them in. It was what they knew best.

* * *

Jamal was at home lying across his bed, thinking about the possibility of going back to prison and where he would run if the Feds indicted him. He knew he could not stay in this country without the risk of being spotted by some damn Good Samaritan.

He received a call from the security desk down stairs. The guard informed him that Candy Melton was in the lobby and that she wanted to come up and see him urgently.

"Send her up."

Jamal walked to the bathroom, washed his face, and brushed his teeth. He hadn't seen Candy since the day he'd put her out of his car and told her to walk home. He had moved since the last time he had seen her. How in the hell did she find out where I live?

Jamal opened the door and invited Candy into his apartment. He offered her a seat, but she declined. "What brings you over here, and how in the hell did you know where I live?"

"Jamal, let me start by saying that I apologize for just showing up at your home like this, but I really need to talk to you about something."

Jamal's face became serious. "Again, how did you find out where I live?"

"I have a friend who works at the cable company. The cable bill is in your name."

"Okay. What's so important that you had to track me down? I hope you ain't come over here for no damn money, because I ain't giving you shit."

Candy sighed and turned away briefly before resuming eye contact. "I wish it was something like that, but it's a little bit more complicated."

"What do you mean?"

"Jamal, I think you need to get tested for HIV."

"What the fuck are you saying?"

"I was seeing someone else at the same time I was seeing you."

"And?"

Candy didn't say anything but looked away again.

"Okay, what does that have to do with me?"

"Yesterday the damn guy showed up at my apartment and said that he thinks I should get tested." Candy now had tears in her eyes.

"Does he have AIDS?"

"No, but he says that he is HIV positive." She wiped her eyes with both hands.

"That's the same shit in my book."

Tears slowly rolled down Candy's cheeks. "I haven't been tested yet. Jamal, I'm scared. I don't know what I'm going to do if I'm HIV positive."

"I hope you don't expect no sympathy from me. First of all, you come to my house and tell me that you have possibly exposed me to some bullshit," Jamal said as he walked over to the door and opened it. "Get out of here before I kill your ass."

Candy used her hands to wipe her eyes again as she took a step toward the door. "Jamal, I'm sorry, I swear to you."

"You damn right you sorry. A sorry-ass bitch is what you is," Jamal said as he was about to close the door. After a few seconds of contemplating, he yanked her back into the apartment. "You know what, I can't let you get off that easy." He closed the door. "Who is this nigga spreading this shit?"

"His name is Raoul."

"What kind of name is that? Is this mu'fucka Spanish?"

"I think he's half Dominican or something."

"Where the fuck does he live?" Jamal asked.

"I don't know?"

"Bitch, don't lie to me."

"I ain't lying."

Jamal grabbed her arm and twisted it behind her back. "Don't fuckin' lie to me."

Candy's face became flushed, and she struggled to get away. But Jamal was too strong. "Jamal, let my arm go. You're hurting me."

Jamal scooped Candy up and carried her into the bedroom, closed his door, pulled a handgun from underneath his pillow, and waved it in her direction. "You're going to tell me where this nigga lives, or else you ain't gonna have to worry about no fuckin' virus."

"He lives near the university."

Jamal cocked the hammer on the handgun. "We're going to pay this Raoul a visit."

"Why are you doing this, Jamal? You don't even know if you got the virus or not."

"I just want to see how the nigga looks in case I have to kill his ass later. I swear to you, Candy, if I got the virus, somebody is going to die," Jamal fumed.

Candy's pupils expanded. She stared up at Jamal while lying on her back.

"Get the fuck up and take me to this mu'fucka."

m CHAPTER 23 m

RAOUL WAS A SMALL-TIME crack dealer who pretended to have more money than he actually had. According to Candy, she had met him in the club one night, and he had propositioned her to have sex with him for a thousand dollars. When they arrived at the hotel room, he then confessed to having only five hundred. She was pissed, but she still took the money. They then started having sex on a regular basis. Candy admitted that she had actually started enjoying their sexual escapades so much, she stopped charging him because she wanted it just as bad as he did.

Raoul's townhome was in a quiet neighborhood lined with huge oak trees. Jamal pulled in the driveway with his headlights off. He didn't want any attention from the neighbors.

Jamal and Candy walked up to Raoul's doorstep and rang the bell.

A few minutes later Raoul opened the door. He was a short man with curly hair and a thin mustache. "Candy," Raoul said, then looked at Jamal.

"Raoul, this is Jamal," Candy said.

"What's up?" Raoul offered his hand.

Jamal left it dangling. "You tell me. What's up?" Jamal said.

"What's this guy's problem?" Raoul asked Candy.

"Jamal thinks he may have been exposed to the virus because he and I were once involved."

"Okay," Raoul said.

"Is that all you can say?" Jamal said.

Raoul shrugged. "What do you want me to say?"

"Raoul, can we come in?" Candy asked as she looked around. "I know you don't want your neighbors to hear all your business."

"I don't want this motherfucker to come in my house."
Raoul stared at Jamal. "I don't like his attitude."

Jamal shoved Candy aside and walked up to the doorway
and brandished a stainless steel handgun. "I think you need
to let us in."

Raoul stepped back.

"Jamal, put the gun away," Candy pleaded.

Jamal and Candy entered the house. Candy closed the
door.

"Mu'fucka, you better convince me that I might not have
the damn virus, or else you going to hell tonight."

"You're going to get out of my house making threats."

"Listen," Jamal said, pointing his finger in Raoul's face.

Raoul knocked his hand down.

Jamal struck Raoul with the butt of the gun across the
forehead. Blood spurted in every direction. Raoul fell
backward, and the back of his head hit the floor.

Jamal stepped back realizing some of Raoul's blood had
gotten on his shirt. He rested over Raoul, pinning his arms
to the floor using both knees. He stuck the barrel of the gun
in Raoul's mouth. "Imagine how close you are to death."

"Get off him or I'll call the police, Jamal."

Jamal made eye contact with Candy. She was standing by
the doorway with the phone in her hand. He realized he had
too much at stake. He really wanted to kill Raoul. Even
though he wasn't certain he had the virus, the thought itself
was troublesome. He knew he had been exposed because he
and Candy had never used protection. He saw fear in
Candy's eyes, and tears had begun to well up in Raoul's.
Jamal's mind then shifted to Dream. How would he tell her
he had exposed her? She would definitely leave him at the
worst point of his life. He thought about Dawg who was
awaiting trial. His friend needed him to stick around at least
until he found out his fate. He knew that if he killed Raoul
he would have to leave town immediately, and he wasn't

quite ready because he hadn't been charged with anything. He pulled the barrel of the gun from Raoul's mouth and slapped him with the butt of it once more. Jamal darted out of the front door got in his car, and drove away.

* * *

The next day Jamal called a local doctor's office and scheduled an appointment for an HIV test. When he got to the receptionist's desk, he was told to pay a hundred dollars since he didn't have health insurance. After he filled out the questionnaire about previous illnesses, the doctor came out and escorted him to a back room.

With a clipboard in hand the doctor studied Jamal's paperwork. "HIV testing, huh?"

"Yeah," Jamal answered.

"Do you think you've been exposed?"

"No," Jamal lied.

"Do you want the results to be public record?"

"I have a choice?" Jamal asked, surprised.

"Yeah. Since you paid for the test out of your pocket, you have that option. If you had health insurance, we would have had no choice but to make it public record. Sometimes this information is sold to databases and can even end up on the Internet."

Jamal was shocked. He couldn't believe that paying a hundred dollars would ensure so much privacy. He wondered how many people were actually infected with the virus, living life as if they weren't. Jamal was glad he had this option, because he definitely didn't want Dream to find out. She couldn't know whether the results were negative or positive. He didn't want her to know that she had been exposed. "I don't want anybody to know," Jamal said.

The doctor then asked Jamal to sign a consent form. Shortly afterward, a nurse entered the room and withdrew a sample of blood from Jamal's left arm. The nurse told him to sit in the lobby and that the results of the test would be available in twenty minutes. "The doctor will call you back and go over the results with you," she said.

Jamal sat in the lobby wondering how everything had gone so bad at once. What did he do to deserve such bad luck? He had always thought of HIV as a gay man's disease. He'd stayed clear of homosexuals while in prison. He was a real man and he prided himself in being a real man. He couldn't believe that being HIV positive was so much a possibility. He glanced at his watch and twenty minutes had passed, so he approached the receptionist. "Excuse me. The nurse said the doctor would be calling me in twenty minutes."

"Whenever the doctor is ready he will call for you," the receptionist said.

"What's taking the doctor so long?" Jamal asked.

"I don't know," the receptionist said. "Just have a seat, Mr. Stewart, and I'm sure someone will be with you shortly."

Jamal returned to his seat; ten minutes passed and he still hadn't heard from anyone. He stood from his seat and eased out of the front entrance.

* * *

Mark was confident that they would win the trial. The prosecution had sufficient evidence against Dawg. Besides the recording, Mark had purchased drugs directly from Dawg. He was relieved that the trial would be over soon. He wasn't glad that Dawg was about to go to prison for a long time. He actually thought Dawg was a decent man who hadn't had the guidance he needed to be a well-rounded person. Mark sometimes found it hard to separate his job from personal feelings.

During the past winter months, Mark had talked to Dawg extensively about his family, his future, and his goals. Dawg had told him he didn't want to be involved in drug dealing for the rest of his life. He had aspirations to own his own business someday. He had told Mark that he wanted to have a carwash or a lawn service; something that didn't have a lot of overhead.

Dawg's mother was a hard-working woman employed by a local nursing home in downtown Charlotte. She was a maid and had worked there for the last fifteen years without missing a day, according to Dawg. Mark was almost certain he would see Dawg's mother in the courtroom.

Steven Davis was only twenty-eight years old, facing at least twenty-five years behind bars if convicted. The only way he would get less than the mandatory twenty-five was to testify against Jamal and Angelo. Mark didn't expect him to do that. Dawg and Jamal were like brothers. they had a special relationship. Mark knew the trial would be an emotional one, but he had a job to do.

Dawg's jury of peers consisted of ten middle-aged white men, one white woman, and a black woman, Mable Johnston, who listed her occupation as a Sunday school teacher. The judge was Theodore Owens, a sixty-eight-year old Republican from Mississippi. He was often selected in drug cases and had a reputation for giving the maximum sentence allowed.

Mark sat behind the prosecutor's table. Dawg, along with his attorney, sat at a table adjacent to the prosecution. His mother, Patricia Davis, was a light-skinned, heavyset woman with a natural haircut. His attorney, Michael Conner, was very capable and well-respected in the legal community. Two weeks after Dawg's indictment was issued, Michael had negotiated a ten-year plea agreement, which Dawg quickly declined, a move that made absolutely no sense to Mark. Now the stakes were higher, and today Michael would have to fight for Dawg's life.

Once the trial began the prosecution began an all-out attack. Their witnesses included Ruff, Mark, and a car salesman. Jennifer was testifying in exchange for a reduced sentence. Mark was later called to the witness stand to testify about five kilos of cocaine that Dawg had sold him. A car salesman testified that Dawg made a large cash down payment on a Mercedes. All the testimony corroborated, and great details were given about the money and the cocaine with which Dawg had been associated. The next day the prosecution called a surprise witness, Psycho, an inmate from Dawg's cellblock.

"What the hell is he doing in here?" Dawg shouted.

"I need order in this court," Judge Owens demanded. He slammed his gavel hard and peered down over his glasses. "Mr. Conner, you need to talk to your client about how to conduct himself in my courtroom."

Michael turned to Dawg. "Listen, we don't want to upset this judge. You need to get a hold of yourself."

"I just want to know why in the hell is this guy on the witness stand."

"Do you know this guy?"

"Yeah, he is in my cellblock."

"Let's just see what he has to say," Michael said before apologizing to the judge for Dawg's outburst.

For the next forty-five minutes, Psycho testified that Dawg had told him about trips to California to pick up large sums of drugs. He said Dawg told him about large quantities of money that he and Jamal had made weeks before the arrest. He ended his testimony by telling the jury about thousands of dollars Dawg had allegedly spent on cars, women, and jewelry.

After four days of testimony and rebuttal, the trial ended. It took the jury only thirty-eight minutes to return with a verdict. The judge asked everyone to rise. The jury foreman, a middle-aged white man with a large brown birthmark on his balding forehead, was then instructed by the judge to announce the verdict. "We the jury find Steven Davis guilty as charged as to count one, guilty as charged as to count two; and guilty as charged as to count three."

Mark had mixed emotions about the verdict. He was happy that he had been effective in doing his job, but at the same time; he was sad that another black mother would lose her son to the prison system. He glanced over at Dawg who was hugging his mother tightly as she wept.

The sentencing would be put off for another six weeks, and again, Mark would have to be present to see Dawg and his mother.

* * *

Jamal and Dream were on the way to his apartment when he had received a call on his cell phone from Thomas Henry. He listened in silence as Dream drove. A huge frown suddenly covered Jamal's face as he absorbed the bad news.

"What's wrong?" Dream asked.

"My lawyer just received information that Dawg was found guilty and that the grand jury is scheduled to meet in a couple of weeks. My phone records and my credit report have been subpoenaed. He said it was quite likely that Angelo and I will be indicted soon."

"What does that mean for us?" Dream asked.

"It means the marriage is off. I've got other things to worry about—like, my ass," Jamal said, without looking at her.

"Is your attorney sure that the grand jury is going to try to indict you?" Dream had already assumed that she and Jamal would never get married. Her plan of an extravagant, beautiful church wedding was simply a dream.

"He's never lied before," Jamal replied. His attorney had worked with a lot people in the prosecutor's office. Thomas was connected, and he could find out about any ongoing investigation.

"So what are you gonna do?"

"I need to get some of my things out of the apartment. I can't stay there anymore."

When they arrived at his condo, Jamal quickly gathered some clothes and personal belongings.

"So where are you going tonight?"

"I don't know," he said, glancing at her briefly before shoving some of his belongings into several laundry bags.

"Do you think it's necessary to leave tonight?"

"Yeah. The last time they got my ass, it was about four in the morning. The Feds are some sneaky mu'fuckas," he said.

Twenty-five minutes later they rode without saying a word to each other. The CD player was barely audible. Dream didn't know what to say. She didn't know what to do. She had never experienced anything quite like this before. She didn't want Jamal to go to prison, but she had made up her mind that she was not going with him. She felt she had already been involved with his criminal activities a little too much. She had dealt with criminals before, but only petty ones. Jamal was in a class by himself, and she loved him.

"So you really don't know where you are going, huh?"

Jamal adjusted his seat and leaned back. "Not right now. But I know I will probably end up on one of the Caribbean Islands."

"You're just gonna live the rest of your life running? How long do you think you can do that?"

" I have a phony birth certificate and Social Security number. After I get a new passport I think I'll be set," he replied. He felt comfortable telling Dream his plans. He didn't feel she would ever tell anyone.

They pulled into a CVS drugstore. Jamal needed razors to shave his head. Andre Von would be a bald guy with a clean-shaven face.

After exiting the store, Jamal heard someone call out his name. He turned and met Patricia Davis, Dawg's mother. He had only seen her twice since he had gotten out of prison. "Hey, Ma," Jamal said as he hugged his friend's mother. Her eyes were red and puffy.

"I guess you heard about Steven, huh?" she said softly.

Jamal felt remorseful about his friend being locked up, even though he knew Dawg's mother wasn't accusing him of having anything to do with it. It didn't feel right to him that he was free and Dawg was locked up. "Yeah, I heard about him," Jamal said, before dropping his head.

"We just gotta keep the faith. It's cloudy right now with my son locked up like an animal, but I know the Lord is gonna bring us some sunshine. Just like after your mama got killed. It was cloudy for a while. We didn't think we were going to make it, but we did."

Jamal raised his head. "What did you just say?" His voice was thick with emotion.

"I said right after your mama was killed, we didn't think we were going to make it but we did."

"My mama was killed?" Jamal asked, looking her directly in her eyes.

"Oh, my God," Mrs. Davis said, covering her mouth. "You didn't know that your mama had been killed, did you, baby?"

Jamal's mouth flew open. His lips went dry, and his eyes became misty. "How was my mama killed?"

"I'm sorry, Jamal. I'm really sorry, baby." She grabbed him around his shoulders.

"How was she killed?" Jamal demanded as he stepped away from her grip.

"Your mama was killed in a fire. She burned up in an abandoned house trying to keep warm. I'm sorry, baby, I really am. I told Steven to tell you. I guess he didn't know what or how to say it." Her voice was sincere.

Jamal dropped his shopping bag and stared at the ground. His only flesh and blood was gone and he had lost his best friend to the judicial system. He had met the love of his life and now he had to leave her. The possibility of being HIV positive haunted him. For the first time he didn't have any direction. Patricia grabbed his hand and took him in her arms again. "It's gonna be okay, baby. The Lord is on our side." She patted him on the back lightly.

Jamal lowered his head before kissing her on the cheek. He pulled ten-1-hundred-dollar bills from his wallet and gave them to her. "Make sure Dawg has money while he's downtown in the jail." They hugged. He gathered his shopping bag and walked slowly to his Mercedes. The night air chapped his already dry lips, and the dashing sounds of the traffic in front of the store grew louder. Car brakes screeched and sirens from far away rang out. The world and the people in it were busy. In no way slowing down, the world had moved on, without Mary Stewart. Sixteen steps seemed like a ten-minute walk, but he finally arrived at his car.

"I saw you with that lady. What was that all about?" Dream said.

Tears rolled down Jamal's face. "That was Dawg's mother. She just told me my mother was killed in a fire."

Dream turned from his gaze without responding.

"Did you hear me?"

"Yeah, I heard," she said in a barely audible voice.

Jamal reclined his seat and covered his face with his hand. "I guess you just don't give a flying fuck, huh?"

Dream leaned into him, putting her head on his midsection. "Baby, you know that's not true. It's just . . . "

He sat up and they made eye contact. "What were you about to say?"

She turned away and noticed Dawg's mother pulling out of the parking lot in a silver Pontiac. "I already knew your mother had been killed. The private eye that Keisha knows found out."

"Why in the hell didn't you say something to me?" he yelled.

She didn't know what to say. She felt horrible for hiding the truth; she simply had not known how to tell him. "So much was going on with Dawg's trial and everything. I didn't think you needed something else to worry about."

He grabbed her arm and made her face him. "You didn't want to worry me? We are talking about my mother here. This ain't something that could have waited. Didn't you think I should know?"

"Baby, I'm sorry. I should have told you. But put yourself in my position and tell me what you would have done. Your boy, Dawg, must have known for years, and he didn't tell you. So I'm not the only one who couldn't find the words."

Jamal placed his head on the steering wheel and sobbed. "I ain't got nobody now. Dawg is going to prison for probably the rest of his life, and my mother is gone. To make matters worse, the Feds are trying to send me to prison, too."

Dream patted his back while he sobbed. Finally when she saw that he wasn't able to drive, she took the wheel, and Jamal sat on the passenger side. He reclined with his arm across his face. His crying was unbearable. Dream had never seen a grown man cry like Jamal, but she had not lost one of her parents either.

ɱ CHAPTER 24 ɱ

WHEN DREAM PULLED UP in front of her apartment building it was only 8:00 P.M. She glanced over to see if Jamal was okay.

He was silent.

"Jamal, are you gonna be alright?"

He sat up and lit a cigar. "I'm okay. I just had to get myself together."

"So I guess you're getting out of town tonight, huh?" she asked.

"Yeah, can't stick around here," he said as he rolled the window down and blew out his cigar smoke.

She felt awkward talking to him. She didn't want him to leave, but given the circumstances, she knew he had to. "I guess you'll call me when you get where you're going, huh?"

He nodded and leaned into her, giving her a peck on her jaw.

"Give me a real kiss," she demanded.

He leaned into her; their parted lips met, and they kissed passionately for about three minutes. His lips were wet and succulent, and Dream's whole body was shivering when she finally pulled away.

"Please stay the night with me," she pleaded.

He grabbed her hand and stroked it gently. "I want to, believe me, but I gotta go, baby. I can't rot in nobody's jail."

She hesitated. "Well, I'm coming with you."

He looked at her strangely. He couldn't believe what he was hearing, but then again, she had surprised him before when she offered to bring product back on the plane. He really didn't want to put her life in jeopardy, but he didn't have anyone else he could count on. He really did need her.

"I love you, Jamal, and I want to be there for you."

He leaned closer and hugged her. "I'm going to need to get you a fake ID if you're going to go with me. Is that okay with you?"

"Whatever you want me to do, I'm with you. I love you."

Jamal pulled his cell phone from his pocket and called Cedric. "Hey, man, I need an ID today for my girl."

"I can get you one, but it's going to take a couple of days. I'm in Vegas right now."

"I can't wait. Do you have anybody who can get me one? I got a thousand dollars. I need one today."

"Jamal, I want to help you, man, honestly, I do. But that's going to be impossible because I'm out of town."

"When you get back in town, do you think you can make a couple of passports? I got somebody else working on it, but I trust you a little bit more."

"Jamal that 9/11 shit has made it damn near impossible to make a passport you could safely get by with," Cedric said.

"Motherfuck!" Jamal yelled into the phone before ending the call.

"What's wrong?" Dream asked.

"I can't get you an ID. You're going to have to use your own name for a few days."

They quickly went inside her apartment and gathered a few of her belongings.

A few hours later, they pulled into a Super 8 motel in Greensboro and checked in under her name.

As soon as they were settled, Jamal called Angelo and told him about the outcome of the trial. He told him what his attorney had said about the Feds seeking indictments on the both of them as well.

"So how much time is Dawg looking at?" Angelo asked.

"At least twenty-five years, but that's not what I called to talk about. I need to see you for business."

"Come on out tomorrow and I'll fix you up real nice."

* * *

The next day Jamal shaved his head bald. He went to the Department of Motor Vehicles with the documentation he'd received from Cedric. When he came out, he was officially Andre Von, and that was the name he used to check into the airport.

* * *

It was six o'clock when Jamal and Dream got off the plane in California. She rented a car, and they stopped at a mall where Jamal purchased two Samsonite briefcases. They checked into a hotel suite near Mission Beach. Jamal told Dream not to unpack. They would be going to Los Angeles later that night. She didn't ask why.

At 7:45 P.M., Angelo arrived at their hotel room. They hugged as they greeted. "We're still standing," Jamal said.

"I know that's right," Angelo said chuckling. "I want to keep standing."

"Getting down to business. I need about ten kilos."

Angelo looked at Jamal suspiciously. "You're going for the gusto, ain't you? That's a long way from your usual."

"I've gotta get paid. The stakes are high, man. I don't know if I told you, but I'm trying to get the fuck out of the country."

Angelo walked toward the door. "Give me about four hours, and I'll be back with what you need."

When Angelo left, Jamal asked Dream to help him fill both of the briefcases with newspaper. She became suspicious. In the past he had put his money in the briefcases. "Why are you putting newspaper in there?" she asked.

"I ain't got a whole lot of money, and I need to get my hands on some fast," he said, looking away from her.

"I thought Angelo was your friend," she said, trying to make eye contact with him.

He turned and faced her. "See, in this game, you don't have any friends. Dawg was the only real friend I ever had. Now that I've lost him and my mother, anything goes."

"So you don't think Angelo is gonna open the briefcases and see the newspaper?"

"No, because each will be covered with $25,000. That's fifty grand."

She looked confused. "Why are you doing this? I don't understand."

"Honestly, I don't want to do this. But at this point, with everything going on, I don't give a damn about Angelo. I got to make sure we're okay."

She dropped her head, not knowing what to make of Jamal's disloyalty.

* * *

Less than five hours later, Angelo arrived with a huge green duffle bag. He and Jamal went to the kitchen, and Angelo opened the bag and dumped the product on the table. Jamal took a huge knife from the drawer, cut the wrapping off one of the kilos and used his finger to scoop a little bit of the coke from the wrapping and tasted it.

"That's the best in Mexico," Angelo said.

"Yeah, it tastes good and my tongue is numb as hell."

"Where's the money?"

Jamal went to the den and came back with the two briefcases in hand. "Here you go, $165,000."

Angelo cracked each briefcase open, saw the money, and closed them. "Well, I guess this concludes our business. Make sure you stay in touch with me and let me know what you're gonna do. If you decide you need something else, call me."

* * *

As soon as Angelo left, Jamal and Dream got in the rental car and drove to Los Angeles. An hour later Angelo called, but Jamal didn't answer his cell phone. He just sent the call to voice mail and laughed. "What a sucker."

Angelo called ten times before they reached Los Angeles. They checked in the Doubletree Hotel, under the alias Andre Von.

They slept until noon the next day. The temperature was in the mid-eighties, and the sky was fairly clear. Dream wanted to sit out by the pool and take in the sunshine, so they sat at a table next to the pool, shaded by an umbrella. Dream looked troubled and Jamal wondered why. "Baby, what's wrong?" he asked.

"Oh, nothing. I was just wondering where do we go from here," she said.

"Right now, I don't wanna think about that. I just want to enjoy the west coast," he said, sipping pineapple juice.

"I really don't want to think about it either, but my parents are probably worried."

"Relax, baby. Let's just enjoy L.A. Let's do a tour, maybe check out some of these movie stars' homes or catch a Lakers game."

She smiled. "I would like that very much. I love Kobe Bryant."

They traded in their rental car for a convertible Jaguar. Dream loved the Los Angeles scenery with the beaches, palm trees, and mountains. In Hollywood they dined at Roscoe's Chicken and Waffles. Jamal ordered smothered fried chicken, livers, and giblets. Dream ordered a chicken breast with waffles. They both ordered orange juice. Shortly after the food arrived, R & B singer Brandy sat at a table adjacent to theirs. When Dream caught Jamal staring, she slapped him playfully. "Okay, Jamal, you can stop gawking."

"Ain't nobody gawking. Now you know if Wesley Snipes or Taye Diggs, was in here you would be all in their mouth," he replied.

"Damn right. I ain't gonna lie I would. But they're not here, so it ain't fair for you to be looking at that heifer."

"You're a hater."

"I'll be that."

* * *

After they left Roscoe's, they took a tour bus through Beverly Hills. Dream looked in amazement at the big mansions. She felt like she was at a taping of Lifestyles of the Rich and Famous. From the tour bus they also saw the landmark Hollywood sign. The tour ended at the Hollywood Walk of Fame. Dream took a picture beside the Eddie Murphy and Wesley Snipes stars. "Keisha ain't gonna believe that I was actually at the Hollywood Walk of Fame," Dream said before ordering Jamal to snap more pictures.

The Lakers beat the 76ers in double overtime. It was 12:08 P.M. when the game was finally over. Jamal and Dream headed back to the room.

Dream got into the shower and came out wearing a leopard-print thong. Jamal was lying on his back in his boxers. She lay next to him. Surprisingly he didn't respond.

"What's wrong, baby?" she asked as she sat up on the bed.

"Nothing. I'm just not in the mood," he said as his mind went back to Candy. Then he thought about the day he had left the doctor's office before getting the results of the HIV test.

"That's a first."

"I was just laying here thinking about prison and how much I hated it."

"I can't imagine being locked up with somebody telling me what I can and can't do," she replied.

"It's rough, and the funny thing about it is, I ain't even been out long." He looked uncertain about what lay ahead.

Dream didn't hear the confidence she had once heard from him, and for the first time since they'd left Charlotte, she wondered if she had made the right decision.

*　*　*

Jamal woke up around 6:00 A.M. He called the airlines and found that there was a 1:00 P.M. flight from L.A. to Charlotte. When Dream awakened, he told Dream they would be flying back to Charlotte. "Are you crazy?" she asked.

He frowned. "What's wrong?"

"I am not about to go through what I went through the last time. Did you forget that you're being watched? By now you might even be charged."

"No, I didn't forget. I have a new ID, remember?"

"You do, but I don't, remember? My name may be on some sort of watch list by now."

Jamal hadn't thought about that possibility. After all, Dream had been harassed by the DEA in the San Diego airport as well. "We can always drive," he suggested.

"How long will it take to get back to Charlotte?"

"We can do it in about two and a half days if we hurry, but I ain't in no hurry. We still haven't visited The Mall of America like we had planned."

She looked confused. "Do you think that would be a good idea? I mean, with the drugs we got on us, and with Angelo probably after your ass now, shouldn't we just go somewhere and get settled?"

232 •   K. Elliott

He laughed. "Don't worry. I've done this before. Nothing is gonna happen to us."

Within the next hour, Jamal wrapped the product in fabric softener to kill the scent. He also painted JUST MARRIED on the back of the car. He knew that people, including police, were receptive to newlyweds. Dream giggled when she saw the car. "Jamal, you are crazy."

"I gotta do what I gotta do to be safe," he said.

"It's creative. I can definitely give you that."

* * *

The next morning the DEA picked up Tony Jennings and brought him in for questioning. Tony had always been fairly comfortable in the interrogation room, but today he appeared really uneasy as Mark and U.S. District Attorney, David Ricardo hammered away with questions. "Do you know why you're here?" Mark said.

Tony shrugged. "I ain't got no idea. Why am I here?"

"Do you know Jamal Stewart?"

"Yeah, I know Jamal."

Mark took a seat beside Tony and looked him directly in the eye. "We just received word that you have been extorting him and Steven Davis."

Tony turned from Mark and breathed heavily. "I don't know what you're talking about. Did Jamal tell you that?"

"Actually, Jamal hasn't been arrested yet. Did you or didn't you do it?" David asked.

"If we find out you did do it, you know you're going to prison for a long time. There's a good chance you'll be in jail with some of the same people you helped us bust," Mark said.

"If I admit to it, what will happen then?" Tony asked curiously.

"We know you had someone helping you who worked with us. We need to know who assisted in this corruption," Mark said.

"Agent Tolliver helped me. He supplied the information to me that I used to bribe Jamal and Dawg with, and this ain't the first time we've bribed big drug dealers," Tony said.

Mark and David looked at each other. "Jeremiah," they said in unison.

* * *

It had taken Jamal and Dream three days to reach St. Paul, Minnesota. Many travelers seemed to take notice of the JUST MARRIED sign on the window. Complete strangers rode by honking their horns in congratulations. A couple of cops even drove by and gave them the thumbs-up. They checked into a Hampton Inn in Bloomington, Minnesota. After they were settled, Dream called Keisha from the hotel room phone. She knew Keisha would be worried.

"What in the hell are you doing in Minnesota?" Keisha asked.

Dream knew she must have looked on the Caller ID to figure out where she was. "I'll be home in a couple of days."

"You better come on back. I spoke with your mother the other day, and she is about to file a missing persons report if you don't show up. You need to give your parents a call."

"Whatever you do, don't let them file a report. Let my mother know that you spoke with me and that I'm alright."

"What am I suppose to do when she asks me where you are?"

"Just tell her I wouldn't say, but I assured you that I was alright."

"You know they're blaming Jamal for your disappearance, don't you?"

"What?" Dream said as she sat on the edge of the bed.

Jamal looked on wondering what had happened.

"Yeah, they're accusing Jamal of abducting you, and debating whether they should go to the police."

"You can't let them do that. You have got to go over and let them know I'm okay. Promise me that."

"You got my word. I'll go over and let them know."

After they hung up, Dream lay on her back and stared at the ceiling. "What's going on now?" Jamal asked.

"Nothing. My parents are just worried about me since they haven't heard from me in a while."

"Maybe you should call them."

"I'll just see them when we get back to Charlotte."

"Have it your way, however you want to do it. In the meantime let's go to the mall. You have got to see it. You ain't gonna believe the size of this thing."

m CHAPTER 25 m

THE MALL OF AMERICA had 525 specialty stores and four major department stores: Macy's, Bloomingdale's, Nordstrom's, and Sears; a huge amusement park; and a wedding chapel. Dream was completely astounded by the size. "This thing is unreal. I have never seen anything like this in my entire life. It's gonna take us forever to walk around this mall."

"I know what you mean. I heard someone say the last time I was here that seven Yankee stadiums will fit in here," Jamal said.

Dream and Jamal walked around for about two hours, visiting at least twenty different stores. Leaving Bloomingdale's, they saw the wedding chapel. The Chapel of Love was beautifully decorated. The pews were all white, and the walls were decorated with elegant floral arrangements. There was no difference from a real church. Wedding ceremonies and christenings were performed daily. Jamal and Dream looked at each other upon entering the chapel.

"Let's do it," he said.

"I don't know. Do you think we should, especially since we don't know what the future holds?"

He looked into her eyes. "Let's not worry about the future, because whatever is gonna happen is gonna happen. I know I said earlier that I didn't think we should get married, but I want to do it, because honestly this may be my last chance." He knew that he would probably leave the country if he didn't get killed shooting out with the police, but he had been fortunate enough to find someone whom he truly loved, and marriage was something he wanted to do before it was too late.

"You really are serious, aren't you?" Dream blushed.

"Yeah, I am."

"I guess we can do it since the car already says we're married," she said, laughing.

The attendant's name was Meagan. She was a tall blonde with a lean frame. She showed them the various packages, including music, photos, and flowers whenever requested. They were surprised to learn that the chapel even had a bridal boutique.

"You mean I can pick out a wedding dress?" Dream asked as she beamed with excitement.

"Yes, our designers include Jessica McClintock, Alfred Angelo, and a lesser known company called U.S. Angels. What size are you?" Meagan asked.

"I'm a size six," Dream replied.

Dream decided on a ravishing, cream strapless, floor-length Jessica McClintock gown with a flared bottom. Jamal chose a black-and-gray Hugo Boss, single-breasted, three-button tuxedo.

"You two make a lovely couple," Meagan said with a bright smile. "Now, do you guys have a marriage license?"

Dream and Jamal looked at each other. Neither had thought about a marriage license. "How long does it take to get one?" Jamal asked.

"There is a five-day waiting period if you're from Minnesota. Where are you guys from?"

"North Carolina," Jamal answered.

"Well, I can probably get you guys one today. Fill out these papers, and I'm going to need a copy of your birth certificate and your driver's license."

"Excuse us for a minute," Jamal said as he pulled Dream aside. "Listen I forgot that I don't have my real ID. There is no way we can do it unless you want to marry Andre Von."

Dream looked down at her gown. She had really hyped herself up for a wedding ceremony. Though she would be getting married in a mall, this was supposed to be her day, but there was nothing they could do. "I guess I can take this dress off now, because I don't have my birth certificate either."

"Let me talk to the attendant. Maybe we can go on with the ceremony and just pretend we're really getting married. We really don't know what's ahead for me anyway."

Jamal stepped over to Meagan. "Listen, I don't have my ID," Jamal lied, "but I was wondering if we could go ahead with the ceremony without the license. We're more interested in the symbolism. We don't actually have to be married for real."

She looked at him oddly. "So you just want to go through the motions?"

"Yeah," Jamal replied.

"I don't think we've ever done this before," Meagan said.

Jamal pulled $300 from his pocket and handed it to the attendant. "It's really important to my girl that we go through with this. Do you understand?"

"I'm sure I can work something out with my boss," Meagan said as she folded the money and put it in her pocket.

Ten minutes later." By the powers vested in me, by the state of Minnesota, I unlawfully pronounce you husband and wife," the minister said.

Jamal, Dream, and Meagan all burst out with laughter.

* * *

Jamal and Dream arrived in Charlotte two days later. Jamal checked into an Innkeeper motel, and he finally turned on his cell phone to check his messages. Angelo had called repeatedly with death threats. The last message was from Thomas Henry. He said it was urgent that they spoke.

When Jamal called him, he learned that he had been indicted. "What? When did this happen?" Jamal asked.

"Actually it happened yesterday. As soon as I learned about it, I called you, but your phone wasn't on."

"What do you think I should do?" Jamal asked

"The last time I spoke with you, you already had your mind made up on running. I personally think you should turn yourself in. We may be able to beat it since your friend hasn't informed on you."

"You think so?"

"I don't know, but we have a good chance. If you run you're going to make it worse. I tell you what, I'll get a copy of your indictment and see exactly what's going on, then I'll call you back."

"Cool," Jamal said.

* * *

They returned the rental car and Jamal asked Dream to rent him a white Toyota Camry—a common car that could easily blend. Dream drove while Jamal slumped down on the passenger side so nobody would see him. He had her to drive to Boulevard Homes, a local housing project where he could have his cocaine cooked into crack, doubling his amount of product. Jamal had always prided himself on not selling crack. He felt it was for the lower level guys, he told himself. Money came fast selling crack, but the prison time was much more severe. Jamal tried to stay away from it, but since he was already wanted by the Feds, he now wanted to make as much money as possible.

Groups of teenage boys were huddled underneath the streetlights. Wine bottles and beer cans littered the streets. Crack pipes could be found sporadically. Windows in many buildings were boarded up. They stopped in front of Building 12. Jamal got the product out of the trunk and they entered the building. He tapped lightly on the door of Apartment C.

"Who is it?" a frigid voice asked.

"It's me, Jamal."

An old woman with a prosthetic arm opened the door. She smiled, showing an array of yellowish teeth. "Come on in."

The apartment was dingy-looking. Cigarette butts and dirty clothes covered the floor. Jamal and Dream stepped inside. "Minnie, this is my girlfriend, Dream," Jamal said. Dream forced a smile.

"Have a seat," Minnie said.

Jamal grabbed a shirt from the floor and placed it on the sofa before sitting down; Dream chose to remain standing.

"I need you to cook some coke for me," he said.

"How much?"

"About two kilos today, but there will be more as soon as I get rid of this. You know I'm going to take care of you."

Minnie smiled. "Let's go to the kitchen."

The kitchen did not have a refrigerator or a stove, nor did it have any kitchen utensils or a place to sit. A microwave, a hot plate, and a small Styrofoam cooler with dingy water sat in the corner. Dream cringed as soon as they entered the kitchen. She had never known of anyone to live in such conditions, but it was no big deal to Jamal.

"Okay, let's see what you've got," Minnie said.

Jamal took two brick packages and placed them on the table.

When Minnie opened the kitchen cabinet and grabbed a large Pyrex dish, roaches leaped out at her — big ones, small ones, white ones. Some even had wings.

Two hours later, when the crack was finished cooking, Minnie excused herself while Jamal sat on the floor gathering the product. Crack covered the floor and a foul smell hung in the air.

After Jamal had gathered everything, he put a little portion aside for Minnie. He figured she could make some extra money. They had waited for twenty minutes and still there was no sign of Minnie. Finally Jamal called her name. She didn't respond.

They entered the living room. Still no Minnie. Jamal remembered she had excused herself, so they headed to the bathroom.

"Minnie," Jamal yelled again, but still no response.

Flick, flick, flick. Jamal opened the bathroom door; it was very dark inside. Flick, flick, flick. He heard the sound again, but this time it was followed by sparks of light. When Jamal turned on the light, he almost gagged at the sight before him. The frail old lady sat on the edge of the corroded bathtub holding a crack pipe to her mouth with the prosthetic limb. She had a cigarette lighter in the other hand. Jamal became disgusted. Suddenly he thought about his mother and how she had been addicted. Minnie kept flicking, oblivious to their presence and unaware that the cigarette lighter was out of fluid.

* * *

When they left Minnie's house, Jamal ordered Dream to drive to a Bojangles restaurant on the west side of town. They were in the parking lot only five minutes when the white Infiniti Q-45 drove up. Dream recognized the man immediately. He was the same guy who had fired at her and Charlie Irving. Rico was his name.

Rico jumped out of his car and got in the backseat of the Camry. "What's up, Jamal?"

"Rico, this is my girlfriend, Dream."

Rico smiled without saying a word.

Dream glanced at him, but didn't say anything. She knew he hadn't recognized her. All this time Jamal had been supplying Rico, who was supplying Jessica's mother, who was busy stealing her husband's car and not attending to her child's well-being. She began to understand how the product trickled down into the community. She suddenly realized that she may have even brought some of the drugs to Jessica's mother, indirectly.

"I need your help on some things," Jamal said.

"Whatever, man, I'm with you."

"I need you to help me move some product, man. The Feds are looking for me and you are about the only one I can trust. So I need you to move as much as you can, as quickly as you can."

"Bring it on," Rico said.

"Do you have any money?"

"I didn't bring any."

Jamal handed Rico a small paper bag. "Here's two kilos. Call me when you're done."

Jamal and Rico slapped hands before Rico got out of the car.

* * *

Keisha was both surprised and happy to see Dream when she walked into her office. "Girl, I'm glad to see your crazy ass," Keisha said as they hugged.

"I'm glad to be back," Dream said, smiling.

Keisha's eyes grew serious. "Tell me what's going on now."

Dream turned from her friend's gaze before speaking. She didn't want to hide anything from Keisha. She was glad she had come to see Keisha because so much had happened. She needed someone to talk to, and Keisha would be much easier to talk to than her parents. "Jamal has just been indicted by the Feds."

Keisha raised her eyebrows. "Well, I hope you'll stay away from his ass."

"He pretty much knows we don't have a future together. I just want to be around him until he goes away."

"Goes away? What do you mean, goes away? Where is he going?" Keisha asked.

"I think he's going to leave the country?"

"Where is he going to go?"

"Honestly, I really don't know."

"You're not going to go with him, are you?" Keisha asked.

Dream looked at Keisha oddly. She realized that Keisha no longer had faith in her judgment. "Hell no, I ain't going with him. Do you think I'm crazy or something?"

"I was just asking. You did go clean across the country with that crazy-ass nigga, getting your parents all hysterical."

"You know what? I can handle my parents. Don't you worry about my parents."

"Call them to let them know that you're okay."

"I'll go see them." Dream replied.

"When?"

"Whenever I feel like it."

Keisha placed her hands on her hips and sighed without responding.

* * *

At 8:00 A.M. Mark and DEA agent Ken Clarkson knocked on Dream Nelson's door. Ken was a tall, blond man with a square jaw. He had been with the agency for six years. He was replacing Jeremiah while the agency investigated Jeremiah's possible misconduct.

Dream opened the door wearing a white robe. "Can I help you?" she asked.

"Yes, ma'am. My name is Agent Mark Pratt, and this is my partner, Ken Clarkson. May we come in?"

Dream stepped away from the door. "Come on in."

Both of the agents stood in living room, while Dream sat on the sofa with her arms folded.

"What can I do for you?"

"Ms. Nelson, I'm not gonna take up much of your time. My sources have told me that you are involved with a guy named Jamal Stewart. Have you seen him lately?" Mark asked.

Dream frowned. "What's going on?"

"Ms. Nelson, as of now Jamal is wanted and we are trying to locate him," Ken said.

"I haven't seen him," Dream said.

"Are you sure?" Mark asked.

"What reason would I have to lie?"

"I have documented information that you took a plane out to San Diego this weekend, and I also know that you have traveled with Jamal a couple of times to California."

Dream hesitated before speaking. "So are you calling me a liar?"

The two men stood. "We're not saying you're lying. In fact we don't know whether you are lying or not. All we know is that if you are withholding information, you will be charged. And if we get this guy without your help, he may decide to give us information on you and whatever your involvement may have been. You may very well find yourself on the inside looking out. Have you ever been incarcerated, Ms. Nelson?" Mark asked.

Dream frowned. "Hell no, and I ain't gonna be either," she said candidly.

"Let's hope not," Mark said. He opened the door and they left.

* * *

"Fuck you, mu'fucka!" Jamal yelled into the telephone.

"You gonna pay me or you gonna pay the fuckin' doctor!" Angelo yelled.

"I ain't paying you shit. I already told you this," Jamal said as he rose from his hotel bed.

"What made you flip on me, man? I loved you like a son." Angelo said.

"You are the cause of all this shit. Your man turned out to be a fuckin' informant, and that bitch, Jennifer, told on my man. Now, all I know is that my best friend is facing twenty-five minimum and you think shit is supposed to be all love. It ain't happening."

"I'm sorry, man. I ain't know Ruff was going to go out like that. I really didn't. As far as that bitch . . . you know a bitch will be a bitch. That ain't no reason for you to pull the shit you did."

"I went to prison without mentioning you the first time. You said it yourself you owe me." Jamal said.

"If you go to prison, consider yourself lucky, because I plan on sending you to hell, mister. You just fucked me out of close to $115,000," Angelo said before hanging up.

Jamal hated his relationship with Angelo had to end. He was a man Jamal once loved like a father. He thought they would be friends forever. Angelo was a guy that Jamal trusted, and he would bet his last dollar that he wouldn't cooperate with the police. Jamal didn't feel good about double-crossing him, but he knew his troubles were Angelo's fault. Besides, Angelo had plenty of money; Jamal did not. He had to do what it took to get the funds he needed to run from the Feds.

It's all Ruff's fault, Jamal thought. If only he had let somebody know that he had been busted, they could have gotten him a high-powered attorney. Ruff might have done three or four years, and they could have made money forever.

Jamal remembered the old men in prison with the canes. Some were sick and in wheelchairs. Others had emphysema, cancer, and other chronic illnesses. Some had been locked up for forty years. The world had moved on without them. Some had children they hadn't seen in twenty years or more. Some had grandchildren they had never seen and would never see. A life sentence in federal prison meant being carried out in a pine box. Only then, if you still had family, would they be able to get your body.

It was all Ruff's fault. He would have to pay.

m CHAPTER 26 m

AROUND 12:30 P.M., Jamal heard a knock on his room door, and he quickly ran to it and looked through the peephole. It was Dream carrying a McDonald's bag. He was pleasantly surprised. "Baby, "I'm glad to see you." He kissed her forehead.

She smiled. "Yeah, I figured you might be hungry, so I brought you some food." She placed the bag on the small round table next to his bed.

"Yeah, I am. I was just about to go out and get me something."

She handed him a Quarter Pounder with cheese some fries, and a medium Coke. "I hope you like what I got you. I didn't know what else to bring."

He put some ketchup on his fries and chomped away. "Right now, I'm hungry. I'll eat just about anything."

She sat across from him. "Jamal, do you think anybody knows you're here?"

He looked at her suspiciously. "Not unless you told them. What made you ask me something like that?"

She looked at the ceiling before answering. "I had a visit this morning from the DEA."

He placed his burger on the table. "The DEA?"

Their eyes met. "Yeah, they wanted to know if I had been in contact with you."

"What did you tell them?"

"Jamal, baby, I didn't let them know anything, but they knew I had been to California." Her eyes were sincere and he believed her.

"Yeah, they probably checked the flight records."

"That's what I thought," she replied.

"I've got to get the hell out of here in a hurry."

"Have you decided where you're going?"

"Yeah, I'll probably end up somewhere like Toronto or Jamaica for the time being, I think I should be able to go there with my fake birth certificate and ID."

Dream looked sad. Reality had begun to settle in on her. Jamal was serious about leaving and there was nothing she could do to help him. She would probably never see him again. "Give me a kiss, baby."

Jamal stood, walked over, and leaned toward her. He wrapped his arms around her and they kissed. "I got to handle some business," he said as he pulled away from her.

She looked into his eyes. His face was intense and she had never seen him look that way before. "What are you about to do, honey?"

"I've got to get rid of some more of this stuff, and I have to make sure I take care of the mu'fucka who is responsible for putting me in this predicament."

Dream rose from her seat and walked toward him. "Baby, don't get yourself in more trouble."

"It's too late for that, it's all or nothing," he said, avoiding her eyes.

Jamal pulled the mattress back on the bed and pulled out a chrome handgun.

Dream took a step back when she saw the gun. "What in the hell are you doing? Put that thing away." she ordered.

He put the gun in his waistband. "There is something I've got to handle. This mu'fucka has made my life miserable, and I intend to do the same for him," Jamal said before storming out of the room.

* * *

It was nine o'clock and Jamal had sold more of his product, though he still had a lot left. Things weren't moving as fast as he would have liked. He had to be extra cautious now. Since he had been charged. He didn't know who knew he was on the run, so he had to take things slowly, even if it meant having his product longer than he had anticipated.

He wheeled the Toyota Camry to the west side of town. He pulled into an Exxon gas station, filled the tank, and bought a pack of cigars. When he got back in the car, he lit a cigar and began to plot his mission.

He slid the Tupac Me Against the World CD in the player and selected "If I Die Tonight." Ruff would pay for what he had done, Jamal thought. He had never killed before, and he never thought of himself as a killer. However, he knew that the only way he would be able to live with the fact that his best friend was in jail was to take Ruff out. He thought about the concept of death and God. He felt he was too young to die. He didn't know if there was a hereafter, but if there was, it had to be better than life in this world. As far as he was concerned, he was already in hell.

He pulled to the end of Ruff's street, put his cigar out, and turned off his headlights. He didn't care about covering his tracks. He was wanted already. He stepped out and jogged up to Ruff's doorstep.

Ruff came to the door wearing a pair of blue Old Navy boxer shorts with no shirt. He was startled when he opened the door. "Jamal, what are you doing here?" He took a step back inside the house and attempted to shut the door.

Jamal stuck his foot in the doorway and grabbed Ruff underneath the chin. He pushed Ruff backward and closed the door.

"What the fuck is wrong with you?" Ruff asked.

Jamal grabbed Ruff's puny neck and applied pressure. "Now, I know you didn't think you wouldn't see me again, did you?"

"Why are you doing this?"

"I think you know the answer to that," Jamal said.

"I ain't have nuthin' to do with Dawg getting locked up," Ruff said desperately.

"I think I've heard enough from you, Ruff, and I know the cops have heard enough from you," Jamal said. He threw Ruff on the floor. He pulled the gun from his waist and quickly pumped three bullets into Ruff's temple.

* * *

Jamal Stewart was still at large, and one of the would-be witnesses against him had been mysteriously murdered. Mark sat at his desk frustrated. He knew Jamal had something to do with Theodore Ruffin's death, though the Charlotte homicide detectives said they didn't have enough evidence to pin the murder on Jamal yet. Mark had worked on this case long and hard, and he wouldn't be satisfied until he got some kind of closure.

Mark had begun to become disheartened until he received a call from his old friend, Don Gonzales, of the San Diego DEA, informing him that Angelo Morgan was headed to Charlotte. Angelo had not been charged with anything. Mark hoped Angelo would lead him to Jamal.

Mark had only seen Angelo's mug shot, which had been taken in the early eighties while Angelo was in federal prison. Though the picture was old, Mark had no problem spotting Angelo when he got off the plane. He looked the same as he did in the picture, only his hair was gray. Mark and Ken followed Angelo to a downtown hotel where they observed him meeting with two other black guys at the front desk.

Angelo checked in and took two pieces of luggage to his room. Mark and Ken waited out in the parking lot, hoping Angelo would come down and lead them to Jamal. Angelo never left the hotel that night.

Mark and Ken finally got tired of waiting. They left.

* * *

It was 2:00 P.M. when Keisha arrived at Dream's apartment. She had left work early because she was still worried about her friend. They made margaritas while Dream told Keisha about the visit from the DEA. She mentioned Jamal's vow to get even with the person responsible for putting him in the predicament. "He showed me a gun, and I think he may have killed this man. He was definitely mad enough to kill the last time I saw him."

"I know you're going to stay the hell away from him now," Keisha said.

"He should be leaving any day now. It won't be a matter of me staying away from him. He is gonna be leaving me."

"Have you seen your parents yet?" Keisha asked.

Dream ran her finger around the margarita glass and licked the salt while avoiding her friend's eyes. "I haven't gotten a chance to see them yet."

"I'm going to tell your mom what's going on if you don't get your ass over there and see them."

"I'm gonna go see them today. There's no need for you to go and make matters worse."

Keisha took a quick drink from her margarita before speaking. "I'm just worried about you, that's all. This Jamal nigga is a serious motherfucker."

Dream looked at Keisha briefly before turning away. "I know. I don't know why I didn't see it coming."

"I tell you what, these brothers out here got some serious issues. It's just hard to tell what kind of things they're into. . . I mean, I met this guy downtown the other day, Rashad. The nigga is fine as hell. Chocolate complexioned, nice hair, nice teeth, and a body to die for. But he is one of the biggest liars I have ever met in my life."

"What did he do?" Dream asked curiously.

"Well, for one thing, he is unemployed, but he told me he worked for American Express as a financial analyst. Lie number two: he said he didn't have any children. He has three babies' mamas and also got some fucked-up credit; just filed bankruptcy two months ago."

Dream burst out laughing. She could always count on Keisha to cheer her up. "Girl, you are too much. How did you find all this out?"

"My private investigator. I have to check all these niggas out now. I have to be careful that I don't get involved with no madman."

Dream became sad. She began to think about her past with men. Somehow she could never pick a decent man. When she was younger, it was fun hanging out with petty criminals and thugs, but now she was in the midst of a serious conspiracy. She believed it would be better if Jamal left the country, since the Feds had knowledge of them being a couple. If Jamal went away, she could go on with her life—a simple life as a middle school history teacher.

She wondered what had happened as she looked at Keisha. Why had she fallen in love with such no-good men? She had even neglected her parents lately. She had not seen her mom and dad for weeks. She decided it was time she paid them a visit. "Keisha, will you go with me to see my mom and dad."

Keisha reached over and placed her hand over Dream's. "Whatever you need me to do, I'm with you. Stop looking so sad. It's gonna be alright. Have faith."

* * *

Janice and David Nelson smothered Dream with hugs and kisses as soon as they laid eyes on her. "My baby is safe and sound," Janice announced.

"Yeah, and we're gonna make sure she stays that way," Keisha said.

Mr. Nelson held Dream for a long time. Though she felt as if her parents were treating her like a baby, she was glad to get all the attention. Being in her daddy's arms made her feel like a little girl again.

Janice had prepared lasagna and garlic bread. Keisha, Dream, and the Nelsons all sat at the dinner table eating. Everybody was kind of uncomfortable at first. Nobody wanted to talk. Dream knew there were many questions that her parents wanted answers to. She knew they deserved an explanation for her disappearance. She could feel her mother's penetrating eyes. "Mama, I know you've got some things you are dying to ask me. What do you wanna know?"

Janice eyebrow's rose. "Now, baby, whatever you choose to tell me, I'll be okay with it but somehow I know that Jamal boy has something to do with your being away without contacting us."

Dream turned, avoiding her mother's eyes.

Mr. Nelson spoke. "Don't be too hard on her, Janice. The main thing is, our daughter is back, and she's safe."

"That's right," Keisha said.

Dream turned to face her mother. "I will admit I made some bad choices."

Mr. Nelson bit into his garlic bread. "We have all made some mistakes, baby. Like I said before, the main thing is that you're here, and you're alive."

Dream smiled at her father. "Thank you, Daddy."

"What you thanking me for?" Mr. Nelson asked.

"Just for being there for me."

* * *

Keisha, Dream, and her parents all went into the den to watch the six o'clock news. Dream and Keisha glanced at each other when a mug shot of Jamal flashed on the screen. The news anchor said Jamal was armed and dangerous, and wanted for a number of criminal offenses, including the first-degree murder of Theodore Ruffin. He then went on to say that if anyone had any information concerning the whereabouts of Jamal Stewart, they should contact the police.

Dream turned from Keisha and just stared straight ahead. Though she was surrounded by her family and her best friend, she felt alone. She felt guilty because she had known Jamal was preparing to commit murder. Now he had taken a life, and she knew this would forever haunt her.

After a minutes of silence, Janice finally spoke. "Do you know where Jamal is?"

Dream met her mother's glance. "Actually, I don't. I haven't spoken to him today."

"If you knew, would you tell somebody?" Janice said.

Dream stared at the floor. "Honestly, I don't know," she said finally. She wanted to do the right thing. She knew Jamal was a criminal and that he needed to be brought to justice, but she didn't know if she could turn him in. She still loved him.

"He's a murderer baby. You can't go on protecting him," Janice spoke softly.

Mr. Nelson walked over and sat beside his daughter on the sofa. "Baby, if you know anything about Jamal's whereabouts, I think you should tell the police. It's just the right thing to do before he kills someone else."

Dream looked into her father's serious eyes. He looked worried. "Daddy, honestly, I don't know where Jamal is."

He rubbed her knee gently. "I believe you."

Dream stood from the sofa. "I think I better leave."

* * *

Jamal was napping in his hotel room when he received a call from Rico for more product. They would meet in the IHOP parking lot on Independence Boulevard. Jamal quickly jumped up from his bed, slipped on some sweatpants and a pair of running shoes. He headed out of the door with the product tucked underneath his arm. He scanned the parking lot on the way to the car. There seemed to be no immediate threat.

Rico had been kind of slow moving the product, but he was the only person whom Jamal could trust to do business with. When Jamal pulled out of the parking lot, a dark-colored SUV appeared from nowhere and seemed to be tailing him. He quicky changed lanes, but the SUV switched lanes as well, flicking its high beams. Jamal could barely see the road.

A half-mile later, he approached a busy intersection and the truck pulled alongside him. Jamal saw the two men in ski masks inside the truck. Spontaneously, Jamal whipped the car onto the median of the road and leapt from it.

The two men fired repetitively as Jamal darted through a maze of cars.

* * *

At 11:00 that night, Dream lay awake in her bed. She had tried to force herself to doze, but she simply couldn't rest. Her emotions were getting the best of her. She was depressed, and the little bit of self-esteem she had left was quickly diminishing. She was saddened by the fact that her parents acted as though they no longer trusted her, and she felt stupid for failing to investigate Jamal a little more carefully before dating him. She tried not to think about him. She focused on returning to her summer job at the Sylvan Learning Center.

At 12:30 Dream was startled by a loud knock. She got up, put on her robe and a pair of slippers, then quickly ran to the door. She opened the door slightly with the security chain still attached.

Jamal stood before her shaking. Mud and grass covered his body and face.

"I think you better leave, Jamal. Too much is happening with you. I can't live my life on the edge with you anymore."

"Open the door, please. I've been shot at."

"And the first place you come is here?"

"You're the only one I've got right now. Please open the door."

Dream deliberated a few moments before opening the door. "What happened to you?" she asked, stepping aside after releasing the chain lock.

"I was going to meet Rico when two men pulled up in a dark green SUV and opened fire. I had to hop out of the car and run."

She folded her arms in disgust. "So I guess I need to report the rental car stolen."

"That's up to you. I mean, I get shot at and all you can think about is a damn car?"

"Jamal, what do you want me to say? I'm sorry it happened. Who do you think did this to you?"

He wiped dirt from his face with his shirt. "I don't know. Maybe Angelo had something to do with it. I received a call from him earlier today and he threatened to kill me."

"How did he know where you were staying?"

"I can't be sure."

"So what do you need me for?" she asked.

"Actually, I need a place to lay my head tonight, but you act like you have an attitude with me or something. What have I done?"

"What haven't you done? You've stolen from your friend, and according to the news, you've killed a man. Have you forgotten you're a wanted man?"

A sudden hardness appeared on his face. "Have you forgotten that you were with me when I stole from Angelo. You ain't no fuckin' angel. You know what? I don't need to stay here," he shouted as he turned toward the door.

Suddenly he turned around with his handgun and pointed it.

Dream's eyes grew wide and she began to tremble.

"You're coming with me. Put on some clothes."

"Jamal, don't do this to me," she yelled.

"Bitch, you enjoyed the benefits of the game, now you gotta pay just like everybody else."

She looked into his eyes again. He was serious and she was afraid for her life. She put on a pair of jeans and a sweatshirt and they left.

* * *

Three days later, Mark lay on the sofa with the remote control in hand searching for the evening news. On channel three the huge mug shot of Jamal Stewart was shown. The news anchorman called Jamal a one-man crime spree, stating he was armed and dangerous. He was wanted on a host of charges that included kidnapping, drug conspiracy, and murder. Crime stoppers offered a ten thousand dollar reward for any information that led to Jamal's arrest.

Mark turned to channel 9. A huge picture of Dream Nelson was on the screen. The anchorman said Dream was a twenty-five-year-old middle school teacher who was believed to be with her boyfriend, held against her will. The setting changed to Spaugh Middle School. One of the reporters interviewed the principal. A short, bald man with a pink face said Ms. Nelson was a studious employee and that he had spoken with her just before school ended for summer break. He went on to say that he was saddened by her disappearance and was praying for her return.

Channel 36 showed David and Janice Nelson standing in front of their home holding a picture of Dream in a cap and gown—her college graduation picture. David said she was their only child. He wanted her to know, if she was watching, that they loved her very much. Janice begged for anyone with information concerning the whereabouts of their daughter to please come forward. Midway through her speech, the tears came streaming down her face.

Disappointed, Mark turned the television off and stared at the ceiling. He felt as if he had not done his job. His heart went out to the Nelsons. He wondered what was going on with Dream and Jamal, and he wished she had listened when he had spoken with her. It was too late now. Dream was gone, perhaps forever. He said a short prayer for her before dozing.

* * *

The next day, as soon as Mark walked into his office his phone rang.

"Hello."

"Mark, David speaking. I have some good news."

"What is it?"

"I've just received some information concerning the whereabouts of Jamal Stewart."

"Oh yeah?" Mark said as he walked to the other side of his desk.

"Yeah, his attorney called and apparently he saw the girl's parents on the news and it touched him so much that he is willing to help us nail Jamal."

"Isn't it unethical for an attorney to divulge information about a client?"

"Not if it concerns an ongoing crime. Who cares about ethics, anyway? This guy is scum."

Mark hesitated before speaking. "I just hope the girl is still alive."

* * *

Dawg stared blankly when the judge gave him a life sentence. Mark looked on, actually feeling sorry for Dawg's mother. He had been trained not to let his emotions get in the way of his job, but he always seemed to find himself getting kind of emotional when women were involved. He was only human. He would tell himself he had a mother, and he definitely didn't want her to go through anything remotely like what Steven's mother was going through, because essentially the judge had just killed Steven. He would never be free again to roam the streets. Mark was happy about the fact that he had been instrumental in getting drugs off the street, but he was disappointed that a black mother had just lost a son.

ɱ CHAPTER 27 ɱ

A WEEK HAD PASSED since Jamal abducted Dream. While evading the Feds they had stayed at several cheap motels before finally settling in at a Ramada Inn in Davidson, North Carolina, outside the Charlotte city limits.

Dream woke up at 6:00 A.M. while Jamal was asleep. She still couldn't believe what had happened to her. She couldn't believe that she hadn't seen this dark side of Jamal. The man whom she thought was the love of her life had turned out to be nothing but a gangster. Angelo was looking for Jamal to kill him and the Feds were pursuing them. She knew nothing good was going to come out of this situation. "Damn," she cursed herself. Not for being stupid, but for being in love with a dealer.

Two hours later, Dream pulled the curtains back and peered down into the motel parking lot. The lot was empty, except for her Mercedes and two pickup trucks.

"Do you see anything suspicious?" Jamal asked as he sat up on the bed.

She turned and faced him. "No, just the same two trucks that was here last night."

"How did you sleep last night?"

She frowned. "How in the hell was I supposed to sleep? The Feds are after you, remember? Plus Angelo is probably looking to kill your ass."

Jamal stood and placed his hand underneath her chin. "Listen, Dream, baby, I'm sorry but this is the way it has to be right now. But I swear to you, it's gonna get better. I got my lawyer working on us some passports under aliases. As soon as he gets them, we're off to one of those third-world countries, and we can live like a king and queen." He walked over and pulled a huge duffel bag from underneath the bed. "I got close to five hundred thousand dollars in here. Do you realize how good we can live in another country? Like I said, we'll be on king and queen status."

She pulled away from him. "I don't want to go to a third-world country. I wanna be with my friends and family."

He became angry. He stepped toward her and grabbed her wrist. "You see, bitch, it don't work like that. You're all in, and you may as well get used to it."

Tears filled her eyes. "Jamal, you're hurting me."

"And damn it, you're pissing me off." He grabbed her by the hair and flung her to the bed.

"What you gonna do now, Mr. Big Man, beat me?" she yelled.

"Listen to me, damn it." Jamal sat on the bed and gently held her hand. "Dream, everything is going to be alright. I promise, babe."

She wanted everything to be okay. She wanted everything to be like before, but she knew it never would.

His cellular phone rang. He grabbed it from the dresser.

"Where the hell are you?" Thomas asked.

"Now, I know you don't expect me to tell you no shit like that," Jamal replied.

"So, you don't trust me? I'm the one who's supposed to get the fuckin' passports, remember?"

Jamal paced the floor nervously. "It's not that I don't trust you, I just need time to think."

"Where's the girl?"

"She's with me." Jamal said as he glanced over at Dream, she was still sobbing.

"Well I hope you know her picture is being shown on the news."

"For what?"

"Her parents are saying you kidnapped her."

Jamal stared blankly. His problems were piling up. He felt like a man walking aimlessly on the edge of the Grand

Canyon, waiting for the slightest hint of wind to force him over. "Can we meet somewhere?"

"Where?"

"The Waffle House on South Boulevard at midnight."

"The Waffle House it is."

* * *

Jamal sat on the edge of the bed with his chin resting in his hands, as if he were contemplating something drastic.

"What's going on now, Jamal?" Dream asked softly.

"They're trying to say I kidnapped you."

"Well, you are holding me against my will."

"Would you listen to me?" he pleaded. "I would never do anything to hurt you. I love you."

"I love you, too, Jamal." Dream grabbed his hand. "But we can't go on like this. I mean, it's not the Feds I'm worried about. It's the contract on your life that concerns me."

Jamal sighed. He was more concerned with the Feds than a contract on his life. "Baby, you're right. Tonight I'm letting you go with my lawyer."

"That's good, but what about you?"

He looked away. "I'll be alright. Trust me."

She leaned forward and kissed his nose. "I'm gonna always love you, Jamal Stewart."

"I'll always love you, too," Jamal said as he picked her up and carried her to the bed. They kissed passionately and explored every crevice of each other's body. Neither wanted the feeling to end; both knew it would be the last time they made love with each other.

* * *

At 11:00 P.M. they rose and showered together like they had done so many times before. The mood was pleasant. They played with each other the way they used to. He

262 • K. Elliott

sprayed her with cold water and she squirted shampoo in his eyes.

"Damn it, Dream. My eyes are burning."

She laughed. "Come here, let me kiss them."

"Get away from me, crazy ass girl." He pushed her away and they exchanged smiles.

* * *

They left the hotel at 11:35. On the way to the Waffle House, Jamal called Thomas Henry to make sure he would be there. When they pulled up, they heard cars screeching to a halt. Several vehicles had formed a barricade. They were surrounded by FBI, DEA agents, and local policemen. "Put your goddamned hands up!" a burly DEA agent yelled.

Jamal knew everything he had worked so hard to build was about to end. The passenger door opened and a huge DEA agent yanked Dream from the car.

"Jamal, get out of the car," another agent demanded.

Jamal looked behind him. There was nowhere to run. There were at least fifteen officers. He wondered where they had come from. It seemed as though they were rising from the ground. He grabbed his gun from underneath the seat. Jamal fired four shots through the windshield, killing only one officer. He suddenly became overwhelmed by the return fire. The shots flew from all angles, striking his head and chest, taking his life. Jamal's body lay slouched in the seat as his eyes protruded.

The ambulance arrived. The firemen arrived. Media ran rampantly. The police taped off the scene. Dream had been struggling to answer questions from Agent Pratt, but when she saw the coroner bring out a body bag, reality hit her. Jamal was gone forever. "They didn't have to kill him," she moaned. "Please don't go away from me, Jamal. Please don't go." She ran up to the coroner's van but was ordered to step away as Jamal's body was loaded and the door was closed. When the coroner drove away, she dropped to her knees and cried.

* * *

Angelo and his two goons had been apprehended at his hotel room on weapons charges. Since Angelo was a convicted felon, it was simple for the grand jury to return an indictment on him. His plea agreement was fifteen years, which was like a life sentence to him because of his age. He had pled guilty and was shipped to a federal prison in southern California.

Jeremiah was subsequently indicted for obstruction of justice and was fired. Most of the cases he had been involved in had a good chance of being overturned. The U.S. Attorney's office was not too happy about that. David Ricardo would later recommend that Jeremiah be sent to a federal prison and placed in the regular inmate population where he knew he would be slapped around once word got out that he was a former federal agent.

* * *

Dream pulled to the side of the road and sat with her head resting on the steering wheel. She felt nauseous and felt as if there was a metal wrench churning inside her stomach. It had been two hours since she'd left the doctor's office, and she still had not made it home. She didn't want to go home; she wanted to end her life. She knew something was wrong after she'd received a call from Doctor Sinclair saying it was very necessary that she saw him immediately. Two weeks prior to the phone call, she had taken her annual physical required by the school district.

She had lost the desire to live the minute Doctor Sinclair told her she was HIV positive. That would be the last thing she would remember. He had tried to tell her everything was going to be all right and that life would be okay for her if she received the proper treatment. He had even told her about support groups that would make her HIV-induced world easier, but before he could say anything, Dream stormed out of the room crying. Her life had been ruined because of Jamal. She figured it had to be him, because he was the only one she'd had unprotected sex with. Did he even know he was HIV positive? How did he get it? Maybe he had been a closet homosexual, or maybe . . . he got it from the stripper. "Damnit," she said as she slammed her fist against the dashboard. "Why in the hell did I get involved with a character like him?" she asked herself. School had just started three weeks before, and things were starting to look up for her again. She was teaching American history, and had her own homeroom class. She absolutely loved her kids. She had started seeing DeVon again, and they were actually talking about marriage and starting a family one day.

After Jamal had been killed, she thought for certain she would pick up and move on with her life. She had actually felt blessed to be alive. She knew that she could have very easily ended up in a prison like Dawg, or could have been killed like Jamal. Now, after receiving the news from Dr. Sinclair, she didn't feel she was fortunate after all. In her mind, Jamal was the lucky one. His life was over. He had not suffered, nor did he have to live with the stigma of being HIV positive. How would she tell her parents? How would she tell DeVon? She was glad she had not had unprotected sex with him.

Dream opened the glove compartment and got the sleeping pills—she swallowed seventeen of them and started crying again. Fifteen minutes later she was unconscious.

An hour later, a state trooper found her slouched behind the steering wheel of her car and called the ambulance. She was then rushed to the emergency room, where her stomach was pumped.

* * *

David and Janice Nelson entered Dream's hospital room with flowers and balloons in hand. Dream sat up on the bed and made eye contact with her parents. She didn't know what to say or do. She didn't know how much they knew. Her father approached the bed and gave her a hug. "Baby, it's going to be okay, your mother and I will be here for you."

Dream knew immediately that they knew about her being HIV positive. Dr. Sinclair must have told them. Suddenly the tears came. "D-daddy, how did you find out?" she struggled to say.

"After we received the call from the hospital, saying you had overdosed, I called Doctor Sinclair and I asked him if he knew why you would try to take your life; I knew you had been to his office yesterday. He was kind of hesitant to answer my question. He told me he had given you some bad news that he couldn't share with me. So I drove over to his office this morning and demanded he tell me. Reluctantly he did."

"Baby, we will always love you," Janice said as she leaned forward and kissed Dream.

Someone tapped on the door. Keisha and Dream's student, Jessica Irving, appeared. They rushed to Dream's bedside and hugged her.

Dream smiled when she saw Keisha. She knew that no matter what, Keisha would always be her friend. Dream knew she had made some mistakes, and seeing Jessica made Dream realize that though her life would no longer be the same. There were still many reasons to live. She had a purpose that was far greater than teaching history. She would now teach her children life skills. These were the same skills she and Jamal had lacked. She had learned from her experience, and she felt she needed to pass her lessons along. She wasn't going to give up. She would live every day to the fullest, thankful for her friends and family, and enjoy what the Lord had given her. At that moment she realized she was loved, and DeVon or any other man no longer mattered. She wasn't worried about whether or not DeVon would accept her and her condition. She closed her eyes briefly and thanked God.

* * *

Mark was slouched in the seat of a U-Haul truck with a USA Today covering his face. From afar, he observed the huge stucco mansion of his latest subject, Tommy Dupree, a twenty-six-year-old black man, short and round, who loved cars. A new Lincoln Navigator and a Lexus LS 400 were in the driveway.

An hour later Tommy came out. He was wearing a green-and-white sweat suit. He was draped in diamond jewelry, and two women clung to his stubby arms. Placing his newspaper on his lap, Mark fired up the ignition as he wondered where his new investigation might take him. He wondered how Tommy's story would unfold.

A word from the Author

Hopefully you enjoyed this work of fiction. The story you have just read was not written to condone or condemn anybody's behavior and none of the characters in the book are good or bad but simply living their lives or playing the hands that they were dealt. I'm not a criminologist or psychologist but an observant artist trying to paint an unbiased picture. If you learned something from the story fine if you didn't hopefully you was thoroughly entertained. Post all your comments about the story on Amazon.com and Barnes and Nobles.com or visit my website at **www.k-elliott.com**

About the Author

K. Elliott resides in Charlotte, North Carolina. He has participated in and completed various creative writing courses at both Central Piedmont Community College and Queens University. In 2001, Elliott received a scholarship that allowed him to attend the North Carolina Writers Network Conference. Elliott was also a finalist in 2001 Keystone poetry competition.